BETTING ON HOPE

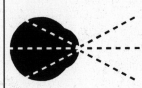

This Large Print Book carries the
Seal of Approval of N.A.V.H.

A FOUR OF HEARTS RANCH ROMANCE,
BOOK 1

BETTING ON HOPE

DEBRA CLOPTON

THORNDIKE PRESS
A part of Gale, Cengage Learning

GALE
CENGAGE Learning·

Farmington Hills, Mich • San Francisco • New York • Waterville, Maine
Meriden, Conn • Mason, Ohio • Chicago

GALE
CENGAGE Learning®

Thorndike Press® Large Print Christian Romance.
The text of this Large Print edition is unabridged.
Other aspects of the book may vary from the original edition.
Set in 16 pt. Plantin.

LIBRARY OF CONGRESS CATALOGING-IN-PUBLICATION DATA

Clopton, Debra.
    Betting on hope : a four of hearts ranch romance / by Debra Clopton. —
Large print edition.
        pages cm. — (Thorndike Press large print Christian romance)
    ISBN 978-1-4104-7807-8 (hardcover) — ISBN 1-4104-7807-6 (hardcover)
    1. Large type books. I. Title.
PS3603.L67B48 2015b
813'.6—dc23   2015000897

Published in 2015 by arrangement with Thomas Nelson, Inc., a division of HarperCollins Christian Publishing, Inc.

Printed in Mexico
1 2 3 4 5 6 7 19 18 17 16 15

To my family: your love, your smiles, your hugs — that's the "good stuff" and I'm so blessed and forever grateful to have each and all of you in my life. I thank God every day for each of you.

1

"*What* have you gotten me into, Amanda Jones?"

Staring at the rough-looking building, Maggie Hope clutched her cell phone to her ear and fought down a hot flood of panic. "The sign says the *Bull Barn*. What *is* this place?" she gritted through tense jaws.

Rustic was an understatement for the faded wooden building sitting on the outskirts of Wishing Springs, Texas. It had dark windows and a long plank porch supported by columns made of knobby tree trunks. The steeply pitched red roof sagged in the middle. It was a dive, a shack.

"Calm down, Mags," Amanda croaked, the flu causing her to sound like an eighty-year-old smoker, instead of the intimidatingly elegant, thirty-five-year-old bombshell who was the key ingredient of the most popular morning show on Houston's local channel. She coughed. "It may look a little

7

rough, but it's the cowboy *and* local folks' hangout."

"But — it's deserted. Lonesome. If it's a hangout, where is everyone?" It didn't look like a place anyone would want to hang out in. Especially Maggie. Dives brought back memories she worked hard to forget.

The TV station's van was the only other vehicle in the white rock parking lot — and that only added to her distress, which in truth was more about the TV camera than the clapboard building that looked like a leftover of the Wild West days.

She swallowed the lump in her throat. She wanted to go back home and write her daily advice column, "Gotta Have Hope," in obscurity. But . . . not happening. Amanda was delirious to have offered Maggie as her stand-in for this important interview with champion Quarter Horse rider, trainer, and ladies' man, Tru Monahan.

Tru Monahan!

Maggie was a writer, not a reporter. She wasn't comfortable being in front of people — it brought back memories of the worst times of her life . . . not only a time of shame and embarrassment but also a time when her life fell apart. But none of that mattered to anyone but her, and since the same conglomerate owned both the news-

8

paper and the television station, Maggie hadn't been asked to do this. She'd been told.

Amanda sneezed. "The show asked for the interview to be done when there was no one else around. Small-town interviews tend to be harder when locals are involved. It's better for you this way." Amanda's hoarsely whispered words ended in another croaking cough.

"Amanda, you sound terrible." Sympathy won out over Maggie's nervous breakdown.

"I feel awful," Amanda wheezed. "I'm going to sleep now. You let those red heels do the walking and get in there, girlfriend. You can do this."

"But —," Maggie blurted, but the line had gone dead.

Maggie's hand tightened on the now useless lifeline to her friend.

She glared into the rearview mirror and cringed at her overdone blue eyeshadow. Her cheeks were too pink, too, and her lips sticky with gloss. Amanda had assured Maggie that for the camera she needed a little more color than was normal.

A camera.

Clammy fingers of panic tightened around her windpipe. Maggie squeezed her eyes shut and counted to ten . . . calm did not come. It was a wonder she hadn't broken out in hives or something on the two-hour-long drive over here.

"Gotta Have Hope" was a dream come true for Maggie and it was because of Amanda's recommendation that she even had the job. No one truly knew what a blessing the advice column had been for Maggie. A lifesaver, really. As Amanda had been to her when they'd first met several years earlier.

She owed Amanda . . .

Even so, Maggie figured this gig was going to be the full sum of her debt owed. Yup, paid in full was getting stamped on that bill. Amanda was always looking out for her, but she didn't know about the fool Maggie had made of herself in her freshman year during the school play. Freezing up, then knocking down the *entire* set in her panic . . .

Everyone laughing . . .

And then the aftermath — a chill filled Maggie. What if she made a fool of herself in front of *thousands* of TV viewers?

"Stop," Maggie huffed, glaring at herself in the mirror. She was not that insecure kid anymore. Not the kid whose home life was so messed up that she could barely hide it from everyone her seventh grade year. The kid who'd tried to lose herself through acting as an escape from reality only to fall apart that night on stage. The clumsy kid who left the stage in tears only to arrive home to find police hauling her father away.

The night of that play, Maggie's life changed from bad to worse.

No, Maggie didn't do limelight well. It brought back far too many bad memories that she was still trying hard to wipe away.

Maggie closed her eyes and inhaled slowly. She'd found out the hard way that she wasn't meant to be in the spotlight where there were things she couldn't control.

But none of that mattered because her bosses believed this would be good for her floundering advice column. They wanted her readers to see the person behind the column. Ha— they might discover that was a really bad idea when they saw her in front of that camera. She'd probably freeze up, throw up, or all of the above.

Stop. Just stop.

"Positive thinking here, Mags. You *will* do this and you will do this *well.*"

Pulling from the well of determination that had gotten her out of that life and into the life she had now, Maggie opened the door of her baby blue Volkswagen Bug. Fear never got her anywhere.

June heat slammed into her along with the scent of something tasty roasting inside the awful building. Okay, so at least that was a positive sign. She reached across the seat and grabbed the red high heels — bought specifically for this interview. Amanda swore they'd give her courage and confidence. Carefully, she set them on the chunky, white rocks of the parking lot and then slipped her feet into them.

She might be a lot of things, but chicken wasn't one of them. Sure, she'd once been afraid but she'd learned to push through her fear. And that was exactly what she was going to do now.

She reached for her red leather folder — something else Amanda said worked for courage — slung her large purse over her shoulder and stood in a decisive movement of decision to give this her all. Her hand trembled as she smoothed her flowing skirt, but she ignored it, then slammed her car door and took a step toward the Bull Barn.

The rumble of a large engine had her glancing over her shoulder. A shiny, black four-wheel-drive truck whipped into the parking lot the same instant a whirlwind swept across the dusty ground. Maggie's skirt had been swishing gently about her knees, now it caught air and attempted to do the Marilyn-Monroe-thing and fly up over her head. Maggie let go of her folder and desperately grabbed for the dancing skirt.

She managed to clamp it down just in time but dropped her folder.

"No," she gasped as it hit the ground and the papers with Amanda's prewritten interview questions instantly swirled up into the whirlwind like birds freed from a cage. Fumbling to gather her skirt hem in one hand, she grasped at flying pages with the other. The white gravel Texans were partial to did not get along well with her heels. She knew she was making a ridiculous spectacle of herself wobbling and tottering as she watched her interview fly into oblivion.

She couldn't do the interview without Amanda's questions.

Her long blonde hair swept across her eyes just as a man's wide, tanned hand reached over her shoulder and plucked a page fluttering in front of her from the air.

"Got it," said a deep voice as its owner stepped past her and continued to snatch pages from the air one at a time with quick, coordinated movements.

Relief surged through Maggie as she watched the long-legged cowboy swoop the last one off the ground and turn toward her.

The championship-size buckle at his hips gleamed in the sunlight in competition with the white smile slashing across his face.

Oh my.

Maggie's stomach nosedived straight to her toes.

Photos had failed to do Tru Monahan justice.

Beneath his black Stetson, the chocolate dark hair brushing his collar was richer looking, his jaw stronger, and his high cheekbones more prominent than they'd seemed on television or in the tabloids. And his eyes . . . Maggie's breath caught when her eyes collided with his. Warm, deep, rich amber reminding her of maple syrup held up to the light. They were simply incredible — *he* was incredible.

Her ankles melted and she wobbled again when his lips shifted from the dazzling smile into the signature half grin that caused the skin around his eyes to crinkle enticingly. That expression enhanced a bunch of commercials and even appeared on a variety of equine products he endorsed.

That grin had won Tru Monahan a horde of female admirers across the country.

And Maggie was not immune. Her pulse went ballistic in response to all that dazzlement and the ground shifted — okay, so maybe that was her imagination, but she felt it nonetheless.

"I'll carry these for you," he said, tucking the folder beneath his arm, his expression relaxing as he focused his full attention on her. Which was a little overwhelming.

The wind fought her skirt, and her hair tickled her nose as Maggie swallowed the lump firmly situated in her windpipe. "Thank you," she croaked — she actually croaked — *Oh, just shoot me now and be done with it.* "I'm in a bit of a bind at the moment." Sometimes the truth was the only way to go.

His gaze drifted to her ironclad grip on her runaway skirt, which was still fighting for freedom.

"It would be my pleasure," he drawled, his grin twitching. "Can I help you?"

Maggie just stared at him like she'd never seen a good-looking man before.

Her hair slapped her in the face — a much-needed wake-up call.

"N-no. I'm fine. Just fine," she gathered her skirt closer and smiled stiffly while sweeping her hair out of her face with her free hand. Forcing her shoulders back, she took a couple of steps toward the restaurant, teetering dangerously on her heels once more.

Tru walked slowly beside her, his black boots crunching the rocks that were in cahoots with her shoes to do her in. After a few treacherous steps, he touched her arm. "I don't want to get in your business, but I'm thinking maybe you should hold on to my arm before you go flying across this rock and skin'n up those pretty knees of yours."

Maggie halted, staring at him. His Texas drawl did funny things to her insides. Okay, so maybe she shouldn't have told Amanda that she thought Tru was the best-looking male on the planet, when her friend had first mentioned interviewing the cowboy. She'd made that statement back when *Amanda* was supposed to be doing the interview.

Maybe if she'd kept her mouth shut, Amanda might not have suggested Maggie substitute for her.

Tru crooked his arm in invitation and the warmth of his gaze radiated through her.

"I'd say no," she said, her voice annoyingly breathless. "But then I'd probably fall flat on my face, so thank you." She slipped her arm through his and wrapped her fingers around the corded muscle of his forearm.

She felt really ridiculous clinging to her interviewee as they headed toward the porch. The man smelled like leather and sunshine and something spicy that drew her like a hummingbird to sugar water. She had to fight the urge to lean in and inhale.

When they made it to the steps, she was thrilled. "Thank you for rescuing me. I was courting disaster out there." *And now too.*

"Always glad to help a lady in distress."

"If you're around me too long, you'll risk getting overworked."

His eyes twinkled. "I definitely might have more than I can handle where you're concerned."

She stumbled on the step — the cowboy was *flirting* with her.

Worse — Maggie choked on a gasp — he thought *she* was flirting with him.

"P-probably not," she assured him, stepping quickly away from him, happy to have the smooth wood porch beneath her feet and space between them. "I'm fairly boring on most days, quartz gravel and heels aside."

He grinned at her words and monster-size butterflies did loops behind her rib cage.

"I have a feeling that's not true." He held out the folder with the pages he'd stuck back inside. "These are yours, I believe."

"Thank you, again." Maggie's fingers grazed his as she took the folder and sparks tingled up her arm. Her cheeks burned. No doubt about it, she was the most unprofessional interviewer the *Houston Tribune* could ever have chosen for this assignment.

He pushed open the heavy door by the glass panes in the upper half. Fighting conflicting emotions, she brushed past him — being sure not to touch him. The delicious coffee-scented, cool air from the inside swept over her, soothing her heated skin.

Coffee — that's what she needed. A strong cup of courage.

Safely inside, she finally dared to let go of her skirt and it swayed gently just above her knees as she glanced around. She was relieved, for a moment at least, to have something other than Tru to focus on. The film crew was set up off to the side of the diner, busy checking equipment while waiting for Amanda to come in and take charge. Only Amanda wasn't here, and Maggie had absolutely no idea what to do. Hopefully someone else would be able to show her the way.

Tru moved to stand beside her. "Looks kind of vacant. Are you here for lunch? I think they're holding off opening 'til after that." He jerked his head slightly in the direction of the cameras, but said nothing about them interviewing him.

"Um, no," Maggie said, startled by his question, only then realizing he had no idea who she was. "I'm here for the interview."

"Oh. You're getting interviewed too? I am, but to be honest, I'd rather be home riding my horse."

A laugh bubbled from her. Of course he didn't know who she was. He was expecting Amanda, and everyone knew what she looked like. "As odd as it is to believe, I'm here to interview you, Mr. Monahan." She held out her hand and tried to look more professional than she felt. Tried to ignore the way her gaze kept wanting to stick to him like a stamp to an envelope. "Maggie Hope, filling in for Amanda Jones — she's ill, I'm sorry to say."

She lifted her chin, hoping to convey confidence. Of course there was an upside to the entire fiasco in the parking lot. She'd caught her skirt just in the nick of time. Otherwise, she'd have climbed back into her car and hit the road to Houston out of mortification.

At least at this point she could still look the cowboy in the eye.

Tru was losing his touch. He found himself staring into the spearmint-green eyes of the gorgeous blonde with the dimples — and a

19

very nice set of legs. Normally he could pick a reporter out of a crowd at fifty feet — there was a certain aggression in their eyes.

Not vulnerability like he'd thought he'd seen in Maggie Hope's eyes. He'd never seen this one coming.

This woman had none of that, and in her own words, two left feet. She'd been a mess out there. A cute mess, but a mess nonetheless.

It was hard to believe a popular show would send a reporter who looked as unprepared as this woman did to tape an interview that would be viewed by thousands. Was it an act to get him off his guard? He didn't consider himself a big deal, but he had won the National Quarter Horse Finals again, and when you added in his unfortunate tabloid debacle, he knew he was news right now. As bad as he hated it.

And the station could send out whomever they wanted to do the interview.

"Hey, Tru." Big Shorty, the owner of the Bull Barn, approached from the back of the diner, sauntering over with a grin on his weathered face. An old cowboy himself, there was no mistaking the teasing light in his eyes. "Any later and you'd have missed your own interview."

Tru shook his hand. "I got held up for a

20

moment." He glanced at Maggie. "Besides, there's no need getting here early for the setup. Wouldn't want them to think I had nothing better to do."

"We all know that ain't the case. Just like they asked, I got folks run off till eleven o'clock, but then they're gonna be bustin' in here to find out about the interview." He leaned in close. "Of course I got a couple who won't take no for an answer, and they're stuffed back there in the kitchen pretending they ain't here." He winked.

"I expected as much." Tru was pretty sure he knew who would be eavesdropping on the interview. Clara Lyn and Reba from the Cut Up and Roll hair salon were likely doin' a little snoopin' for the scoop. They were lovable, but did tend to go overboard when it came to getting things firsthand. "It's okay," he chuckled. "I don't care one way or the other — I've had snoopier people trailin' my steps." His sponsors had set this up and wanted him to do the interview in a local hangout. They thought it would be good PR. Besides that, the Bull Barn just sounded catchy to them. Tru hadn't minded that at all.

Shorty was a good friend. All their lives Tru and his brothers had hung out here, listening to their granddad and his buddies tell rodeo stories.

He was more than happy to throw some good PR Shorty's way by having the interview at his place.

"Mr. Monahan, sir," a guy with a mike stepped from the group across the way and motioned to him. "We're ready for you. I need to get this set up, if you don't mind."

Tru hiked a brow at Shorty. "Talk to you later."

"Don't be looking all put out over this. I see that beautiful little gal about to interview you. Maybe you should invite her to lunch when this is over."

Five minutes ago that had been an enticing possibility, however, now that Tru knew Maggie Hope was a journalist, not a chance. His life was public enough without asking for more trouble. Been there done that.

He enjoyed his privacy and had given it up only because as a co-owner of the Four of Hearts Ranch with his two brothers, Bo and Jarrod, he needed good publicity for the business. When the trainer of the ranch's horses was also a champion on a champion horse — 'nuff said. A cowboy did what a cowboy had to do to bring in the business. Especially with the debt that had been owed on the place after his dad's death.

Tru didn't let his thoughts linger there

too long; it wasn't a good place to be before he sat down for an interview. There were a lot of folks 'round town who knew what his dad had done. Tru's jaw tensed thinking about it. Almost two years had passed and his anger was still as hot as it had been the day he'd learned how bad his dad's gambling had been. Two years since he'd seen the hurt in his granddad's eyes. Pops had worked his fingers to the bone to build this ranch and watched all of his sons but one die while he was doing it. All but Joe, Tru's dad, and he'd very nearly destroyed everything Pops had lived for anyway.

Truth was, it took the united effort of Tru and his two brothers to dig the ranch out of the hole it was in — and they were still digging but had managed some success while paying the debt down. Tru's part in that equation was the Quarter Horse business and the sponsorship his success had brought to the table. Endorsement money paid bills, and while he wasn't George Strait, the money he made from his sponsors was a big part of the equation.

But sometimes . . . like now, he was just weary of the whole thing and wished he could — what? Disappear? Be his own boss and not have so much of his life dictated by his sponsors?

Or maybe find a wife . . . start a family. His future wasn't his own right now. His dad had made sure of that.

Pops's dreams were in his and his brothers' hands.

He pushed the bitter thoughts of his dad from his mind. Now was not the time to let himself be hijacked by things that couldn't be changed.

He focused instead on the pretty reporter across the room. Though his insides had warmed at the touch of her hand and the sparkle in her eyes, that was as far as it went. She was a journalist, a profession he just didn't trust — there was no way on this green earth that he was letting his boots shuffle her way any time other than this interview.

As if hearing his thoughts, she turned and those soft green eyes shot sparks all the way to the tips of his Tony Lamas.

Trouble. Tru recognized it like he anticipated his horse's misstep in going after a calf. He tugged his hat low, met those amazing eyes, and knew straight up he was going to have to fight for focus or he might just forget Maggie Hope was a reporter.

2

"Back off, bucko," Jenna Olson warned. Clutching the toilet plunger in her hands like a baseball bat, she willed herself not to puke as she glared at the hefty drunk blocking the exit of the truck stop restroom. Jenna might be short, sixteen, and pregnant — *big time* pregnant — but she was nobody's pushover.

"I'm not afraid to use this plunger, mister," she said fiercely, true enough but she sure wished it was a bat, or better yet, a steel pipe.

As if giving her a pep punch, her baby kicked her in the kidney. Jenna didn't know if she was having a girl or a boy, but the baby kicked like a linebacker. Resolve filled her. Clutching the plunger tighter, she nodded agreement with her little fighter. Jenna's eyes never wavered from the bloodshot ones that were making her skin crawl as they studied her. This wasn't going to be pretty;

she just had no plans to be the victim.

Most girls her age would have been terrified, but if Jenna had ever been afraid of anything, it had been beat out of her a long time ago by her dad — until she threatened him just like she was threatening this foul-smelling piece of junk with his tobacco-stained smirk.

When he took a swaying step forward, Jenna's heart skipped a beat or two and her adrenaline kicked up a notch, thrumming through her veins like an Amtrak. She had more to protect than herself now, and she couldn't fail.

She had a precious baby inside of her and no man was laying another hand on her or her baby ever.

"C'mon, lil' girly. You —"

"I'll scream and hit you so hard you'll see stars," she yelled, as he lunged. Thankfully he was so drunk, he staggered. Jenna might look like a small whale, but she could still move, and she sidestepped him. When his greasy hands grabbed for her, she swung the plunger with all her might. It whacked him in the face and the dull reverberation shimmied up her arms. If it had been a bat, he'd have been knocked out cold. Instead he stumbled back, slipped in a puddle of water on the tile floor, and slammed his head on the grimy sink.

At first Jenna stood frozen to the spot as he started to fall like a tree in the middle of the woods, but she didn't stay to see him hit the ground. She spun and ran, grateful when the cool air of the morning hit her heated skin.

She scanned the parking lot for a cattle trailer. Boy, was this place full. Two cowboys in the truck stop diner had been discussing the cattle they were carrying down the road to Wishing Springs. Her luck seemed good today, because that was where she was trying to get. She'd slipped out back to the women's restroom, figuring since her bladder had a baby sitting on it she better prepare for the journey.

She'd been trying to leave when the drunk had come in. He'd been watching her and had obviously followed her out.

Yet, her good luck returned, and she finally spied the dusty silver Dodge hitched to a long cattle trailer filled to the hilt with bawling cattle. Relief washed through her so sweet it made her breathless. Though maybe the breathless part came from the fact that she was seven months pregnant. Moving as quickly as she could, she faltered when a stabbing pain stole her breath. Had she strained something with the force of her swing?

By the time she reached the trailer, she hadn't come up with any great ideas on how she could get inside. Whew, cattle did not travel politely — she had to hold her nose at the stench. It was a mess in there, but if she had to, inside was where she would get. Easing to the back of the truck, instead, she peeked into the bed. *Yes.* There was a tarp spread out over something lumpy. Whatever it was filled the back end and large sacks of feed secured the tarp.

Ignoring the pain radiating through her, Jenna hiked her short leg up to the high bumper then hoisted herself over the tailgate and into the bed. Just as she made it, she spotted the two cowboys crossing the lot toward her. She wasted no time crawling under the tarp and burrowing as deeply as she could beneath it. Curling around her baby, she bit back a cry of pain and prayed the cowboys didn't need to look under the tarp.

Maggie stared at the camera that would film everything she did from the moment they said roll, or whatever it was the cameraman would say. Was it *action*? He'd shout it then snap that chalkboard thingy. No, that was movies — there were no "do overs" on this interview. They could cut and splice, but they only had what she could give them.

Her mouth went dry and she pressed a hand to her stomach. *No pressure — and no throwing up, Maggie.*

Her stomach rolled as if taunting her. This would *not* be a repeat of her seventh grade play disaster. She'd finished that fiasco off by knocking over the castle set — it crashed to the ground like a row of dominoes and she tossed her cookies right there on the knight in shining armor's feet . . . she'd done it again when she'd arrived home. Threw up on the policeman's shoes. She glanced at Tru Monahan's shiny boots and was glad that this interview would be done sitting down.

Taking a deep breath, she watched as he took the seat across from her in the booth. Behind him sat a swarm of rodeo photos, many of them signed. The cafe even had light fixtures made out of galvanized feed buckets, branding irons bent and welded together to form lamp shades, and sought-after stirrups that just happened to come from the Four of Hearts Ranch stirrup business run by Tru's brother Bo — Amanda had given her a little background. The Monahan brothers had a lot going on.

Tru met her gaze across the scarred wooden table, seeming to shut out the signed photos of him filling the wall beside them. The camera crew had clearly chosen this booth on purpose.

"Are you ready?" the cameraman asked from behind the heavy camera sitting on the tripod just a couple of feet away from them.

Tru tipped his head toward her. "Shoot away when you're ready."

Sighing inwardly, Maggie gave her best smile to the camera guy and hoped it didn't look as puny as it felt. She met Tru's waiting gaze once more — ignoring the tickling sensation in the pit of her stomach. She glanced at Amanda's list of questions, thankful she hadn't had to come up with her own.

She looked up just as the camera guy gave her the signal and they were on . . .

"What's she sayin'?" Clara Lyn Conway asked, elbowing Reba Moorsby in the ribs in her attempt to get a peek out the kitchen door at the interview. "It isn't every day we get television people in Wishing Springs, and I don't aim to miss a minute of it."

Reba bumped Clara with her ample hip and shot her a perturbed look. "You're shorter than me, bend down a bit and we can both see what's going on."

"For cryin' out loud," Clara harrumphed, hunching down to squint through the crack. "The poor girl looks jumpy."

"That's what I think. But what young woman wouldn't be looking into the eyes of that hunk of burnin' love? It is an undeniable fact that our little town can produce some great stock when it comes to cattle, horses, and fine-lookin' cowboys."

"It's the water," Clara Lyn whispered, straining to hear the questions.

"Agreed. Did you ever think Tru Monahan would grow up to put us on the map?" Reba asked.

Clara Lyn chuckled. "There was a time I wasn't sure that boy would grow up. After his cancer, reckless was his middle name."

"I don't blame him for having a live-like-you-were-dying attitude. I'm just glad he got over it. Or *lived* through it."

"That's the truth," Clara Lyn said. "Look, that poor reporter is practically sweating bullets."

"I know. She's having to look at those papers more than she is looking at him. Oh, shhh, here she goes again. I think."

"About time too."

As they watched, the reporter finally

found her place and started reading the question.

Her voice shook at first. "You have had a fantastic year repeating your reign as champion," she said. "To what do you owe your success?"

Shorty was standing in the dining room with his arms crossed, watching the private interview. Suddenly he moved over into Clara Lyn and Reba's line of vision, his big bulky form totally blocking everything.

Clara Lyn couldn't believe it.

"Get out of the way, Shorty," she and Reba hissed in unison, shoving the door wider and sticking their heads out the opening just in time to see Tru give the reporter a crooked grin.

"Hard work and a great horse."

"Oh, goodness," Clara fanned herself. "That drawl, grin, and twinkle together should be outlawed."

The reporter's gaze locked with Tru's.

"You," she faltered, biting her lip for a moment, obviously overwhelmed by their hometown cowboy. "You trained your horse, didn't you?"

"I can't believe it," Clara whispered excitedly. "She didn't look at her blasted notes for that question."

"It's about time," Reba snorted.

"I did," Tru answered, with ease. "I'm a trainer before I'm a rider. A good horse makes any cowboy look better than he is."

"Ha," Clara exclaimed in a hushed exclamation.

"Shhh, Clara. They'll hear us."

"That boy was born in the saddle —"

Shorty turned and glared at them, Clara and Reba yanked their heads back into the kitchen, the door swung closed and Reba hit a metal pan with her elbow, sending it flying. It clattered on the wood floor like cymbals.

Shorty came barreling through the door. "What is going on? Y'all are supposed to be quiet. They'll hear you. Now, if you two can't hold it down, then you're going to have to leave."

Clara Lyn scowled up at the lumbering man. "Okay, our lips are zipped. Now get out there and let us get back to the interview. And stay out of our way."

Looking skeptical, Shorty obeyed, backing out of the door with his finger to his lips.

Clara Lyn and Reba took their positions and continued watching — this was the most excitement they, or Wishing Springs, had seen in a decade and they planned on having firsthand knowledge of the event to pass on to their friends and clients over at

33

the Cut Up and Roll hair salon. Why, Pebble Hanover, owner of the Sweet Dreams Motel, whacking that rascal Rand Radcliff on the head with a mop and calling the cops didn't even come close to this. Not close at all. Drunk as a skunk the old coot had been, and trying to steal a kiss, which he'd been most assuredly sorry about when he woke up behind bars the next morning with a lump the size of Texas on his forehead.

Nope, this was news, and if they had to be quiet then they'd suffer through. Girls had to have some excitement in their lives and this was about as good as it got in Wishing Springs.

Yes, indeed, Clara Lyn thought excitedly, things were looking up.

Maggie's hands shook as she turned the first page of questions over and stared at the second page while Tru's last statement rang in her ears. *"I'm a trainer before I'm a rider. A good horse makes any cowboy look better than he is."* Nothing could make him look better than he already did.

The thought only flustered her more. She wondered if he could see how out of her element she was. The pages shook and she closed her eyes knowing that she was flubbing this interview. If the station wasn't able

34

to use this, then she was doomed. She scanned the questions and laid the papers flat, hoping the camera didn't catch her shaking hands or the rattle of the pages. Silent moments were ticking by as she tried frantically to find her way among the questions. *Where was my place?*

"So you write a column for the newspaper?"

His question was unexpected. Her head shot up. Tru was smiling calmly at her. Her mind went blank. "Ah, wh—"

He dipped his head, his eyes holding hers. " 'Gotta Have Hope.' Right?"

He was interviewing *her.* Saving her from the dead space she'd left open — but still *she* was supposed to be doing the interviewing. Maggie felt about as tall as the saltshaker sitting on the table. Surely they could shelve this disaster and send Amanda out here when she was well. What they should have done in the first place. Her making a fool out of herself was not going to do the rankings any good for television or her column. He chuckled, leaned forward, and laid a hand on hers. Maggie's eyes flared wide with shock. A small, sharp gasp puffed from her from the tingling warmth of his touch.

The camera zoomed in on their hands —

she saw it on the monitor.

"It's okay, Maggie, you can relax. Why are you so nervous? I'm really not a scary guy. At least not that I know of. Kids don't cry when I come in the room or anything."

Relax? Ha! "I'm not scared," she said, knowing almost the entire population of Houston would see him holding her hand. There was no touching in an interview. His touch, firm and warm, looked comforting and calming to the cameras when in fact it had thrown her system into utter chaos and had her stomach erupting in fire-winged butterflies. Fireworks were exploding in her skull.

She could hardly breathe for the "smoke."

On the one hand she was amazed by her overpowering attraction toward him and angry that he was overstepping boundaries and turning his well-known charm on her for the camera!

That slow smile spread across his face — he knew she was scared and so did everyone else.

Speak, Maggie. "Well, just a little. I mean —" she gave up trying to smooth over the situation. After all, they could edit this out. "I'm a writer. I don't normally do interviews. My friend got sick and they sent me. I am so sorry about this."

He chuckled softly. His thumb was making tiny, soothing circles on the back of her hands. It was not helping her calm down in the least.

"It's okay," he assured her. "When I did my first interview, I was a nervous wreck, but it comes with the territory, and I got better. I just learned to relax and be myself." He nodded toward the camera like it was his best friend.

And it was. Maggie knew the camera behind her was zooming in on him. The man was gorgeous and she'd eat her shoe if he'd ever been nervous in his life. He looked at that camera like he looked at her. He had a way of making a woman feel like she was the only woman in the room, and she knew from seeing him in other interviews that that look translated through the camera lens.

He chuckled. "Breathe, Maggie. Come on."

Maggie sucked in a breath, willing herself to pull her hands away and gain control of this debacle. She'd let everything go south. She snatched her hands away and grabbed up the papers, snapping them on the table to straighten them into a pile. A question came to her and she blurted — "You must be a really great horse trainer. Who did you learn it from?" In her rush, she came off sounding like a school kid eager to share the correct answer to a problem.

He leaned back in the booth. His expression said he was laughing at her fumbling questions, like anyone else who watched this would be doing. Anger flashed through her. As irrational as it was to be getting mad at the man, it was all she could do not to glare at him across the table.

"My grandfather taught me," he said calmly, oblivious to Maggie's urge to whack him with the red folder of questions. "He had a knack of spotting a horse with potential to be a great Quarter Horse. And that was half the battle. People waste their time taking a horse with no inclination and trying to force them to cut."

Maggie had seen Quarter Horse competitions occasionally on TV and after Amanda had first booked this interview, they'd pulled up YouTube videos of Tru himself competing. Because of this she knew Quarter Horses weren't called "cutting" horses for nothing. They were lightning quick on their feet, moving in a way that would stop a calf from getting past them and driving it where the horse wanted it to go. If the rider wasn't competent in moving with the sudden direction changes of the horse, then he could easily end up in the dirt. Riding and staying in the saddle took great skill.

"It doesn't look easy to do. It sounds like you had a great teacher," she said, proud that she managed to sound calmer than she felt.

"The best."

"I'm sure you had the talent that it takes to be as great as you are too. Do you think your grandfather had the ability to spot that in a person like he could with a horse?"

He grinned. *Why was he grinning so big?*

"He taught me everything he knew, but Pops was so good, he could take a novice and have them riding like a pro in a few weeks."

"Really. *Anyone?*"

"Sure, it just takes know-how and want-to. And a good horse."

"That seems like it takes away from your grandfather's ability."

He shook his head. "No, not at all. Pops had talent and he taught me everything he knows. You need to know what you're do-ing. Because of what he taught me, I could take a novice and do the same thing."

"That seems like a pretty strong declara-tion. I don't think anyone could teach me to ride, much less *stay* in the saddle on a cutting horse." A chortle of disbelief escaped her.

He leaned in, placing his hands on the table between them. "Maggie, you are much too hard on yourself."

"I am just honest. I know my limitations."

His eyes dug into hers. "I could teach you to ride a cutting horse."

"Wanna bet?" Maggie gasped, shocked by her uncharacteristic words. What was she doing?

Tru's expression lit up. "Sure. You up for it? I'd enjoy bringing out the cowgirl in you."

"Cowgirl —"

"He could do it too!" Someone exclaimed as the swinging door of the kitchen suddenly flew open and two sixtyish-looking women lunged forward into the room.

"You could do it," they gushed together.

One was slightly plump with big eyes and pale silver hair that looked freshly done in the latest Betty White style. The second was taller with brown hair cut short and just finger combed behind her ears. Both of them wore big grins and wide eyes.

Everyone in the room turned to stare at them. It was obvious they'd been caught eavesdropping on the interview.

Shorty had swung their direction, storm

clouds in his expression.

"Oops, *sor*-ry," singsonged the Betty White look-alike as they both grimaced apologetically and waved at the camera which was now pointed their way.

Silence rang momentarily in the room as they backed up through the door, still waving, and disappeared into the kitchen.

A frowning Shorty stomped after them.

All the while the camera kept filming.

It was a regular circus. However, Maggie was at least relieved that their bursting into the room saved any more conversation about Tru teaching her how to ride. This interview had run its course — straight down the tubes, it had gone. It was time to wrap it up.

"Admiring fans?" she asked.

He was smiling, not appearing the least bit surprised by the event. "Friends. That's Clara Lyn and Reba from the Cut Up and Roll hair salon. They and the rest of their buddies keep Wishing Springs in the know about everything." His contagious grin had the camera crew laughing.

"They do sound like fun."

"Oh, you can say that again. They're full of mischief. Falling out of the kitchen in front of a TV camera while eavesdropping is normal for them."

"Well, on that note, I think we'll wrap this up." She wanted out of there. Home and quiet solitude. And no camera.

And no Tru.

"Wait," he said. "I hate to leave everyone thinking we can't get you to ride a cutting horse. Let me at least introduce you to my horse. Amanda had wanted me to show him off for the camera. He's out in the trailer."

"No," she snapped too harshly, completely taken off guard. Amanda must have forgotten to tell her about this part.

"Come on now. The viewers would probably enjoy seeing him. He's a beauty. You're not afraid of him, are you?"

"I'm just not comfortable. I'm a city girl, after all."

His eyes warmed as they seemed to take in everything about her. "You certainly are. But, at this point I know the viewers out there would love to see you at least pet my horse."

Maggie swallowed hard and sweat dampened her armpits at the thought of stumbling out there on those rocks again with a camera rolling. And she wasn't good with animals. A horse was big.

Before she came up with a way out of this new kink in the plan, the overbearing cowboy was out of his seat and holding out his hand to her. There seemed no gracious way out of this fix other than to agree. Her hands clenched. She plastered on a fake smile — a cover for the urge to scream in frustration. She glanced at the cameraman — her last hope to stop this, but he already had the camera hoisted to his shoulder with a goofy grin. His helper was waving his hand in a circle that she knew meant "go with the flow."

Maggie slapped her hand into Tru's and shot to her feet. She had a very bad feeling about this . . . very bad indeed.

A few minutes later, tottering back across the rocky parking lot with the camera crew trailing, she gripped Tru's hand *and* her skirt as her hair whipped across her face. She was certain that no one on the face of the earth had ever looked more unprofessional.

"Crimson is my horse's name. He's a great horse," Tru said as they rounded the end of the trailer. "Don't run off. I'll unload him."

"Unload him?" Maggie laughed nervously. Running off was the best idea she'd heard all day. "But, y-you don't need to do that."

"Sure I do." Tru already had the trailer gate open and was stepping inside.

Maggie watched in disbelief. This interview had gone to the birds — or horse. Tru untied the powerful-looking animal and led him out into the parking lot. Maggie's insides quaked like an earthquake. She had never been good with animals. Small or large. The instant the horse emerged from the trailer, it spotted her and yanked hard at its rope with a loud nicker.

Maggie jumped back — too quickly — her blasted high heels wobbled, and that was all it took. She fell back and hit the ground like a cow crashing on an ice rink.

It was pathetic, painful in more ways than one, and a show of her complete klutziness.

Alarm rang through her as her gaze flitted to the wide-eyed cowboy, then shot to the camera.

It was pointing straight at her.

3

Tru headed back to the ranch after the interview. His conscience stung with regret for the way it had ended. He still couldn't believe Maggie had fallen like that. She'd told him she'd never been around horses, but he hadn't expected her to be that afraid. She had vehemently denied any fear, but nothing else explained the way she'd jumped back at the jerk of Crimson's head. That fear and those red heels had been hard on her pride, not to mention her backside. She was tough, though, no tears.

Only steam pouring from her ears as she'd glared fire and brimstone up at him.

Her quick recovery and the way she'd joked on-camera about her clumsiness had saved the interview from going south like a runaway bronc.

But her anger at him became evident when the camera stopped rolling and she tossed those shoes off and stalked barefoot across the rough rock to her car. That had to have bruised the bottoms of her feet, but she was obviously too angry to notice, and that made him feel more of a jerk than he already did.

He'd deserved it. He'd taken over that interview and left her no alternative but to go along with him.

But what could he do now?

He drove through the gate of the Four of Hearts and was still trying to find a solution as he drove past his Pops's house, then the barn, and stopped in front of his place. A long, stretched-out single-story house with a low-slung roof and a wide porch in the back. Growing up, this had been the foreman's house. Nothing fancy, but it suited Tru just fine.

One day, if he married, he'd build something bigger, something more suited to a woman, but there was a big "if" on the end of that thought. An "if" he was hoping to find an answer to in a couple of weeks after he heard from his oncologist. But right now, he had a ranch to run and a reputation to build for him and his horse program. A program he planned would last long after this time spent competing for championships that would keep sponsors knocking at his door and paychecks coming in.

He was on the road a lot, and he'd seen what that kind of life did to many families. And he'd been thinking about family a whole lot lately. Not that he could do anything about it right now with all these responsibilities to the ranch and his sponsors.

For now, his Pops's ranch being safe from foreclosure or takeover was priority.

"How'd it go?" Bo, his little brother by a year, asked, leading a bay horse out of the barn.

Tru closed the door of his truck and met him at the round pen. "It was interesting."

Bo shot him an appraising look. "Not the answer I was expecting. You hate interviews."

"Still do, but —" Maggie holding her skirt in a tornado of wind, her blonde hair and interview pages whirling about her. She'd looked about as put out when he'd driven up as anyone could have been staggering about in those red high heels. He smiled thinking of that first sight. Those fancy shoes were more worthless on that chunky white rock than a pair of spurs without boots. Though he had to admit her legs looked amazing in them.

"But what?"

Tru scrubbed his jaw. "My interviewer

wasn't a reporter. She got roped in to doing it when the real reporter called in sick. She was different."

"How so?"

"I have to admit it was the first interview I actually enjoyed." He told Bo what had happened and how she was a mess asking the questions until he got her riled up on camera and she started asking her own. Bo threw his head back and laughed when Tru told him about his stupid remarks. And her challenge. He didn't say anything about her falling. The odds of the town not finding out after the local ladies told the tale were low, but it wouldn't be because he repeated it. He knew the station would delete that portion from the interview, along with much more — like him taking over asking the questions. They'd salvage what they could and hope for the best.

"A bet? Not your smartest move ever," Bo said, having stopped grinning the instant Tru mentioned it.

"Don't I know it. You should have seen her, though. She was flustered so much I felt bad for her. And then she tossed out that 'you wanna bet' line and I just reacted."

"I can already see the camera crews following y'all around," Bo teased.

Tru's smile turned into a scowl. "That's

48

not happening. They'll cut all of that. The station won't want their reporter falling apart on camera, and that was exactly how Maggie looked."

"Maggie, huh? Did you get her number?"

"You don't let up, do you? She lives in Houston. And she's a writer for some column in the *Tribune*. I did not get her number. Despite not being a TV reporter, she's still in the journalism profession."

Bo's left brow cocked. "A column, huh? Hey, maybe she'd write a column on you, big brother. Make you famous again."

"Funny." Tru knew his brother was ribbing him about his stupid move of the year, dating a high-strung actress that he'd met at a charity fund-raiser of one of his sponsors. He'd ended up on the tabloids more times than he'd wanted, and the last time it had been a big mess. One that he could only blame on himself. What had he expected from a media-hungry starlet?

It had ended badly when he'd tried to end the relationship, taught him a big lesson, and made him more grateful for his home than ever. He was glad to be back where he belonged for a little while; here on his ranch, on the soft disked earth of his arena with his horses.

He didn't make mistakes with horses.

That wasn't always the case with people.

As he'd proven once more with Maggie Hope.

The truck slowed, bumped roughly from the pavement, and came to a halt.

Jenna waited beneath the tarp, holding her breath. When she heard the truck doors slam, she prayed the cowboys wouldn't need anything from beneath the tarp. Seconds ticked by that felt like minutes.

She was cramped from being in the rough truck bed balled up like she was, but she was farther down the road and that was all that mattered. The voices faded away as the cowboys walked away from the truck, and after a few minutes, she knew she had to take a chance and see where they were. Slowly, she eased the tarp from over her face. All was clear, no sounds anywhere near. Groaning involuntarily with stiffness — being curled up for more than two hours would do that — she eased up and peeked over the edge of the truck. It was a good thing the roads they'd traveled had been in good shape because rough roads hurt like a son of a gun.

They'd stopped at a gas station and it was pretty deserted. She didn't have a clue where they were but, thanks to her little baby, Jenna's bladder was about to explode. She had to go.

Hoisting her considerable bulk over the tailgate, she hurried to climb to the ground then ducked behind the trailer out of sight of the windows of the convenience store. She wanted to go find the cowboys and just ask them straight up if they'd give her a ride to the home for pregnant girls, but she hadn't been having much luck on this trip. The men she'd run into were not hero material. Her life in a nutshell.

Her stomach growled and she tried to remember when she'd last eaten. She'd managed to swipe a piece of uneaten toast and a strip of bacon off a plate of leftovers at the truck stop the night before, before the tired waitress had gotten around to clearing the table near her. But other than that, she hadn't eaten anything for at least twenty-four hours. Before catching this ride, she'd hidden in the back of a hay hauler and slept curled up between the bales when the truck had stopped at the truck stop for the night. It had been a pure stroke of luck that she'd overheard that the cowboys were heading this way.

Though Jenna had strained something in her side when she'd swung that plunger, the sharp pains had subsided and she no longer feared that she might be in labor.

Or at least she hoped she wasn't.

Easing down the length of the cattle trailer, she kept her head down, stuffed her hands in the pockets of the bulky sweatshirt she wore, and walked from the protection of the trailer toward the building. Hopefully, if anyone saw her, they would assume she had walked up — from where she wasn't sure, since the ragged station and convenience store looked to be out here alone at the crossroads.

Jenna followed the sidewalk along the side of the building hoping the restrooms were on the outside. The old store looked like it had been converted from a gas station way before her time, so maybe . . . yes. There was the tiny one-room restroom and it wasn't locked. Relieved, she slipped inside and slid the bolt on the door. To her surprise, the place, despite appearing rustic on the outside, was clean — sparkled, in fact.

It was like heaven.

Jenna knew her chances of sneaking back into the bed of that truck were not good. She'd just have to figure something else out later. Right now she couldn't resist the chance to scrub some grime off of her face and body. She sniffed the soap and closed her eyes — pure bliss . . . especially when the soap dispenser was full of that pink soap that smelled like bubble gum.

And the paper towel bin was full.

If there was one thing Jenna had learned, it was to take advantage of the good things when they came along. Because more than likely it would be a long stretch of the bad before "Mr. Goodlife" showed his head and anything good happened to her again.

Turning on the hot water, Jenna sighed with pleasure, stripped off her shirt, and draped it over the doorknob, then she filled her hand full of the bubblegum scented soap.

This was definitely one of the better things in life.

At least her life so far. She wanted more for her baby than what she had to offer, and finding the ad in the newspaper for Over the Rainbow had been exactly the miracle she'd been praying for. When she'd gone to the library and looked it up on the Internet she'd known this was where she could find help for her baby.

It *had* to be a good place. It just had to be.

She couldn't believe anything else.

Jenna held tight to the idea that if she could just get to the home at Wishing Springs everything was going to be okay.

She just needed to get there.

Two miles from the Bull Barn, Maggie was still seething over the interview when she spotted a teenage girl walking slowly, haltingly, down the shoulder of the road. She was small and wore a bulky sweatshirt, but something about the way she walked, kind of a waddle, had Maggie believing that the girl was pregnant. The kid's face was beet red and she held one hand pressed to her side, like she had a catch in it.

What was the girl doing all the way out here?

As she drove by the girl, Maggie continued to watch her in the rearview. Saw her turn as if to watch Maggie pass her by with a look so lost and alone that icy fingers of the past grasped Maggie's heart, squeezing tight, sending a chilling ache through her. Maggie had once been a teenage girl lost and alone needing help. Her foot had already stepped to the brake, when suddenly the girl bent forward, then crumpled into herself and sank to the ground.

Maggie's foot slammed hard on the brake, tires screeching. Images of herself alone, in trouble, and in need crashed into her with the force of her foot on the brake. Spinning the car around in a sharp U-turn, her heart racing, Maggie pulled to a halt on the shoulder not far from the young woman.

The girl had not passed out, and was watching her from where she sat. It crossed Maggie's mind that this could easily be a setup, a scam, but she couldn't think about that right now. Her gut told her this kid needed help.

"Hi," Maggie called, jumping out of the car and hurrying toward the girl. Thankfully there was no quartz gravel anywhere to be seen, and so she could actually move without breaking her leg. "Can I help you?"

The girl had curly brown hair, the kind of curls that were big and loopy and sprang out haphazardly around her face. Her eyes, huge pools of green, looked dull with pain. She couldn't be more than sixteen — seventeen at the most. Maggie was thankful she'd stopped.

"I'd tell you that I didn't need any help, but that would be a lie, and I'm trying to cut back on them."

Her dry wit made Maggie smile. "Then I'm here to help. I'm Maggie," she said, crouching down beside the kid.

"Jenna," the teen managed and gritted her teeth at the same time.

"Where do you hurt, Jenna? You're pregnant, right?"

Jenna nodded. "I'm not having contractions, I don't think." She closed her eyes, her soft brown brows meeting in the middle as she fought off the pain before looking back at Maggie. "I've had a long twenty-four hours."

There was defeat in Jenna's voice and Maggie got the feeling this girl didn't often let strangers or anyone see this side of her. That had Maggie all the more determined to help her.

"Here, let's get you in the car. I'm taking you to the hospital."

"No."

Her cry was so sharp Maggie froze. "Okay. So what do you want to do?"

"I have to get to this place." She dug a neatly folded piece of paper from her pocket and handed it to Maggie.

"It's a home for pregnant girls. I need to get there before I go anywhere. They can help me."

"But I'm worried you need help now." Maggie took the paper and had to tear her gaze from the fierce plea of Jenna's eyes. *Help me* they cried silently.

"If you're not taking me there, then I'll wait right here till someone who will stops to help me," Jenna said, grit filling her eyes and her voice.

The paper turned out to be a newspaper clipping with a picture of a house and an address for a home for unwed mothers, Over the Rainbow. The address was here in Wishing Springs.

Looking at it, Maggie made a decision. "Okay, then let's get you in the car and we'll plug this in my GPS and get you there pronto."

Relief washed over Jenna's expression. "You're not just telling me that, are you?"

Maggie's heart clutched. How badly had this girl been hurt in her life? "I wouldn't lie to you. I promise."

"Then help a poor whale up."

Maggie chuckled and placed her hands beneath Jenna's arms, spread her high-heeled feet wide for stability, and with Jenna's help they heaved her to a standing position.

"Whew. I thought I was down for the count on that one."

The girl had humor. "Naw. You're made of tough stuff. You'd have gotten up and walked to this place if I hadn't shown up."

They were almost to her car now and Maggie pulled the door open and Jenna sank into the soft cream leather seat.

"This is so nice," she sighed, snuggling back against the seat.

Maggie noticed she looked pale and hurried to get to her side and plug the address into the GPS. It came up, and to her happy surprise, the home wasn't too far down the road. "Did you know you were this close?"

"An old man working at the gas station back there told me it wasn't too far."

Maggie put the car in gear and did another U-turn to head back down the road. "How did you get out here? Did you hitch-hike?" The very idea horrified Maggie.

Trepidation filled Jenna's eyes, reminding Maggie again of the uncertainty she'd felt at that age after she'd fled one of her mother's boyfriends for the last time and knew she was better off striking out on her own rather than being a sitting duck in the apartment with her mom. Maggie had lived with her mother's disdain all of her life. Knowing she'd been unwanted from birth had always been something Maggie was aware of from the first moments that she could recall. That knowledge had helped Maggie finally realize that leaving was her best option because there would be no protection from her mother. Especially when she was doped up and partying. No help. No sympathy. And so Maggie's only choice had been to run away. She shut down the flood of memories and focused on the girl.

Jenna looked her way after a few beats of silence. "I got someone I know to take me to a truck stop, and I listened to conversations in the diner till I heard someone talk about heading this direction. I had watched what trucks they'd gotten out of, so then I tried to find a way to ride. When I found a truck going the right direction, I'd stow away till the next stop."

Cringing, Maggie imagined this pregnant girl fending for herself. There was more to the story, she could see it in her face, but she didn't press. She'd just met Jenna; it didn't matter that when she looked into her eyes, she felt like she'd known her all of her life.

The GPS signaled the next driveway was the one they were looking for.

Turning onto the long drive, they headed toward the pretty house that sat at the top of the hill.

It was the same as the advertisement.

Jenna had held her side the whole ride, and a glance her way confirmed that she was silently enduring pain. Maggie was thankful they were here. She pulled to a halt in front of the house.

"I'll go see if there's anyone home," she

offered and pushed open her door, almost tripping over herself hurrying to get out. Truth was, Maggie didn't know much about having a baby. She was twenty-five and hardly ever had the opportunity to hold a baby, much less change a diaper or know how to take care of a pregnant woman — or girl in this case.

She needed help and she needed it now.

That didn't mean she didn't have a hopeful heart about kids, though. Maggie wanted kids. A whole houseful of the little darlings so she could love on them and be loved by them. Nothing in this world was sweeter to Maggie than that dream. Only problem was, she was going to have to find a man who could give them to her, and that was the hard part. First she had to find one she could let herself trust. And trust didn't come easy for Maggie.

Even with her runaway thoughts and in her rush up the sidewalk, Maggie noticed the red geraniums filling pots beside the door, welcoming visitors to Over the Rainbow. This appeared to be a welcoming place. She pushed the doorbell and glanced back at the car. Jenna had gotten out and was standing beside the door holding onto the doorframe as she bent slightly, obviously in pain. Maggie feared she should have rushed the kid to the hospital. Now no one was going to be here and Maggie could just see herself having to deliver a baby right there in the grass.

"Come on. Open. Pleas—" the door opened and there was a woman standing there. "Yes. Thank you. I have a friend, a girl I picked up on the road, and she was coming here and —" Maggie pointed toward Jenna. The woman moved forward and stared out the door. "She's in pain and insisted I bring her here."

"Mother," the woman, not more than thirty, called over her shoulder as she wasted no time and jogged down the sidewalk to Jenna.

Maggie felt totally and completely useless as she watched the woman put her arm around Jenna and help her up the path. Another woman, older, yet still small and brisk, rushed from the house and jumped on the other side of Jenna, asking medical questions. Jenna answered her, meeting Maggie's gaze as she shuffled by. Maggie stood in the doorway, not certain what to do, feeling like an intruder now. After all, she'd only driven Jenna here.

"Don't go," Jenna called, looking over her shoulder.

Maggie's heart lurched in her chest and she fought back tears. "I'm stickin' like glue," she said, giving a shaky smile and stepping inside the doorway. "I'll be here if you need me."

Jenna smiled weakly as she disappeared through another doorway, and that tight smile touched Maggie all the way to the darkest corner of her heart. To the spot where the little girl inside of her hid — the scared little girl who had longed to hear someone say those words to her so long ago.

But no one ever had.

4

The knowledge that she might have dumped her career down the drain made for a sleepless night, that and thinking about Jenna. The girl hadn't had the baby and she was in good hands. Peg and Lana Garwood, a wonderful mother and daughter team, ran Over the Rainbow.

Peg looked like she was in her late forties. She was a nurse practitioner/midwife and reminded Maggie of Sally Fields, a pretty brunette, trim and obviously feisty — she took charge of the situation immediately. Lana, her daughter, was a counselor and looked to be in her early thirties — which, if Maggie's age assumptions were correct, meant that Peg had been a teenage mother herself. They ran the shelter/home with love and a mission. By the time Maggie had driven away with a promise to call back and check on Jenna, she'd felt good about the girl's situation. Of course she didn't know much more about Jenna than she had upon picking her up off the side of the road, but she still sensed a kindred spirit. She'd felt good and hopeful for the girl as she'd headed back to Houston.

But as the miles had ticked away, the reality of her situation came racing back to Maggie — she'd done a terrible interview and really had no idea what this meant for her career.

By morning, if she could have, she would have hidden in her apartment for the rest of her life. Instead, she was standing in line at the coffee shop around the corner from the *Tribune* office getting a cup of courage before heading in.

She'd been summoned.

It was going to take a double shot of caffeine to help her face the inevitable disappointment of all of her superiors.

The coffee shop was hopping today. Maggie stood with her back to the wide-screen television over in the seating area. Many of the regulars sat and drank their coffee and ate their muffins as they watched *Wake Up with Amanda.* Maggie never had time or the inclination to sit in the busy place, preferring solitude to do her writing.

The line moved forward and the lady beside her tugged her arm.

"Isn't that you?"

"Excuse me?" Maggie said, not under-standing.

"There." The lady pointed to the flat-screen TV.

Maggie gasped. The interview she'd done with Tru Monahan was playing. *No.*

"It *is* you," the lady declared accusingly, then spun back to watch the interview.

It was playing the part where Tru was holding her hand. Maggie's stomach dropped to her knees. They were showing the entire interview.

Other people had begun to look at her. Herb, the man behind the counter who had been serving her coffee almost every day for the last year, did a double take.

"Hey, Maggie, you're on TV."

"Yeah," she laughed, backing out of the door. "Gotta run," she called, and set out for the office at a fast clip. What was going on? There had been a mistake. There was no other reason they would show that entire interview otherwise.

She caught the elevator and tapped her foot anxiously waiting for the fourth floor. The doors had barely opened when her boss spotted her from across the expansive office from her doorway. "Maggie," she rasped, waving her over.

65

Now in her sixties, Helen Davenport had smoked like a train all of her life and just recently given up the habit. It was a little too late for her skin, which was as wrinkled as a Shar Pei's and her voice was as raspy as gravel in a mixer.

"My office. Now."

Her steps faltering, Maggie wove through the cubicles feeling all eyes on her as she went. This was it. There had been some horrible mistake. She'd now embarrassed the newspaper and the network.

Ms. Davenport closed the door after she'd entered and then hurried to take her seat behind her very large desk. "Sit, sit," she said absently, waving Maggie to one of the two pale blue chairs across from her. She was all smiles — that alone was scary. Helen Davenport rarely smiled.

Maggie sank into the first chair; it was easy since she felt like she'd swallowed a case of horseshoes. She attempted a weak smile, but said nothing. What could she say?

"So, that was some interview."

"About that — I'm so sorry."

"Sorry? Are you kidding me? We all thought the bet you threw out for Tru was pure genius. The station is so excited they aired it this morning. Did you catch it? The phones are buzzing with requests to see Tru

Monahan teach you to ride a Quarter Horse."

Maggie hadn't gotten much past the genius statement. Were they kidding? "But, I was just rattled, and blurted that out because I'd be hopeless on a horse."

"That's what I love about you, Maggie, you never boast. You sell yourself short every time. Let me give you a word of advice. In this business, being humble gets you nowhere. Actions speak louder than words, and yesterday you spoke volumes. You're a hit. Well done."

"But, I don't understand."

Ms. Davenport's crinkled red lips spread wider. "What's there to not understand? This is a win-win situation. This will help your column, because you are going to write about your experience weekly. You'll document as you go and still give some advice. But don't worry, you'll have plenty of space, because we are going to allot an extra slot for a continuing progress report. You and the paper win with better ratings, the station wins with the publicity this is garnering and the follow-up special they'll air in the end, and Tru Monahan's sponsors will win because of the advertising spotlight this will put on them."

"While I do what?" Dread formed like a

lead rock in the pit of Maggie's stomach. She wanted to be completely confused about what her boss was talking about, but the more she'd talked the clearer the picture had become. "You surely aren't expecting to follow up on this bet? It was a silly blunder. He would never agree to this."

"Don't look so bewildered." Helen Davenport stopped smiling, her eyes narrowed. "He'll have no choice but to agree. Just as you have no choice, Maggie. This is golden. You will go there and you'll go there for two months. I'll spell your assignment out clearly. You'll write a weekly article on the town or your training — anything that will grab the reader's attention. You'll find some interesting angle and hopefully give us some juicy insider info on this cowboy for our female readers."

"But —"

"Hold on, I'm not finished. You'll also continue to do the 'Gotta Have Hope' column, answering four letters a week. It'll be good, Maggie. And at the end of the two months Amanda will come out, film you competing in a cutting completion, and do an interview with you and Tru. Then the network will air it as a TV special. Maggie, I'm giving you a major shot here. You'll do this or your column is done."

Maggie's breath evaporated, and she coughed, *"Excuse me? You can't be serious?"*

Had she really said that to her boss?

Ms. Davenport's gaze turned to darts pinning Maggie to her chair. "Perfectly serious."

"But my readership is growing. They're comfortable with how things are."

"Your numbers are stagnant, Maggie. We need something to shake them up. Draw more in."

"But —"

"No buts, Maggie. This is done, so you are either on board or out the door."

Maggie's mouth dropped open. *Out the door?* But what about Tru? He didn't strike her as the type who would take being put in a corner well.

She could not lose her column. She just couldn't.

It was all she had.

No one knew how important that column was to her. There had been a time when she'd felt so hopeless, so alone . . . and now she felt that same desperation in some of the letters she received from readers. She gave them advice. She gave them a sounding board.

She gave them a place to not feel so alone.

She could not abandon them . . . the very idea had her feeling . . . lost.

She — she could not lose her column.

Swallowing the cotton clogging her throat, she met her boss's stare. Slowly Maggie nodded. "What do I have to do?"

It was clear. She was going to go back to Wishing Springs and make a fool out of herself learning to ride a horse that could turn on a dime and toss her in so many directions it wasn't going to be funny. And somehow she was supposed to be able to compete in some kind of cutting trial at the end of two months. *Sure* she would — and she would do it because her job depended on it.

"So you have to go along with this crazy setup?" Jarrod Monahan studied Tru from across the desk in Tru's office. "Your agent actually said you *had* to go along with this?"

Setup was the accurate word, Tru thought, meeting his older brother's skeptical eyes. "Frank said my sponsors see me taking this challenge as a good thing. They've been in talks all evening and morning with the paper and TV conglomerate. They're going to build this up in print and do lead-ins about it on *Good Morning with Amanda Jones* or *Wake Up with Amanda* or whatever the name of that show is. Then I'll pick a competition for Maggie to compete in and they'll film it for a TV special."

"Is that all?" Bo hooted with laughter. Tru ignored him.

"And how long do you have?" Jarrod continued, not laughing.

"Two months. The sponsors are going to spend a lot of money advertising on that time slot."

"You can't get out of your contract?" Bo asked, having reined in his laughter. He was sprawled in the thick leather armchair across the desk from Tru, his long legs stretched before him, his dusty boots crossed at the ankles. He'd been the one who'd called Tru earlier and told him to turn on the TV. His agent had called a few minutes later.

"Ironclad on this. Basically, I'm theirs." Tru's gut twisted and he stared out the window at the barn and riding arena of the Four of Hearts. Frank knew, as well as he and his brothers did, that Tru couldn't walk away even if he could get out of his contract. "They'd take me to court. They wouldn't want to, but this is business and they see dollar signs. Dollars trump everything."

Jarrod had a shoulder propped against the thick mantel and his arms crossed as he

71

studied Tru from across the room. Tru could almost see the wheels churning behind his blue-black eyes while he contemplated the situation — much like he would judge the quality of a herd of cattle before hauling them to market.

"What a mess," Jarrod said at last, his jaw tensing as if he'd found no solution but knew precisely what the future held.

Tru pushed himself to be more optimistic. "I got myself into it. I let my guard down."

Jarrod jerked away from the mantel. "Dad put us in this spot. If he hadn't tried to gamble this ranch away and everything we and Pops have worked for, then you wouldn't be forced to be on the road so much. So don't kid yourself." Of the three of them, Jarrod had viewed the fix their dad had left them in as an unforgivable betrayal, but mostly to their Pops. Tru and Bo hated it too, but Jarrod had hardened like tempered steel.

His brother was right. They hadn't known the mess they were in until their parents died in a small plane crash — only then did they learn their dad had leveraged their heritage to the max and then added on more debt, leaving them on the verge of losing everything.

How a man could lose that much and still

get loans for more had made Tru and his brothers furious.

Even with some fast thinking and then hard work, it had taken them over a year to make a dent in the debt and get the banks off their backs. But if he hadn't already been doing well, and if Bo hadn't already started making a name for the ranch with the stirrups, and if Jarrod hadn't been so savvy in cattle and ranch management, then Tru doubted if the bank would have given them a chance to save the ranch.

As it was, it took all three of them working to pay the debts in order to save this ranch from being foreclosed on and sold off to the highest bidders.

"Thanks to dear old Dad's irresponsibility," Bo said, sarcastically, "you're going to have to sacrifice yourself as a *TV star.*" Always the joker, he winced in mock horror. "If I were you I'd start watching out for those photo jerks hiding in the bushes," he added, hitting too close to home. Tru recalled the night he had found some jerk doing exactly that, trying to get a picture of him and Felicity. She'd loved it. Lucky for Tru, the low-life had gotten his photo and run before Tru had really messed up and punched him in the jaw.

"You're a barrel of laughs, little brother,"

Tru said.

"Hey, I'm just glad it's you and not me tied to those suits."

"Look, I'm not happy about it. But we all know we need the sponsor money. Thankfully it's not that bad." He'd lived through cancer as a six-year-old boy. A rare cancer that had taken two of his uncles before he'd been born, so he knew in the realm of bad things that this really wasn't earth shattering. "Bottom line is I shouldn't have let my guard down with Maggie Hope. I've learned better than most that a reporter will do whatever it takes to get a story. I shouldn't have been taken in by her naive act."

Tru rubbed the back of his neck. He'd been a fool to think just because she looked so innocent and sweet with those big eyes and that "break her neck" act that she wasn't a reporter with the skill set to get a good story, much less a decent interview. The reality was she'd set him up like a pro.

And he'd taken the bait.

And that was what bothered him the most about this entire deal. But nothing could be done about it. He'd dug this hole for himself. His agent had hinted that they'd especially liked the chemistry between the two on camera.

Chemistry — he'd felt it like a lightning

strike. That chemistry had gotten him into this fix. It had also jumped from that TV screen so vividly that he could almost feel it, and she was all the way back in Houston when the show aired. Of course there was the YouTube video that had mysteriously appeared — the cut portion of tape of Maggie's fall after being scared by Crimson. While it had been omitted from the actual interview, those flashing eyes and her refusal of his help to get on her feet and the ensuing sparks had caused a viral sensation. One that he wasn't happy about and he felt pretty certain she hated more than him.

"The sponsors want you to play that up — tastefully of course," Frank had said. "No *Bachelor* reenactments or anything, but . . ." Frank had left it at that.

"But what?" Tru had shot back. He had to draw the line somewhere or the sponsors would dictate his life.

It was a hard place for a man like him to be. But for his Pops he'd do anything.

But he didn't have to like it.

"So how long before it starts?" Jarrod asked, drawing him back from his thoughts.

He met his brother's gaze. "Two days."

He had two days before this fiasco started. Two days before his life was turned into a sixty-day circus.

5

Clara Lyn squirted the steel blue, temporary hair rinse on Greta Hogan's wet kinky perm, then began massaging the color into the woman's thinning hair. The blue rinse made Greta's hair about as blue as her lips had been the day she'd choked on a bite of Reba's maple-cured ham. Boy, had that been a day — Clara Lyn had used her Heimlich maneuver.

Yes, indeed she had. After practicing that life-saving move for years, she'd been proud to say it had worked like a gem. Well, after the initial tense moments of getting Greta out of the styling chair. Greta, no small girl, had been wedged into the chair tight. Clara Lyn had finally gotten her out and her arms wrapped around Greta's middle and started squeezing — just like she'd watched that teacher on the computer show her. One good yank and that piece of ham squirted out of Greta's throat, sailed across the room, and hit Reba square in the face.

Now, Clara Lyn looked at Greta in the mirror, swiped a dribble of blue rinse off her client's forehead, and shot her a knowing look. "We saw it in person. I tell you, that televised version didn't even begin to compare to what we witnessed with our own eyes. It was like the Fourth of July in there when Tru put his hand on Maggie Hope's. The sparks couldn't be disguised."

"True," Reba said. "But she didn't act like she was *glad* she reacted to all that testosterone that boy emits. She practically couldn't get out of Wishing Springs fast enough."

Clara Lyn rolled Greta's short blue hair on the small blue rollers, her fingers flying as she snagged up a section of hair with her rattail comb, smoothed it, and slapped a roller under it. "Maybe so, but Tru was so sweet. That's our boy. Always the gentleman."

Greta gave a knowing look. "There were those tabloid stories, though."

"Pure trash," Clara Lyn harrumphed. "They didn't know what they were talkin' about. Yes, he and that glamour girl were dating, but everyone is entitled to a few mistakes."

"Absolutely," Reba added. "It's so exciting that Maggie Hope is coming here to learn to ride. And she looked so sweet and scared that day. I can't imagine her getting on a cutting horse. Especially after, well . . . she landed on her tush. Those rocks had to hurt."

"Poor girl, had bruises, I imagine," Greta chimed in.

"Just shows she's got spunk." Clara Lyn paused her rolling. "If she can get up after that and make a few jokes she's all right in my book."

Greta nodded. "It'll be entertaining, that's for sure."

Reba didn't look so confident. "She was a little clumsy. That can't work too well with a Quarter Horse."

"Bah, could have just been those cute shoes," Clara Lyn waved off the remark.

"Still, Tru will have his work cut out for him," Reba persisted, then beamed. "But that will mean he will just have to help her all the more. Wouldn't it be wonderful if . . ."

"They fell in love," Clara Lyn finished for her.

"Yes," Reba said quickly. "They did look so good on camera, and he was so sweet trying to help her not make a fool out of herself."

"Could be a romance brewing," Greta offered.

Clara wrapped the last curl, giving both Reba and Greta her best mark-my-words look. "I recognized the chemistry right away. It's going to be interesting."

"And well-deserved. Tru Monahan has done nothing but work his bones weary since his father and mother died," Reba looked sad. "He has a lot on his plate that would weigh a lesser man down, though Tru seems to handle it well. But I worry about him on the road so much. He needs a good woman in his life."

"You're right, Reba," Clara Lyn scowled. "That Felicity loved creating drama for the paparazzi more than she did Tru."

"Exactly," Reba agreed. "I think he got mixed up with her just because he was lonesome."

"I think so too. Him and those brothers of his are all too young to be slaving away like they do," Clara said, leading Greta to the dryer. She placed the bubble hood over her head, still thinking of Tru and his brothers. There had been a lot of sorrow in their family, yet those boys had held on. She'd heard rumors that their dad had had a very bad gambling problem. Rumors, but no one knew for certain.

"We sure could use a little romance around here." Reba sighed. "It would sure liven things up, don't you think?"

"I totally agree."

Just like her, Reba was a sucker for Hall-mark movies and her DVR was set to record every upcoming mushy movie there was. Watching this newest development play out before them would be absolutely divine.

Maggie felt as if her editor and the powers that be had taken hold of the steering wheel of her Volkswagen Bug and driven her full throttle into the tangled underbrush of the Amazon. She once again had no idea what she was doing.

And a week after having her life hijacked, she was still miffed, embarrassed, and confused as she drove through the gates of the Four of Hearts Ranch. The sun blazed vividly in a pale blue Monday sky filled with feathery transparent clouds. She sighed and tried to be positive. Have a little hope.

This was a career booster.

A shot in the arm.

Who was she kidding — obviously it was a career saver, or at least a shot at saving her column. She'd had no idea the paper was thinking of dropping her column. She had a loyal and diverse audience, but when they'd talked, Amanda had reiterated what Helen Davenport had said. She had to increase her audience. Newspapers were all fighting for their lives, and their world had turned just as cutthroat as the television industry.

So, even Amanda was rooting for this to all work out. Her ratings were great but every opportunity was a boost that helped her maintain that status.

Maggie had taken that to heart and tried to be positive while giving the continual negative thoughts a swift kick to the curb.

The ranch was impressive — *like the cowboy.*

She kicked *that* thought to the curb even harder. But Tru Monahan was hard to forget. Hard not to think about. He was also the reason she was now not only on television looking like an idiot but also a YouTube sensation. It was awful — *and good for readership.*

Driving between the massive black pipe entrance of the Four of Hearts Ranch, its name wrought in large letters of metal above her, she focused on the details of the sign. The ranch's brand bracketed the name — a large number four with a narrow heart connected to the straight side of the number.

She'd learned through her research that Tru's grandmother had actually been the designer of the brand.

It was . . . *pretty.* She thought that said something nice about Tru's grandfather that he would let the slightly feminine logo stand. He must have cared for and valued his wife. That gesture spoke volumes to Maggie.

She wondered what it would feel like to have a man, a husband, who valued and cared for her. Maggie craved a loving husband and a house full of kids, but knew that the odds were against her ever having either.

Her family background, the emotional fears, and the subconscious scars she carried all too clearly made that seem like a hopeless dream. Though Maggie refused to let it define her. Her column was about holding out hope that one day those like herself, who were seeking true love and devotion would find it. "Gotta Have Hope" embodied the spirit of hope and believing that true love existed. That there was someone out there for everyone. Maggie just had no trust where men were concerned — she hoped she could open her heart up to the right man when he came along.

Her thoughts flew straight back to the moment in that interview when she'd felt . . . a connection between her and Tru, and she pushed that out of the way again. He was not that man.

Parking in front of the house, she pushed her door open — not giving herself time to even think about not getting out. She stepped out onto the red gravel. Her jogging shoes were much more suited to country life than the notorious red heels. *Those* were in her closet in Houston and would stay there, indefinitely.

She headed toward the front door. She could see a barn out behind the house and past that was a smaller house — a rambling single story of cedar and brick. The main house was white with a large front porch and a solid black door with a heavy brass knocker. The mournful cry of a dog echoed from inside. The wails grew more intense as she crossed the porch and knocked, turning into a frantic mixture of barks and very loud howls. What was going on? This was more than a hysterical pet announcing someone was at the door.

Maggie knocked again, harder. A crash sounded inside. Maggie stiffened. Okay, something was seriously wrong.

She was still trying to figure out what to do when she heard shuffling on the other side of the door and then it swung open and Maggie came face to face with a wide-eyed, lanky older man, in his early- to mid seventies. She hadn't known what she was expecting but this was not it.

His angular face, thin and weathered, appeared very much the face of a cowboy. The resemblance to Tru was unmistakable, though this man's dark brown hair was peppered with gray. Was this his grandfather? Was this "Pops" as Tru had called him affectionately? Not only did he resemble Tru, he was almost six feet tall and it was easy to see that he'd probably carried himself with the same straight-backed posture.

The dog, wherever it was, wailed louder and the older man's eyes grew wider. There was a blankness — a confusion — in their depths heightened by his frantic, panicked expression.

When the dog let out another endless yowl, the man waved his hands for her to come inside. "Help my baby," he said. "Help."

Feeling frantic and scrambled herself, Maggie didn't hesitate. "Is it your dog?" she asked, hurrying behind him as he led the way down a wide entrance hall, then cut left down a narrower hall.

"My puppy."

They entered a room dominated by a gigantic wooden bed. The headboard was made of carved logs and the footboard was nearly as massive. It took up the entire room. The thin man eased to his knees, obviously stiff with age and probably abuse from years of cowboy'n. Not waiting to follow, Maggie plopped down onto the floor. The terrified sounds were so loud now that they were in the room it was a wonder the bed wasn't hovering.

Yanking up the bedspread, Maggie found herself staring at — not a puppy, but the fattest Basset Hound she'd ever seen.

Why, the dog was wedged between the bed and the floor as if the bed had been dropped on top of it. How had it squeezed in there?

"Baby," the frail man said, now that he'd finally managed to get to the floor.

The term sounded so heartfelt that it tugged at Maggie's gut. His gaze reached out to her, pleading. Something wasn't right with this picture. To look at the man you would think he was fine, but his reactions were not right. Could this be dementia? Not that she had much contact with it. Whatever it was, the man needed help.

"It's okay," she urged, patting his arm. "I'll get you your baby."

The dog was now really wailing and yelping like she was poking it with a prod or something. It sounded like it was in agony. The man looked as if he were about to cry. Maggie didn't think twice. She dropped to her belly and scooted under the bed.

She sneezed three times in a row from the dust, causing the dog to scream more — just what she needed. She wedged herself under the bed to get to it. She grunted — not sure who was going to get her out and even more uncertain how she was going to get the plump Bassett Hound free. How had he gotten under here? Crawled under with the hindquarter of a buffalo and then eaten it? Or eaten a whole one?

"Hey, pooch, calm down," she urged, her rump scraping the bed frame as she moved deeper into the shadowy depths. The dog's eyes, white saucers of terror, glared at her.

She sneezed again and the pooch wailed louder. Now almost even with the animal, Maggie inched a little farther under, a tight squeeze for her hips.

"Come on." She reached out to the dog — not her smartest move. Second only to her crawling under the bed. The moment her fingers got close enough, the pooch hauled off and took a bite out of her.

"Ouch!" Maggie jerked sideways, she was so shocked. She was bleeding. The dog growled and suddenly she feared it might be able to come after her now that she was stuck.

Stuck — Maggie grunted and tried to

budge, but when she twisted sideways she wedged her shoulders more tightly between the bed and the floor.

"Come on," she gasped, wriggling, trying to budge. There was no use. Her shoulders hurt.

"Maggie?"

The familiar drawl sent a shot of warmth spreading through her. Hope flared and a fiery adrenaline hit every nerve ending in a euphoric rush.

Gripping her bleeding hand, she cocked her head so that she could see Tru. He stared at her from where he'd crouched down beside her feet. He placed his hand on her ankles and she forgot to breathe.

"Looks like you're having problems," he said, as if she was having trouble tying her shoelace instead of being wedged under the bed like a pig in a blanket.

"Hi." It was the only thing that popped into her brain. It wasn't lost to her that for the second time they'd met, she was in a crazy fix.

"What are you doing?" he asked, that oh-so-amazing grin on his face.

Only then did she realize the dog had stopped its incessant noise. She was getting past the wave of heat that had hit her — adjusting to his touch and the throbbing of her hand was responsible for that. "Um, I crawled under here to help this, this ungrateful mutt because your grandfather was upset. And it bit me. And now I'm stuck."

She glanced at her hand. She was holding it tightly to her chest. Blood oozed from the throbbing doggy-teeth-shaped wound in the flesh of the meaty part of her hand below her thumb.

"Solomon *bit* you?" Tru banged his head on the underside of the bed as he tried to see her hand better.

"Yes, and I'm stuck," she said, grumpily.

"Hang on," he snapped, then stood.

All she could see were his scuffed cowboy boots and jeans so faded they looked as soft as silk. He moved to the end of the bed where she couldn't see him any longer. She was left looking at the now-docile mutt.

"If I lift, can you get out?"

"I think so." The cramped quarters suddenly seemed to squeeze tighter and Maggie's heart raced. She sneezed again and instantly the dog began wailing.

"Okay," Tru called over the noise. "Ready?"

"Oh, boy, am I." It was all she could do not to start wailing right along with the pooch.

The bed lifted and blessed relief washed

88

over her. She didn't hesitate — oh, no, she did not — the instant she could move, she belly-crawled out of there almost faster than the fat, floppy-eared hound.

With a backward glare, the beast let out another long yowl, as if warning her it would like to bite her again. Maggie gave it an I-just-dare-you glare and it ducked around the edge of the door and out of sight.

Blessed silence remained.

"Baby," the bewildered man called and shuffled after the dog.

Tru stooped beside her and before she could stop him he'd taken her hand in his — just like in the interview. Instant heat spread from his touch, licking through her like a wildfire.

She frowned. If it hadn't been for him taking her hand during the interview, they wouldn't be in this fix.

"Let me look at that," he said, seeming not to notice that she wasn't exactly thrilled that he was touching her.

Maggie tried to ignore the way his touch affected her. His eyes narrowed — as if he felt the jolt too. And at that thought Maggie's heart tripped over itself. She looked away. She had forgotten exactly what it felt like to look into those intense golden eyes.

"Come on, let's get you in the kitchen and

clean this up." He helped her to her feet then led her down the hall and into the kitchen.

She fought the urge to pull away. This reaction to him was not going to help her situation.

He took her over to the sink and turned on the water, testing it for warmth before thrusting her wound beneath.

Her breath caught the instant the warm water hit the wound. She winced and bit her lip.

"Sorry." Tru looked down at her, so close she could see the gilded specks in his irises that caught the light from the window like stardust. "This is bad, Maggie. I'm really sorry about Solomon. He's old and not the best-behaved dog. But he's crazy about my Pops and Pops is crazy about him. He senses when Pop is having a bad day and it just makes him act weird."

"I shouldn't have climbed under there," she said, finally, glad her voice sounded almost normal. "I should have been more careful. It wasn't like I didn't know he was in distress."

"It was probably pretty intense. My Pops is in the early stages of Alzheimer's." Bone-deep sadness filled Tru's eyes. He looked away and focused on her hand.

She felt for him.

Tru pulled her arm from the water and reached into the drawer at his knee and pulled out a blue dish towel. Gently he toweled off the water, then wrapped her arm.

"We need to take you to the clinic and have Bertha look at this. Have you had your tetanus shot?"

Pops wandered in and looked over Tru's shoulder at her like a little boy checking out something cool.

"Yes, I have." It hurt like the dickens, but she didn't want to put anyone out or make Pops feel bad, though the doctor really sounded like a good idea. "I'm fine, I'll just wrap it in gauze."

"Nope, you're going to the clinic. Come with me." He led the way through the house to the front door with Pops trailing. "Pops, stay here, Bo will be here in a minute." Tru's heart was heavy with the knowledge that his Pops was getting worse and they might be to the point that he would no longer be able to stay by himself, even though he and his brothers lived so close. Closing the door, he pulled his phone from its holster and punched a speed-dial number.

"Bo," he said. "We've had a little accident at Pops's. Solomon took a bite out of Maggie, and Pops needs you up here. He was a little upset. I'm taking Maggie to see Bertha." He nodded at something Bo on the other end of the conversation said. "Yeah, he's calm now, but I don't know for how long. And put Solomon behind the doggie gate until we figure out what to do about this. We can't have him biting people."

He ended the call and slid the phone back into its case and led the way to his truck. He opened the door then slipped his hand beneath her elbow to help her inside. She was glad of it. Her arm was throbbing now.

She hadn't wanted to come here. Had forced herself to pack her things into her car and head toward Wishing Springs and this . . .

This was not the start of this ridiculous venture that she'd expected.

But like everything else about this deal, it was out of her control.

Maggie didn't do out-of-control very well.

6

Tru drove toward town. He hadn't wanted Maggie here, but he certainly didn't wish her any ill will. Finding her stuck beneath the massive bed he'd built in high school shop class had been a shocker.

"This is all so messed up." Maggie slouched in her passenger seat beside him, pain etched on her pretty features. "If this is a sign of what's to come, then we're in more trouble than I thought."

"I'm sorry you're hurt and I'm getting you to the doc to take care of that, but this isn't exactly my fault. Maybe we should leave this conversation for another time."

"Sure, maybe after we get back and one of your horses tosses me off in the name of fun?" she said, in a dismal tone.

He slid an accusing glance her way. "You didn't have to offer up that challenge like you did."

Her green eyes flared. "You were the one

who touched me. There's no touching during an interview. And then you had to turn those honey-colored eyes so the camera could read your concern."

"Isn't that a pretty way of puttin' it? I was concerned, if you have to know."

"So, the best plan of action would have been to keep that concern to yourself. *Not* let the public see it and put their own spin on it."

"Like I said, you're the one who threw out that ridiculous bet to me."

"I was nervous. And you were the one holding my hand."

He scowled and watched the road. "This is going to be a long two months. Just so you know, I don't want to do this, but my sponsors pay me to do the promotions they want and that includes this. They obviously want this bad, because every one of them are on board. My hands are tied."

"Kind of like you tied mine when you insisted we go outside the Bull Barn and see your horse? I'm in just as deep, or deeper, than you are, cowboy. Have you seen how many people have looked at that video and watched me —" she clamped her mouth tight and stared out the windshield.

Guilt piled on Tru like a mudslide. He'd never called and checked on her after he'd learned that he was going to be forced into this situation. After realizing she'd probably set him up. "Look, I'm sorry about that. I really am. I had no idea. But you set me up."

Her expression could have melted the Antarctic. "Set you up?"

"That bet was premeditated."

"How was I supposed to know you were going to brag about teaching anyone to ride? And do you seriously think I have any interest in getting on a cutting horse after what happened? My coordination isn't my pride and joy. It's embarrassing, but true."

She sounded completely disgusted with herself and authentic. And just like the day of the interview, he found himself wanting to make her feel better. "I thought it was those red high heels. It was a poor choice of attire."

"If the Bull Barn had had a paved parking lot like a normal business establishment, then my shoe choice wouldn't have mattered," she huffed, her cheeks burning prettily.

"I hate to break it to you, but Wishing Springs isn't Houston. We don't find the need to pave every extra piece of ground there is." He pulled into the parking lot — the paved parking lot she noted — of a small red brick building. Health Clinic was written above the door and there was a *closed* sign in the window.

"It's Monday," Tru grumbled, put the truck in reverse, and headed out of the parking lot. "I forgot what day it was. Clinic is open Tuesday, Wednesday, and Thursday." He glanced at her. She might be putting up a good front, but she was in pain. Solomon had bitten her hard and deep, though their arguing had distracted her.

"That's okay, I'll be fine."

"No, you need to see a doctor. Doc Hallaway will fix you right up." Tru turned into a parking lot a half mile down the road and parked between two trucks.

The sign read Hallaway Veterinary.

"But —" Maggie's brows scrunched. "That's a veterinary clinic."

"Yup. That'd be right. Doc's the next best thing. He'll fix you right up. Most folks around here think he's a better doctor than most."

"But —"

"Trust me, you'll be fine."

He was out of the truck and around to her side by the time her feet touched the ground.

"But, but this is a *vet*. An *animal* doctor," she said, eyes huge.

96

"Yes, but he's a very good vet."

The man had brought her to see a veterinarian.

Feeling as if she'd been thrown into a scene of the movie *Doc Hollywood,* Maggie followed Tru inside the animal clinic, feet dragging.

Only because her wound was yelling for attention did she ignore the need to protest — that and she was in shock.

A vet. Seriously?

There was no one behind the reception desk and the place was empty except for two men who jumped up from their seats smiling the minute she walked in.

Obviously twins, each had sandy brown hair, sleepy brown eyes over a long straight nose balanced by a wide mouth and identical grins.

"Hey, fellas," Tru said giving each man a handshake. "This is Maggie Hope. Is the doc in?" Tru asked, sounding distracted as he looked toward the back.

"Maggie Hope?" asked the one in the green shirt. "The reporter?"

"What do we have here?" the twin in the blue shirt asked as Maggie moved to sit down.

"A dog bit me." She didn't bother correcting the reporter comment.

"A dog," they chorused.

"Did you take the dog to see Bertha at the health clinic?" Blue-shirt-twin asked, grinning.

"Funny, Doonie," Tru drawled, looking around. "Where's Doc?"

"He's out there vaccinating a trailer-load of goats."

"I'll be right back." Tru strode around the counter and headed down a hallway and out the door at the end.

The twins introduced themselves as Doonie and Doobie Burke.

"Obviously our parents had a sense of humor," Doobie in the green shirt said.

"I got the good name, he got the weird name," Doonie in the blue shirt added with a grin.

She chuckled despite her throbbing hand. "I love your names." Her mind was working on how to use them in her column. She was going to have to figure out how to approach this next column, how to make it work. Interesting.

"I'm the mayor of Wishing Springs," the one in the blue shirt said. Doonie, she thought. "But me and Doobie own the real estate agency in town."

"That's right," the other man grinned.

"When you need a property, just give us a call."

"I doubt I'll need to buy any real estate. If I do, though, I'll come see you."

Both men smiled again and came to stare intently at her wound.

"That is nasty," one said.

"Doc's got enough needles in here to fix a few horses, though, so you're gonna be just fine," one offered, chuckling.

Maggie was not reassured.

"If it leaves a nasty scar you could make it into a tattoo of a flower, or a Tasmanian devil," the other, Doobie, said or was it Doonie? Maggie was confused.

Their parents must have had a great sense of humor to have given them these confusing names. Maybe that was where they got their quick-witted personalities. Whereever it came from, Maggie was glad to have someone to take her mind off her hand. And the pain in her side that was Tru Monahan.

He reappeared within five minutes followed by an older man with wild, thick white hair and busy eyebrows above penetrating pale blue eyes.

"Well, don't just sit there, get her into my office," the man barked the moment he saw her.

Even if she'd wanted to run — which she

was thinking more and more about doing — she couldn't with the twins at her side. Each one took an elbow and helped her stand — as if she'd walked in with broken legs, not an injured hand.

"How's the pain?" Tru asked, moving aside as she was escorted past him.

She didn't answer him.

The doc waved her to a chair in the examining room while digging for supplies with the other hand. The place looked clean, at least. Dogs barked from behind a door down the hall and there was a whole lot of mooing going on back there as well. If that wasn't enough, about the time she sat down, she heard the distinct pitter-patter of something trotting down the hall. A potbellied pig burst into the room. Trotted right in and looked about as if it had business there.

Knee-high with a white body and big brown spots covering its shoulders, the pig's skin beneath its short hair was a bright rosy pink. It studied her with big brown eyes then pranced over and stuck its pink snout into her face.

"Don't mind Clover," Tru said, grinning. "She thinks she's Doc's nurse."

The doc turned toward her, pushed his glasses up his nose, and took hold of Maggie's hand. He didn't even acknowledge the presence of a pig that had Maggie leaned back against the wall to avoid contact.

The doc unwrapped her hand. "So what happened? How'd you get this?"

She looked to Tru and he answered for her. "Solomon bit her when she crawled under the bed to try and get him unstuck."

"What'd you do to Solomon?" Doc asked, looking incredulously at her.

Clover stuck her snout into Maggie's armpit. "I didn't do anything to him." She pushed the pig away, thankful she didn't get her other hand bitten by a pig this time. She couldn't believe he wanted to know what she'd done to the dog.

"I tried to help it. Pops" — she didn't know Tru's grandfather's name, so she used what she knew — "h-he asked me to." She decided that was easier than telling them that the poor man had been near hysterics.

"That dog is about as gentle as a lamb," Doobie said — or Doonie — she'd forgotten which one was wearing the blue shirt.

"He was upset."

The doc pressed an antiseptic-soaked pad to the punctures and she winced.

"What was he so riled up for?" Doobie asked. She decided she'd had it wrong and Doobie had on the green shirt, not the blue shirt.

"Because he was stuck." Again she didn't know what to say. She glanced at Tru looking for direction on how much to say about his Pops.

"He's claustrophobic, maybe. Who knows," Tru offered with a shrug for the men.

She almost smiled at his explanation and added, "You'd have been upset, too, if you were stuck" *Doobie?* Oh, fiddle, she gave up on which one was speaking.

"I wouldn't have bitten a pretty lady's hand for helping me. I can tell you that much," twin-number-two said, then shot her a wide grin.

Having decided she didn't need stitches, the doc had her hand cleaned and wrapped in no time. A good thing, too, because Maggie's head was spinning from the questions. The twins switched from asking her about her bite to asking her about the interview and the bet.

Tru leaned against the door frame, arms crossed, watching silently. She was left hanging out on a limb all by herself except for Clover who had decided that Maggie's lap was the perfect headrest.

She found out that the twins were friends of the doc and often hung out in his office drinking coffee in the afternoon.

"They're a sneaky couple," Doc told her as he finished wrapping her hand. "They pretend to be each other sometimes — we all know they do — but no one can tell them apart, so it's hard to prove." He looked at her over the rim of his bifocals. "I think they're both the mayor of Wishing Springs and no one knows it."

She laughed. The twins just grinned, not denying or confirming.

Tru gave a short snort of a laugh from across the room.

Though he was helping her out because he obviously felt guilty that his dog had bitten her, their heated discussion had made it clear that he thought she'd set him up. That put another spin on this fiasco.

Set him up?

It was crazy ridiculous.

But what was new? This entire day had been crazy.

When they finally made it out of the vet's office, she had an arm that was feeling much better than it had when she went in — the doc had fixed her up even with the nosy pig snorting around. Thankfully, since she'd already had a tetanus shot, she didn't have to have Doc Hallaway stick a horse needle in her — she figured she'd be grateful for anything at this point.

Honestly, nothing about her arrival in Wishing Springs was as she'd expected. Once they were back in the truck and Tru had turned it in the direction of home, she was also grateful they hadn't been forced to participate in a reality TV show. The dog bite, the vet, the pig, and the twins would have been too far-fetched. No one would believe it wasn't scripted.

Tru just wanted to get back home. He slammed his truck door and glanced at Maggie.

"Well, that was a first," she said, buckling up. "I'm not sure if anyone would believe anything that just happened to me. I was mauled by a pig while a vet cleaned my wound. A wound that I received after I got stuck beneath a bed with a Basset Hound. *Or* that I was the afternoon entertainment for a pair of twins with names that sounded like a a line of purses."

Despite his suspicions about being manipulated by her, Tru chuckled. He had to admit she'd been a good sport about the whole incident. "Well, when you put it that way, you might have a problem. We do try to keep things interesting here in Wishing Springs."

"Try?" She cleared her throat and shot him a look of disbelief.

He found it hard to pull his gaze away and focus on the road. He'd been having trouble ever since he'd found her stuck under his old bed.

The fact that his truck cab now had the faint scent of spring flowers calling to him only added to his dilemma.

He found himself wanting to pull her close, wanting to see if she tasted as good as she smelled. And that was not good, more now than ever. This attraction complicated everything. He might be attracted, but he reminded himself that she very well could have manipulated this dog-and-pony show.

It was too convenient.

How good were the show's ratings? He'd been wondering that since the moment he'd been given the ultimatum that he had to join in on this circus. He suspected she needed PR for her column and this was proposed to benefit her and benefit Amanda's morning show.

Still, he had no proof. He could just be wary and not let her manipulate him further. And, despite the attraction, he refused to do anything that would even begin to appear as if he were having a romance with Maggie. He wanted no part of that kind of circus again. He'd made a bad dating decision by going out with Felicity. Starlets made their living by being in the public eye so he should have thought about the old saying: Bad publicity is better than no publicity. His mistakes had been glaringly showcased by the tabloids when Felicity acted up — especially that last time. Tru didn't like to think about the catfight.

The positive of the whole miserable ordeal was that he'd also realized that in the near future he wanted a family: wife, kids, and a quiet life here on the ranch. One that didn't include a spotlight or a starlet who craved a spotlight any way she could get it — even if it meant creating scenes in public in hopes of attracting tabloids and becoming fodder for their readers.

"I need to explain about Pops." It was time to set the boundaries.

"You don't have to say anything."

"No, I need to clarify a couple of things." He glanced sternly at her. On this he wouldn't budge. "I've agreed to do this, but my Pops is off limits. Whatever you write in that article you're supposed to write, don't put anything about my Pops in there."

"I wouldn't," she said, sounding genuinely insulted. Maybe hurt. "I didn't mention it in the clinic. Just the dog."

"Thank you for not mentioning it. I didn't mean to insult you, it's just hard to deal with when someone you love is . . . going through it."

"I can't even imagine how it must feel." She was looking at him and he found himself drinking her in for a moment. She just seemed so real. Angry at himself, he cranked his truck and backed out of the parking lot.

"His forgetfulness and confusion is taking over, and as bad as I don't want to accept it, it really is Alzheimer's," he said after they got back on the road. "Me and my brothers can't stop it. He does some strange things now and again. But" — he looked at Maggie, his heart aching — "he used to be the strongest man I knew. His mind was quick — sharp as they came — and to see him on a cutting horse was to watch genius in action."

Just thinking about it wedged a lump in Tru's throat. "Pops is — was the best of the best in his day." Sometimes, the man Tru saw now was nothing like the man he'd always known. Always idolized. Always emulated.

But that didn't change the fact that he loved him fiercely. He slowed at the entrance and after he'd turned onto the drive, he stopped before going through the gate.

He held her sympathetic gaze. "I don't

want him in the funny papers. I want him remembered for being the man he worked all of his life to be. I don't want your paper or the show getting laughs at his expense. If that insults you, I'm sorry, but I needed to make sure there is absolutely no misunderstanding."

She studied him. He had never been more serious about anything in his life. "Promise me," he added when she said nothing.

"I promise. I would never do something like that. I think it's admirable of you to protect your grandfather."

They stared at each other, the seconds ticking by.

He swallowed hard and the lump lodged in his throat eased, but the knot in his chest remained. "Good." Pressing the gas, he took them past the main house. "I'll take you to your cabin."

He drove past the barn, the round pens, and his house. The well-maintained road wound through the pasture and down into the river area where the cabin sat in a tiny clearing surrounded by woods. Maggie silently fidgeted in the seat beside him as they neared the cabin. The woman did tend to have a nervous streak. But who could blame her in their situation?

"This is where you'll be staying. It's not

too far away, and yet you'll have your privacy when you want it."

"It's, um, fine." There was a slight hesitation in her voice. "Does it have electricity?"

He laughed. "I'm not putting you in a cabin *that* rustic. Not only does it have electricity but water too. You won't even have to use the river to bathe in."

"Oh, a wise guy. Funny."

He chuckled, feeling a little lighter than he had for days. "The only thing it doesn't have is a washer and dryer. You're welcome to use the one at my house or the one at Pops's place."

"I can do that." She stared at the cabin, making no move to get out of the truck. Absently, she rubbed her arm and looked from the cabin to the woods. "I'm glad you had a place to put me."

"So this is going to work for you?"

She glanced back at the woods and he could have sworn she looked worried about them.

"Yes. It's great. I'll have plenty of quiet time to work."

"Yup." He wouldn't be bothering her, that was for sure.

Within a few minutes they'd gone back for her car and she'd followed him back to the cabin. Then he'd helped her unload her things and carry the stuff inside.

"Like I said, it's rustic. But we like it. Pops built this a long time ago. It hasn't been used in a while. So the cleaning lady came out and got it in shape for you."

Standing near him in the doorway, she stopped to look at the paneled walls, the small stone fireplace, and the furniture made from tree limbs.

"I like the furniture."

"Thanks, I made it." He enjoyed working with his hands. Woodwork intrigued him.

She stared at him. "You made it? Wow. I have to admit that I've always been a little obsessed with twig furniture. And this is gorgeous. I love the way you sanded the limbs to show the grain, rather than leave the bark on like most that I've seen."

Her eyes had turned the color of seafoam and could pull him in in a minute if he wasn't wary.

He was.

He yanked himself upright, realizing he'd leaned toward her, letting her sweet scent of spring lure him in closer.

"I need to go to work," he said, backing toward the door. "After you get settled in, you can find me at the arena and we can go over the logistics of this thing. We're going to set up certain times for lessons. I have other responsibilities — priorities that have to be fulfilled. There will only be so many hours in a day that I can give up."

"That is just fine with me. I'll have plenty to do," she bristled. "I'll be up soon. It'll be better to get this thing going as soon as possible. The sooner we start, the faster the time will go until we're finished."

"Yup." He turned and strode to his truck as fast as his boots would go.

What was it about Maggie that had him wanting to go against every instinct he had? She was like a magnet — or an undertow.

Climbing into the truck, he slammed the door. It was time to put distance between him and trouble.

This could get complicated. The thought rang through him as he drove away . . . as fast as wheels would carry him.

7

They'd put Maggie in the woods.

She was a city girl. She didn't do woods. After unpacking she went to meet with Tru about their schedule. She needed to get that settled and then she had to go grab some groceries in town before the small town closed up tight for the night. She'd also hoped to stop by Over the Rainbow and check on Jenna but there wasn't enough time today. Soon though. She'd thought of the teen and her baby often and wondered how they were doing.

The trip to the barn ended up being fairly short. She parked then walked toward the barn, she scanned the area — looking out for a yard dog that might be waiting around to bite the newcomer. There were a handful of buildings and fenced pens.

A metal building with double doors sat several yards away and drew her attention. The doors were open and she could see what looked like packing boxes. On the wall beside the door was a large sign with the Four of Hearts brand and the word *Stirrups* beside it. She realized that in that instance the brand was there as the logo for the ranch's handmade stirrup line and that must be where they were made. Her curiosity was stirred.

A cowboy came barreling around the corner of the stable as she approached. Maggie gasped and her hand went to her heart.

"Sorry," he said. "Didn't mean to scare you." He had dark hair and a five o'clock shadow that emphasized a square jaw. His eyes were green like emeralds on high octane. "You're Maggie, right?"

"Yes, and you must be one of Tru's brothers." The resemblance was too close, despite the difference in eye color.

He crossed his arms and gave a wolfish grin that caused a dimple to appear playfully. "Depends on who's asking. These days around here, a guy can't be too careful."

She couldn't help smiling at him, his grin was contagious. "I'm Maggie Hope and I'm looking for Tru."

"I was afraid of that. All the pretty ones always are," he said with a wink. "I'm Bo, by the way. Tru's baby brother. How's the hand? Really sorry about that — Solomon's never bitten anyone before."

"It's fine. My hand will make it. He was scared."

"He's a stinker, and thank you for going above and beyond by climbing under the bed to pull him out. I hear you got stuck."

She laughed. "Your brother rescued me."

"Just call him the Lone Ranger. I'm just glad he was able to hoist that hulking bed he built off of you."

He'd built that beautiful monster. "He didn't seem to have a problem." She was suddenly very uncomfortable. She didn't want people thinking she needed rescuing and that Tru was her knight. Bo was teasing, but what if others started thinking the same thing. That is what got her into this trouble in the first place.

"Well, that's good to hear. But then, he took you to see Doc Hallaway and Clover. I'd hold that against him in a heartbeat." Bo flashed his dimples and tipped his hat. "He's in there. Good luck with the riding lesson."

"Thanks," she called as he headed toward one of the trucks, and she went to find Tru.

The afternoon sun was streaming in through the wide rolling doors at each end of the barn. A long wide alley cut down the middle of the building. She'd actually never been in a barn before.

It smelled. Not bad, but musty like grass and probably feed. She was a little startled that it didn't stink. She could see the outline of Tru and a horse in the light. His silhouette was pure cowboy, bent with his back to the horse and the horse's front leg propped on his thigh as he studied the horse's hoof. A flock of pigeons erupted in the pit of her stomach — forget butterflies. She shooed them away.

"No attraction allowed. None," she declared under her breath, daring herself to say otherwise even as her pulse ignored her and kicked into race mode.

He looked up as she neared him.

Oh, man. His rugged good looks made a mockery of her declaration, but that only made her more wary. Tru Monahan could have his pick of adoring women.

"Is it hurt?" she asked, directing her thoughts to the horse. She halted several steps away from Tru, keeping him between her and the horse. The caramel-colored beauty reminded her of Tru's eyes.

"He had a rock in his shoe. It's out now." He placed the horse's hoof on the ground and straightened. "So, how much experience do you have with horses?"

She gave a shaky laugh. "None. That's what I was trying to tell you in the interview. I have never been around a horse. This is my first time even inside a barn. I've always lived within the city limits of Houston, and we don't generally have too many horses roaming around there."

"Ahh, you have a point."

"And I have made no secret that I'm just not the most coordinated person on the planet. God ran out of that long before he got to me," she added.

His lip twitched. "That bad, huh?"

She put her hand on her hip. "You've seen me in action."

"True. But again, the shoe choice makes a difference. You'll learn to ride. I was serious when I said that."

"Excuse my skepticism. It has more to do with me than you."

"Are you always this hard on yourself? Look, it might not be pretty, but you'll be able to ride a cutting horse before two months is up. Even if you are clumsy — your words, not mine."

His words stung, even if he was repeating her.

She carefully stilled her expression, not wanting to show what she was feeling.

"But I'm supposed to *compete.*"

116

His forehead crinkled beneath his hat as he considered her. "Who said competing was all about winning? I never said you'd win. But I never said you wouldn't, either. So, relax, take a breath, and stop beating yourself up before you've even touched your horse."

She could not look away from the mixture of chastisement, challenge, and encouragement in his expression. How did he do that?

The corner of his mouth slowly lifted and he nodded at the horse standing quietly beside him. "Are you ready to meet your horse?" He lifted one of his tanned hands and placed it on the horse's neck.

Maggie noticed the horse didn't flinch, yank its head, or anything. It just stood there. "What's this one's name?"

"This is Stardust. He's a great horse and he'll take good care of you over the coming weeks."

"Oh, is . . .." she paused. "He's the one I'll be riding? I thought maybe you'd have a little short one somewhere."

He chuckled. "Sorry. Stardust really isn't all that big. He's not as quick as some, so I feel like he'll be a better ride for you than Crimson over there."

He nodded toward the horse she hadn't noticed standing by the fence out in the

117

arena. She tried not to hold her bruises against the horse.

"Crimson is high strung, but he's quick as lightning, greasy on his feet. Stardust is an eleven-year-old gelding who has won over twenty-thousand in the nonpro, nonprofessional, division. He'll take care of you if you listen to me and never take your eyes off the calf."

"I assume that keeping my eyes on the calf must somehow keep me stuck to the saddle as the horse does its fancy footwork."

He chuckled again. "Yeah, something like that. Come closer. He won't bite, I promise," he added, and when Maggie remained rooted to the spot, he reached out and took her arm.

The touch of his long fingers wrapped around her arm set alarms ringing. Sighing and stamping down her intimidation, she let him tug her over to stand beside Stardust.

She felt dwarfed.

"Just touch him, he won't mind."

Tru's voice softened as he bent slightly and spoke to her. She glanced at him, catching the glint of sunlight in his eyes. It was suddenly hard to breathe.

"Come on, you can do it."

She yanked her gaze from Tru's to the

safety of the horse's deep chocolate eyes.

The horse was studying her.

Maggie was so flustered by Tru that she lifted her hand and touched Stardust's nose without any more hesitation. It felt surprisingly velvety and when she touched it, he crinkled it up slightly and dipped his head forward as if asking her to continue. She touched the soft hair between his eyes and then gently rubbed the swath of mane hanging from between his ears.

"See, not so bad."

"He's soft and he acts like he enjoys it."

Tru chuckled. "Oh, yeah, he's a sucker for some lovin'."

Like an idiot, she met Tru's gaze again; the cowboy was standing so close. Her heart tipped over the edge of a cliff, dangled there precariously. She hadn't expected him to talk as if the horse were a person — it was sweet. She found herself looking at his lips and then found him staring at her. His eyes shadowed, and suddenly he stepped back as if yanked by a rope.

"Okay, we got that out of the way." He was curt. "So here's how it will be. I can give you a couple of hours first thing in the morning. Then I'll need my midmorning and afternoon for my own work. We may be able to get in a little time in the evenings.

We'll have to play it by ear. That's all I can do right now. Maybe after I get this month behind me, we'll have more time in the next month. But I've got deadlines to meet. You'll have to do some practicing on your own once we get you on the horse."

She bristled at his tone. "That's fine. I've got plenty to do myself." It wasn't as if she were any happier to be here than he was.

"Good. Then, I'll see you in the morning. Six-thirty."

"Six-thirty?"

He shrugged. "Take it or leave it."

"I was just clarifying is all. That's perfectly fine with me. I need to go to town now and buy groceries." More than ready to get out of there, she whirled away and stumbled over her feet — Tru's strong hand grabbed her elbow and steadied her.

"Thanks," she mumbled and kept on walking. Tru was probably thinking she was going to fail miserably at this. Her pride stung a little thinking about it. But in truth, she'd bet he couldn't teach her, so the less they worked, the more things went in her favor. But what would that prove? What would her readers think?

She actually wished she was capable of riding, and riding well.

Ha! That was a laugh and a half. God had

not seen fit to give her what it was going to take to keep herself from being made a complete fool on this venture. She didn't care if Tru was the miracle teacher that he thought himself to be. She didn't have what it took to get it done. She'd overcome a lot in her life, but she still had no confidence in her athletic ability.

And yet, there was that whisper inside that wished she were up for the challenge.

Tru's heart rate slowed with every step closer to the barn exit Maggie took. When only a dust trail was left from her car, he finally breathed. He spent the rest of the afternoon working five different horses. But though he tried to keep his eyes on the calf, he almost bit the dust several times while his mind kept roving to thoughts of Maggie.

Lanky, with those endless legs that carried her with the grace of a dancer one moment, and then turned as gangly as a newborn foal at other times.

The woman was gorgeous by most standards, but it was her cuteness that kicked him in the gut. She hadn't even looked at him when she'd stumbled, not even when he'd steadied her. She'd just kept on going as if nothing had happened. Despite not wanting to find her intriguing, he did.

She'd never been in a barn. Much less on a horse. And she was afraid of them. This was going to be a slow process if he didn't find a way to get her comfortable with Stardust so they could move on from there.

He was going to have to get her to trust the horse and him, in order to pull this off.

And yet he didn't trust *her*. He hadn't always believed that, but it was working out all too well to give her the spotlight. And that was always what he came back around to.

It wasn't much to build any relationship on. Even if it was only a temporary working relationship.

But the fact was they had to get her ready for competition and make his sponsors happy. And he figured her embarrassing herself on camera wasn't what they were looking for. As far as they were concerned, right now, Maggie Hope's ability was going to be a direct reflection of them, since he represented them.

Tru's only option was for Maggie to surpass expectations.

Especially her own.

His phone rang and he was glad for the distraction. He pulled it out of his pocket and hesitated a split second when he recognized his doctor's number.

He'd been waiting on this call. He pressed the button. "Dr. Jenson, how are you, sir?"

"Tru, I'm good. Sorry it's taken me this long to get back with you. So, what do you want to know?"

"I understand because of the chemo that it's a real gamble . . . but I've decided I want confirmation, positive or negative."

"It's time." Dr. Jenson was all about the facts. And saving lives. "I'll put you down for this survivor infertility study. I'm glad you've agreed, Tru. Like I told you when you were a young teen and you and your parents came in for your yearly evaluation — knowing if you were infertile wasn't what you needed then, but would one day be important to you at the right time to know. I'm glad you're joining this study instead of just getting tested. Data saves others."

Tru knew that was what had helped save his life. Every time they learned something new, it could mean the difference in if someone won the battle or lost the battle. "I want to know the truth, and pay it forward at the same time."

They didn't linger on the phone. Dr. Jenson told him he'd receive notification of when and where to report and then they hung up. The doctor had others to call, and

123

not all the calls were good ones. Tru stood still for a moment and studied the horses in the far pasture. And he wondered . . . what kind of call would he get back after he'd done the test?

8

It was getting late as Maggie drove into Wishing Springs. This had been a long day of finishing up last details in Houston, then packing her car for the trip to town in the early afternoon. She hoped the quaint old town had a grocery store that stayed open past six.

She stopped at the intersection with Main Street, but wasn't sure which way to turn. Pressing the gas, she studied the shops as she drove through town. The main area had an array of businesses flanking the street. It looked like many small towns in Texas with a hair salon, a pharmacy, and a diner. She turned onto a side street and saw a law office and beside it, Burke Brothers Realty. And bingo, a little farther down, she spied the grocery store with several cars parked in the paved lot.

"Yes," she sang to her empty seats. "It's still open."

She hurried inside and grabbed a buggy. For now, all she needed were a few basics. She was heading toward the fruit section when she spied a thin man, who looked to be in his late fifties, weaving down aisle two.

The man carried a small grocery basket on his arm and was definitely weaving back and forth with unsteady steps. As she watched he stopped, bent forward, and stared at something on the middle shelf. He swayed forward, then tilted back. His hat, a jaunty little tweed number, sat crooked on his head. He tried to straighten it and instead hit it too hard, knocking it off. When he leaned down to pick it up, he stumbled and hit his head on the stack of canned goods.

On impulse, Maggie headed that way. What was she doing? A glance around had shown no one had a view of the man but her — clearly he was in no shape to shop. How had he gotten to the store? How was he leaving? One thing was certain, if he was driving, she didn't plan on letting him get behind the wheel. How she intended to stop him, she didn't know. But she would.

"Let me help you." She crouched down to grab the cans that were rolling and strewn across the aisle.

The man looked at her with bloodshot

eyes, hazel eyes so pale that they almost appeared colorless with all the red obscuring them.

"Th'k you, madam," he slurred and he went to tip his hat, then realized it wasn't on his head.

She picked it up and handed it to him. He thanked her again, gave a crooked smile, and carefully, oh, so carefully, placed it on his head once more.

"Mr. Radcliff." A young man came around the corner. He wore a red shirt with the store logo on it and grimaced when he saw the mess.

"He bumped the canned goods," she explained, placing two more cans on the shelves.

He sighed and shook his head. "Thanks. I'll get this."

She stood. It really wasn't her place. The drunk man gave that smile again and she didn't know whether to pity him or be angry. She was both. After all people like this were dangers to society. It didn't matter that he looked as harmless as a kitten. If he got behind the wheel, he was as deadly as they came.

"Do, do you have a ride home, Mr. Radcliff?"

"He'll be fine," the teen told her. "He lives

two streets down, and always walks to the store. My boss called the sheriff's office soon as he arrived, though. One of them will come and give him a ride home."

"Oh. That's good."

"He's not always like this." The kid's expression twisted in apology.

Maggie was still wondering about that when an officer walked through the grocery store's automatic doors and headed toward them.

"Rand, come on. You've got to stop doing this," he said, taking the grocery basket from the man's arm. "Let's get you home," he said, and escorted the drunk from the store.

Maggie watched the man go; a sad feeling enveloped her. This incident was far too close to the past she wanted so desperately to forget — everything lately seemed to be reminding her of her past. It was not welcome.

Nothing good ever came from alcohol or drugs. It stole good people away and replaced them with shells . . . sad shadows of their former selves — or worse, replaced them with monsters.

She sighed, pushed thoughts of her past aside, and focused on food and getting back to the cabin before dark.

■ ■ ■ ■

"She's moving, Lana." Jenna smiled. She loved it when her baby moved in her stomach. It was a reassurance that for now, they were together — a fact she would cherish every moment of. It also showed her that her baby was strong and that was good.

Heart pounding, Jenna laid her fork on the plate of eggs and flattened her hand over her large stomach where she felt her baby move. Each time she felt her baby, it was as if the sun had just burst over the rise and into the sky while birds sang a chorus. It was as if morning had come fresh and new, and joyously, each time. Things were so much better here than they had ever been in Jenna's entire life.

Lana turned from the stove and smiled. "She's a bundle of energy like her mom." Kindness in her eyes turned to concern as she walked over and cocked her head to the side, studying Jenna. "Are the eggs still making you nauseated?"

All the other girls had finished eating and left the kitchen. Jenna was having trouble getting anything down again. "A little," Jena admitted, wanting to eat the eggs for her baby's health.

"It's okay, sweetie. Let me take them."

From the moment Jenna had arrived over a week ago, Lana had been kind to her. Peg, her mother and the midwife at Over the Rainbow was kind too, but in a livelier way. Lana was gentle and there was something about her voice and the way she could look at Jenna that made Jenna's heart ache. She was glad Lana was here now to share the moment with her when her baby moved. It was kind of like having a mother who cared. And Jenna always wondered what it would have been like to have a mother who cared like Lana. Or a grandmother like Peg. Or some of the older ladies who came out for game night.

Jenna tried not to think of her mother. Dwelling on thoughts of her own lack of a loving mother did nothing to help her baby, and Jenna was convinced it even upset the baby. Lana had helped her focus on the positives of her actions. She'd taken control of her life and was showing her love for her unborn child by thinking good positive thoughts.

Lana reached for the plate. "You keep the piece of toast and at least get a few bites down."

"I'll try." Keeping one hand on her stomach Jenna took the toast and took a bite, chewing slowly. She'd come this far for her baby, her hand tightened on her stomach and love surged through her. "I'm not going to let a little nausea get me down."

Lana patted her shoulder. "You've got some spunk, kid. And you're keeping your eye on what's good for your baby. I love that."

She'd eat because it was good for baby Hope. One of the first things they'd done when she'd arrived was an ultrasound, and Jenna had learned she was carrying a baby girl. She'd almost not given her baby a name because she knew she was going to give her up for adoption and she was too scared to let herself cross that line of actually naming her child.

But she'd been unable to stop herself in the end. Maggie Hope, in the blue Volkswagen Bug, had picked her up on the side of the road, with her perfect blonde hair and smile and cool red high heels. Maggie had shown her kindness when Jenna had needed it most.

When her baby's life had depended on it.

Because Jenna had been in a really bad way that afternoon. She'd needed someone, and she'd actually prayed that God would send her someone. She never prayed, never thought it did much good. But that afternoon, she'd prayed like she'd never prayed before, because this was about her baby. She knew that even if God didn't care about her that maybe he'd care about her little baby. When that blue car sped her way, hope had sprung up in Jenna. And when it had passed her by, she'd crumbled, but then, it had whipped around and beautiful blonde Maggie had come to her rescue.

It was as if God had sent her baby its very own angel.

Jenna would never be able to forget what Maggie had done. Maggie had given her hope when she thought she had lost it all.

Without even realizing it that day, her baby had become little Hope.

Named for the beautiful woman who'd taken time out of her day to rescue them.

Where had Maggie gone?

Jenna took a bite of the toast and forced herself to swallow it. It made its way into her stomach and some of the queasiness stilled. Food, the sight of it, could make her want to upchuck and then once a little made its way in, she felt better.

She took another bite and a breath. Lana smiled.

"Better?"

She nodded and voiced the question knotting in her chest. "Lana, do you think we're going to find my Hope a wonderful family?"

It was a question she'd asked that first day a little over a week ago. Lana had assured her that she would.

"Honey, I promise, you keep poring through those files and praying about it and you'll come up with just the right family for Hope."

Jenna sighed. Her heart squeezed tight like it was going to explode.

She had to find them. She had to be strong and go through with her plan. Her baby needed more than she'd had.

More than she could offer her.

More than Jenna knew how to give her.

After all, Jenna hadn't been raised up with love and kindness; she didn't want to take the chance of doing it wrong.

And she was just a kid. No home . . . no job . . . no money.

What good would that do her baby?

Little Hope needed a chance to grow up and be . . . be like Maggie. The kind of person who radiated beauty and goodness and kindness.

All the things Jenna wasn't. She was a tough scrapper. Exactly what she didn't want little Hope to have to be. It would be better if she had the opportunity to be a lady.

Like Maggie, in her classy red heels, her funky blue car and that pretty dress that fluttered around her knees when she walked. Jenna wore sweats and oversize T-shirts.

No, her Hope needed a shot.

And it didn't matter that since arriving here Jenna kept having pangs of . . . regret. She was finding her baby a happy home. It was one thing she could do for Hope.

It didn't matter that it was killing Jenna to think about it. She was doing it and that was final.

Maggie had shown Jenna real kindness, and this was the kindness she could do for her baby girl.

And it didn't matter if thinking about it every second of the day made her sick to her stomach. It was happening.

It was done . . . if there was one thing Jenna was, she was tough, so she could do this. She could do this for her baby.

"It's creepy, Amanda. You should hear the coyotes out there howling." Maggie had made it back from the grocery store just before dusk set in. "And at dusk when I got back from the grocery store, there were shadows everywhere, looming out from the woods around this cabin."

Amanda laughed on the other end of the line.

"Stop that," Maggie demanded. "You'd have to be here to understand."

"I'm from Weatherford, right up the road from Wishing Springs, Mags. Remember, I'm a country girl gone city. You're a city girl gone country."

"Ha, I beg your pardon, I have *not* gone country. I'm only here under extreme duress."

"This is so unlike you. Where is the woman with the heart and spirit of a mother tiger? There is something going on here that really has you stirred up, and I suspect it has more to do with that hunky cowboy than those spooky woods. Woods are not spooky, Mags. They are peaceful and calming to the soul. All things you could use right now. Tru really gets to you, doesn't he?"

"No . . ." Maggie had hurried back to the cabin from the grocery store as fast as possible, not certain she could find it in the dark. The last thing she'd wanted was to get lost in the dark and need to have Tru come rescue her again.

"You say that with such conviction." Delight rang in Amanda's chuckle. "You can deny all you want, but I know. I remember your words the first time I told you I was doing an interview with him. You said, and I quote: 'He is the best looking man in the world' "

"I *knew* it. You set me up."

"Well, believe me, I did not get the flu on purpose. But yes, I may have remembered that statement when I suggested a replacement. But you set yourself up for this bet gig. And I, for one, am enjoying it immensely. I can't wait to see what you do with this opportunity."

Truth was, Maggie was tied in knots thinking about the things she was still to face. "I still can't believe that one crazy slip of the mouth puts me in this all-or-nothing position. You and I both know that this is all about Tru. I'm interchangeable with any other female silly enough to open her mouth and put her foot in it like I did. But, like Ms. Davenport said, the clock was ticking on my column's life."

"Your blunder is actually a gift. This at least gives you a shot at redeeming your standings. And increasing your readership by giving you visibility you've never had. And you said yourself, this could be your shot at syndication."

Maggie had been dreaming of being the

next Dear Abby, and Amanda knew this. But it was a farfetched dream. Until now. "Which is another reason why I would never come here to make goo-goo eyes with Tru. Not only am I interchangeable with any other female as far as your television audience is concerned, I'm also interchangeable for Tru. The man's wandering eye has been well documented. So this is all about the health of my column."

Amanda sighed. "Well, one thing about you, Maggie, is you have the ability to cut to the truth of an issue."

"It comes from bad experiences —"

"I've admired you from the moment I met you. You've overcome things that would have broken most people. And that's exactly why the people who read your column stick with you. You give good advice. You really do care about the problems of every person who writes you. All you need is some attention so more people find out how awesome you are."

Maggie picked up the small bag of letters she'd brought with her. Amanda knew more about her than anyone and she understood so much about where Maggie wanted to go but . . . but there was so much Amanda didn't know. And never would. No one would.

She pulled the bag closer and started trying to open it with one hand. So much of what Amanda had said was true. She was blunt sometimes and more focused on giving good advice than anyone knew. But it was as much about her as it was about the readers. For Maggie, there was redemption inside this bag.

Atonement . . .

"You'll be okay, Mags. *And,* you're going to have some very nice *scenery* helping you learn to ride that horse."

Maggie paused opening the bag and focused on the conversation. "Amanda, I am not interested in the scenery."

Amanda only laughed. "Sure, you're not, and that's completely fine. But you can still enjoy the view. Hey, I'm going to let you get on with your letters. And then get a good night's sleep. You've got a busy day coming. Enjoy," she teased and disconnected, but her chuckle echoed through the dead phone line.

Maggie tossed the phone onto the couch beside her. She rubbed her temple. Not only did she have to face her first lesson, but she also would begin to get to know the community that her paper was expecting her to feature over the next few weeks.

Odd as it was, this bet was a gift, and now

she had to find a way to add this town, the television special, and that blundering bet all together to save her column.

But right now, she had letters to answer.

9

Maggie's alarm didn't go off.

Miraculously, at six-fifteen she rolled over, lifted thick lids, and groggily peeked at the glaring red lights of her alarm clock. *Six-fifteen.*

What?

Heart thundering, she sprang to a sitting position. She was going to be late.

She couldn't be late.

Maggie flew out of bed. Tangled in the covers, she stumbled and disengaged from them and finally made it into the bathroom. She grabbed her toothbrush and scrubbed her teeth while yanking clothes from her suitcase with her free hand.

Five minutes later she was speeding — bumping and jerking — down the dirt road toward the stables.

Skidding to a halt, she bolted from her car and didn't stop running until she reached the double doors of the horse barn and spotted Tru.

Smokin' tortillas! What a cowboy sight to see first thing in the morning.

Surprise lit his expression as he saw her — a splash of cold water to her runaway imagination — because it was immediately clear that he hadn't believed she'd show up on time.

"So," she said, trying to sound more upbeat than she felt. "What bone am I going to break today?"

"You're not going to break anything. I promise."

"I wouldn't be so sure about that," she muttered, focusing on the horse she was expected to ride. She'd be lucky if she could hang on.

"Relax, I'm not putting you on Stardust today. You're going to brush him and groom him and get to know him. I want you comfortable with him before I put you on his back for the first time."

Her nerves eased a little looking at the brush he held out to her.

"Slip your hand in here like so," he demonstrated the right way to hold the brush. Turning toward Stardust, he placed the brush on his side and stroked downward. "See, he's used to this, so you don't have to worry. I'd never put you with a skittish horse."

She looked at him. There was sincerity in his eyes, but his proximity made her more aware of the heat coming off his skin.

"Do you trust me?"

"N-*no*. Why should I?" she blurted out. She barely knew him — sure he took her breath away — but that was certainly no reason to trust him or any man. Besides, *how many other females' breath had he stolen?*

"No?" he repeated.

"Don't look so shocked. I don't trust any man as far as I can toss a boulder." Especially one who smelled of fresh soap and tangy aftershave that threatened to distract her. She frowned and held her hand out. "May I try?"

He pulled the brush from his hand and placed it in her extended palm. Their fingertips brushed and she jerked her hand away and almost fumbled the brush.

His eyes narrowed. "You're right. This is about you building a relationship with Stardust."

"Right." Maggie stepped tentatively toward Stardust. "So, like this?"

Stardust looked over his shoulder at her with accusing eyes — as if the horse knew what she'd been thinking about. Hadn't she heard horses were intuitive?

They had instinct. Maybe she could learn a thing or two from them.

She began brushing the horse and he just stood there. Like a good horse.

Doing exactly what Tru had shown her, she concentrated on each stroke, conscious that Tru was watching her.

"That's good," he said. "See, that's not so bad, is it?"

A knot in Maggie's chest that she hadn't even realized was there eased a little.

"It's okay. He likes it," she said. "I'm brushing a horse." With a giddy feeling, she smiled at Tru.

His dark brows dipped. "See, there, what'd I tell you? All you have to do is trust me and it's all going to be just fine."

Maggie stiffened. He tossed out the word *trust* as if it was the easiest, most natural undertaking in the world . . . like deciding to enjoy breathing.

But trust . . . it wasn't something so easily decided.

She stilled her enthusiasm over having touched a horse. She had simply made the first step. She had a long way to go.

And Tru — wasn't he being the hypocrite? After all, he thought she should trust him, but he'd made it clear he didn't trust her. She needed to remember that.

Maggie's expression puzzled Tru.

If he'd expected her to look at him after that statement and suddenly change her position on trusting him, he was wrong. Instead she said nothing, turning her attention back to Stardust.

She didn't trust him. News flash: he didn't trust her either, but it bugged him that she hadn't even hesitated when she'd answered his question.

What in her past had put this chip on her shoulder against men? Because she had said she didn't trust men. He guessed he should be relieved that it wasn't just him, but he wasn't. Right here, right now — this was only about him and about her.

"You could ease up a little, you know," he grunted, irritation pricking at him like a woodpecker. To be honest, he wasn't in the easiest of moods today, and this hadn't helped. Since learning that he'd soon be going through with the test that would tell him if he had the ability to be a father, a biological dad, he was as tense as freshly stretched barbed wire.

He nabbed another brush from the bucket next to the stall entrance and moved to the

other side of Stardust, needing the movement to calm himself. "We've both agreed
to this. You don't trust me or men at all,
from what I can see. And I have to admit
my curiosity about all of that. But the only
thing I can see that I did wrong was to help
you through a rough spot in that interview.
I messed it up; I get that. What I don't get
is your attitude."

She stared at him across the gelding's
back. Those pretty eyes had flared momentarily, telling him she hadn't expected him
to confront her. Just like he hadn't expected
the two-ton cement chip perched on her
delicate shoulder.

He started brushing Stardust, focusing on
each stroke and felt her gaze on him.

"You have a lot of room to talk. *You* think
I set you up."

He met her accusing gaze. "Did you?"

She cocked her head, her expression
suspiciously demure. "Why, Tru, don't you
trust me?"

After the first awkward lesson finally ended,
Maggie headed to town intent on meeting
some of the locals. If she were to write some
of the weekly articles about the town then
she needed to meet the locals. Those were
going to be her focus rather than her train-

145

ing, if at all possible. She hated the idea of writing things about Tru — she wasn't a tabloid writer and she really didn't want to resort to anything that resembled it. If she could find something, anything that would grab attention and be of interest other than Tru Monahan that was what she planned to do.

Writing her "Gotta Have Hope" column would be the same as always, and meant reading emails and answering four of them in the column each week. But she tried to answer as many as she could, and it was exhausting sometimes, because she actually received a lot of mail. So she knew that with the added assignments, she had her work cut out for her if she were to get it all done successfully. And she had to be successful.

She just had to be.

There were so many women out there who had gotten raw deals looking for love. Men too. Love was complicated. Life was, too, and she was proof of that. But despite her own mixed-up past, she'd found that she was good at giving advice or at least helping her audience feel uplifted.

But there was a strong sense of joy that filled her when she was able to help someone look past the pain of a breakup and move forward. To realize they deserved more than they were giving themselves credit for. There was nothing like the feeling she got when someone she'd helped wrote her and told her something she'd said helped them.

She'd grown comfortable with her column. But this new assignment put her in unfamiliar territory.

She had to get to know this town, had to meet the people, and figure out a way to use it to save her column.

As she got out of her car, two ladies moved from the sidewalk across the street, excitement radiating from them as they hustled her way. It was the two eavesdroppers from the interview.

"Maggie," the shorter of the two called, several strands of very chunky, very gaudy jewelry bouncing and jangling as she jostled to a halt. "We wanted to welcome you to Wishing Springs."

"We've been so excited ever since we heard you were coming," the taller woman said, her smile wide as she pushed her blunt, chin-length brown hair behind her ear.

"Hi," Maggie said. This was perfect. "I remember y'all. You were in the kitchen at the Bull Barn during the interview." She remembered them all right — their voices could even be heard on the tape, breathless and animated. She was certain that they'd helped add some excitement to the interview and the powers that be felt it and realized others would feel it too.

One thing had been certain, they'd believed in Tru.

Now they beamed.

"I'm Clara Lyn Conway," the short one said and waved a bejeweled hand toward her friend. "This is my sidekick Reba Moorsby. We co-own the Cut Up and Roll salon. If it's to be known, we know it," she stated with pride.

"We are certain that you'll be a really good rider by the time our Tru gets done with you," Reba assured her. "We're on our way to the Bull Barn for our weekly lunch meeting. Come along. Everyone is dying to meet you."

Maggie's adrenaline started humming and she agreed to the lunch invitation without hesitating. "I came to meet people, so this is perfect."

Reba and Clara Lyn grinned at each other.

"Then lunch at the Bull Barn is where you need to be," Reba said. "How's the hand, by the way?"

Clara Lyn took Maggie's arm and inspected the bandage. "Doonie and Doobie told us they saw you at Doc's after you were bitten by Pops's dog."

Maggie had heard things traveled fast in small towns. "It's fine." She gave an unenthusiastic grin. "He didn't mean anything by it. I shouldn't have crawled under the bed with him."

"You crawled under the bed with him?" Clara Lyn gasped.

"He was stuck."

"The dog was stuck?" Reba asked.

"Yes." She started to clarify why she'd crawled under there and then remembered how Tru didn't want her putting anything in the papers about Pops and his Alzheimer's. She wasn't sure how he felt about the town's people knowing about Pops's problems. "Yes, when I arrived he was under there, and he was wailing, so I was just going to try and help him out. I should have waited on Tru to arrive."

"They said you got stuck."

She looked at Reba. "Well," she swallowed, they were all going to think she was some brainless woman, "I jumped when the dog bit me, and I wedged myself there sideways by accident." There, that should explain it. And she'd said nothing about Pops.

Fifteen minutes later Maggie saw that

149

Reba had been right about lunch at the Bull Barn being the place to be to meet folks. The parking lot was packed. She found an empty spot and then followed the two ladies inside.

Unlike the emptiness on the day of the interview, today there were people popping out of every nook and cranny. All talking ceased momentarily as Big Shorty came up to greet them, then led them toward a table.

Conversation resumed, and folks began stopping them as they passed by. The women asked about the interview. The men — cowboys — didn't say anything. From a table in the corner, either Doonie or Doobie waved. The twin was sitting at the head of a table with several older men and a couple of ladies.

"How's the hand?" he called. "You haven't tried to be puppy food anymore, have you?"

It felt awkward to hold a conversation with the entire diner. "No," she answered.

"Did you start your lessons yet?" someone else asked.

"Isn't that Tru a hunk?" a petite lady said heartily. She was sitting at the end of the table with the Burke twin.

Maggie really didn't know how to answer that. Yes, Tru Monahan *was* a hunk. A hunky ladies' man, making him absolutely,

150

decidedly *not* her type with his womanizing exploits. Then there was the issue of discussing it in the middle of the diner with a pint-size woman well into her seventies, not to mention everyone else in the room listening and grinning at her as they waited on her answer. It was a little overwhelming.

In the end, Big Shorty saved her. "All right everyone, the interrogation is over for the moment. Let Miss Hope get to her table and enjoy her lunch."

Maggie could have kissed the man as he escorted them to a table and handed out menus. The man took care of his clients.

Melting gratefully into her chair, she took the menu and pretended to study it as Big Shorty headed off to get the tea and waters that they all ordered.

The place was buzzing about the column, the TV special, and the riding challenge. Much speculation abounded. Though they were honoring the owner's decree to let her get her meal underway, she soon found herself involved in what was more like a huge family gathering.

The general consensus: the town was genuinely excited about the publicity that she'd generated for their friendly town.

During the conversation, her attention was grabbed by the man she'd seen at the grocery the night before. Today, though his hat sat a little crookedly on his head, he didn't appear to be in the least bit tipsy. Or to recognize her.

"Did you say that was Wishing Springs's city council sitting with Doonie?"

Clara Lyn nodded. "Each and every one."

Maggie couldn't believe her eyes. The man in the jaunty hat, the drunk from the grocery store, was Mr. Radcliff — town *councilman?*

The plot thickened; Maggie was shocked. It wasn't as if people in positions like that didn't get drunk. But still, she was shocked.

He wore a neatly pressed oxford shirt and his hair was combed impeccably, every thick silver strand in place. Yesterday he'd been wearing a rumpled cotton shirt and khaki pants, and when his hat fell off, his hair had been mushed and hanging in his eyes.

Clara Lyn caught her staring at the man. She leaned in close. "That is Rand Radcliff," she whispered. "He's the editor of the *Wishing Springs Gazette.* I'm sure he's going to be wanting an interview from you for the paper. He's a bit of a scoundrel. You know, he tends to tip the bottle a little."

Reba clucked her tongue twice. "When he's not loaded, he's a dear and a good reporter and editor. But . . ."

"It's sad," Clara Lyn picked up where

Reba trailed off. "Real sad." Then with a shake of her head, Clara Lyn turned to Maggie. "So, we read your column. You give things such a hopeful twist. You know, in the beauty shop, I often give advice. People just come in and tell me their life stories. It's not like I even ask. They just do. And Reba can tell you that I do give good advice." She dipped her chin. "I take it *very* seriously."

Reba nodded. "Too seriously, sometimes. She went on a stakeout for a customer once."

"I don't do stakeouts anymore."

Reba glared at her. "That's a good thing."

Clara Lyn blushed. "There are just some things your beauty operator does not need to know."

Reba hiked a brow. "I tried to warn you."

"I know. But my clients are important to me and sometimes I just get carried away."

Maggie was smiling. She couldn't help it. These two were alive with energy and it was very easy to see that they cared. "I take my job seriously too," she confessed. "All these people write to me, and I have this fear that I'm going to say something wrong. So I try mostly to find ways to help them see hope in their situation. It's not like I can actually change their problems. But, God has always been there for me, and I know that in my darkest hours, I had hope. He gave me strength." She paused, letting her purpose fill her up like gas to an empty tank. "There are really good people out there, so I try to shine a light their direction too."

"You do, dear. You do," Reba cooed. "I read that column you wrote two weeks ago about that woman who is the child advocate. She was amazing."

"And she gives hope to those kids out there who need a champion," Maggie pointed out. She could have used someone like Silvia Tatum when she'd been a kid.

"So this other column about the bet, what's it going to be about?" Reba asked.

"I'm trying to figure that out as I go. But I just thought I'd write about the town, and things that are going on here, and of course I have to write something about the bet, you know, Tru and me."

Clara Lyn and Reba looked at each other thoughtfully and then grinned.

"That sounds perfect," Clara Lyn said. "We might be a hole-in-the-road town, according to some, but we are interesting. And I suspect strongly that Tru will give you a *host* of interesting things to write."

Both women beamed at her in a way that put Maggie on alert. "Hold on," she cautioned. "Contrary to what everyone is likely thinking, I am not here for Tru in that manner. And he is not looking at me in *that* manner. So I'm exploring other aspects of the story. Any ideas would be greatly appreciated."

"Well, that is a cry'n shame," Reba huffed. "And I can hold out for 'Tru' love to blossom — get my pun?" She smiled with coyness in her expression.

"Me too," Clara Lyn agreed. "But in the meantime, we are having the Thanksgiving in July celebration in three weeks. You could write about that. Might get us a lot of tourists coming in and a lot of business for a good cause."

Maggie sat up straighter. "Thanksgiving in July?"

Clara Lyn quickly filled her in. Mayor Doonie Burke had come up with the idea last year to help raise money for Over the Rainbow. The festival had booths, turkey frying by the men, and games.

Relief and a rush of excitement filled Maggie as her mind started whirling with the thought of things to plump up the article. It was so much better than what she had before:

Wishing Springs, hometown of hunky champion Tru Monahan. A lovely town with an awesome home for pregnant girls, fat Basset Hounds that bite, and a local veterinarian who'll doctor you up while you enjoy the bedside ministrations of Clover the pig . . .

Thanksgiving in July was *so* much better. Of course she had two months of articles to fill, but at least she had some things to focus on other than just Tru Monahan's hunk appeal.

Two hours later Maggie was actually smiling as she drove back toward the ranch. She'd had fun at lunch. After she'd adjusted to the questions being hurled at her like baseballs from a batting machine. She'd come away looking forward to writing a column that introduced the warm, welcoming town to her readers. This silly bet had a plus . . . she had the power to help the town benefit from a thorn in her side.

That pleased her.

After all, if they were going to have to go through this, then someone should benefit. It might as well be this town. The people seemed genuine. Clara Lyn tended to talk but she seemed to have a good heart, as did Reba.

And then there was Over the Rainbow. During the meal she'd asked the ladies about the home for unwed mothers and found out it had a great reputation. The two ladies who ran it were top-notch, and the girls there got great care.

Maggie smiled and her heart clenched at the knowledge. She'd sensed that poor Jenna had gotten herself out of a terrible situation and had chosen wisely when she'd come here.

Tomorrow, Maggie would go and check on Jenna.

10

"Jenna, girl, you lookin' like you're ready to pop."

"Look who's talking." Jenna grinned at the tall, young black teen who was due three weeks after her. "The only reason I'm bigger than you is because you're three feet taller than me."

Kasandra chuckled. "*Everyone* is three feet taller than you."

They were walking the long drive for exercise and their shadows emphasized the difference in their heights all the more. The girls had formed a tentative friendship, despite that after their babies were born, the odds of them ever seeing each other again were not likely.

Kasandra had her eyes set on college and she had plans. She'd picked out the family who would become her baby's parents and she had no desire to see the baby after it was born. She hadn't even asked to find out the gender.

Jenna understood this was not abnormal. Some girls did this to keep their distance and prevent attachment. Some girls just didn't want to know. Kasandra was just keeping her distance. She was nice. Had come from a good family. Her father was actually a coach. And she'd gotten mixed up with a football player from his team who was heading to play college ball and had a future in the pros. Neither of them had being a parent in their plans.

Unlike Jenna, who put on a happy face and tried to let some of the positive from Kasandra rub off on her. Jenna had no plans, other than making sure her baby got a shot at life. After that was accomplished, she didn't know. None of it was important right now.

For what seemed like forever, Jenna had just been living one day at a time, avoiding her dad's wrath as best she could and enduring it more times than not. When she'd learned she was pregnant, it had been the first time she'd thought nine months into the future.

Hope's daddy was a mechanic's helper who worked at a garage on the corner down the road from the apartments where Jenna used to live. He'd been nice. He used to give her a soda when he'd see her passing by.

Jenna had eventually met him late one night and she'd given in to the tenderness he'd shown her. But that had been all of one night. She found out the next day he had a wife and a baby already.

And he'd actually laughed at her when he'd realized she'd thought their being together had meant something.

Six weeks later she found out she was pregnant, and her dad found the test. He'd beaten her so bad she had hardly been able to move afterward.

That was the night Jenna had known it was up to her.

And she'd started searching for a way out for her baby.

She and Kasandra had just made it back to the house when the unmistakable sky-blue Volkswagen turned into the drive.

Joy sang through Jenna. She couldn't believe it. Her knees weakened. *She came back.*

She tried to hold back the emotions going nuts inside of her. With what seemed like superhuman strength, she lifted the heavy door and sealed her emotions safely away behind a similar door that protected her heart from the pain others could inflict on her. Not many people held that power any longer. Because she'd saved her and her baby, Maggie Hope was one of those few.

"That's that woman who brought you here, isn't it?" Kasandra asked, watching the little car speed up the hill.

"Uh-huh," Jenna mumbled. *She had come back.*

When the car came to a halt, Jenna swallowed the elephant that was clogging her throat. It stuck in the center of her chest and hurt something awful as Maggie got out of the car smiling. She was as beautiful as Jenna had remembered.

And with all that blonde shiny hair, she really did look like an angel.

"Jenna," she called. A radiant smile caused Jenna's heart to kick into a fierce pounding.

"Aren't you gonna say something?" Kasandra asked.

"It's so good to see you," Maggie said as she came to a halt two feet away. "You've made it through another week. I am so glad. You look great."

She was talking fast. Her green eyes misted when her gaze traveled to Jenna's stomach and then back to her face. That made Jenna have to blink hard. Her eyes burned while the elephant in her chest started doing jumping jacks. And still, Jenna couldn't speak. If she spoke, she might cry, and Jenna did not cry. She didn't.

Kasandra elbowed her and held out her hand to Maggie. "Hi, I'm Kasandra. You got to forgive my girl here. She doesn't talk much."

Maggie shook Kasandra's hand and looked kindly at her. "Nice to meet you. When are you due?"

"Any time is fine with me, but officially in about five weeks. It sure is nice to meet you. I've got to head on inside. Nature calls — you know, with this child sitting on my bladder, it calls more than I'd like." Kasandra shot Jenna a questioning look then hurried inside.

Jenna knew she had to speak. "You came back."

It wasn't exactly what she'd meant to say. Her instincts were to keep her emotions hidden, having learned it was safer that way, but this meant the world to her and . . . there was just no hiding it.

Maggie stood very still, staring at her as if she wasn't sure what to say either. And then she grabbed Jenna and hugged her.

The action took Jenna by surprise . . . causing her eyes to burn with the need to cry. Her chest ached and she breathed in the scent of flowers, a soft fresh scent that wrapped around her and made her dizzy. Faded memories of being held by her mom enveloped her. Memories so old and long ago that Jenna sometimes thought she'd imagined ever really being hugged by her mom. Maggie would be about the age that Jenna's mom had been when she'd died. Jenna had been about three. Just barely old enough to remember.

Maggie let her go after a moment, wiping her eyes as she stepped back. "I am just so happy to see you. I have thought about you so much. You are a brave girl, Jenna, and you had me so worried."

"You've thought about me?"

"How could I not? When I found out I was going to have to come back to Wishing Springs, seeing you and your baby — if the sweetie was born yet — was the best part of coming back."

Jenna couldn't believe that. "Honestly?"

Maggie laughed. "Scouts' honor. Is there somewhere we can sit and visit? I'd love to learn all about how you're doing, and if there is anything I can do for you."

It was more than Jenna had ever expected. "There's a patio table on the deck."

Maggie smiled. "Perfect."

It was perfect, but Jenna couldn't believe it — not yet anyway. She led the way around the house and they sat down at the table on the big deck. She wasn't sure what to talk about, but Maggie started asking questions about Over the Rainbow and Jenna relaxed. Maggie seemed like she was completely avoiding any questions about Jenna's background. It was like she knew that Jenna wasn't comfortable talking about it. Instead she talked about what had brought her back to town.

Jenna laughed. "You actually get to learn how to ride a horse? That's the reason you're here?"

"That's the plan. I'm going to give it my best shot anyway."

"That's sweet. I love horses."

"Maybe you can come out and see them one day."

"I'd like that," Jenna said. "I'd like that so much."

Dear Maggie,

It's been three years since I lost my husband. I'm fifty-two years old and my friends tell me it's time for me to start dating again. To "get a life." But I don't want to. I can't imagine ever loving someone else. But they keep pressuring me. Is there something wrong with me? They tell me I'm just scared. Do you think so? I know my husband wouldn't want me to be alone, but . . . I just don't feel ready. No one seems to understand. You seem like you really care. And though I was shocked to see how young you were when I saw you on *Wake Up with Amanda,* I feel like somehow, you have an old heart, and might be able to offer me some advice. Some hope as you always seem to do in your letters to other readers.

Thanks for your advice,
Hopeless in Central Texas

Maggie held the letter, letting the words sink into her. After a moment she placed it in a small stack of letters that had similar comments and worries. One of the letters was from a thirty-year-old widow who'd closed herself off from everyone for almost a year. Another was from an eighty-one-year-old who'd lost her husband of sixty-three years.

Maggie would answer these as a group in her column. She'd been startled by the increase in mail that she'd started receiving. Ever since they'd announced the challenge there had been an upsurge to her letters. It was encouraging and daunting seeing all those emails. There were hundreds of them.

In the end, she'd just dug in and started reading.

It took time to weed through the crazy letters, the bizarre letters, and the occasional sicko letters. But then there were letters like Hopeless in Central Texas's. Letters that filled her with an overpowering need to answer.

Pulling her computer near, she began to type.

Dear Hopeless in Central Texas,

Your letter touched me. I've received several this week where readers are feeling similar emotions. Though I've never been married, I can tell you that my heart is hopeful that one day I'll feel the kind of love you and the other ladies have expressed to me in your letters. The gift of a love like this is not something to take for granted or to leave behind quickly or easily. I can only imagine the hole that must be left in your heart. My first reaction to your friends urging you to "get a life" was one of frustration. You had a life, and you have a life now . . . it may not be as full as the life you shared with your loved one, but it is still a life full of memories that you aren't comfortable stowing away yet. Or maybe those

166

aren't the right words. Maybe I should say you aren't comfortable sharing space with new memories. To me, I think you'll know when the time is right. You, and only you, will know. Let God lead you. And when the time comes, you'll be prepared to face the new emotions that will come with stepping out and daring to seek a new life. Though I'm young, I've had my own sorrows and hardships. I've had to sometimes push myself to make changes and to be brave and I've felt no shame in moving slowly as I've felt ready. I've had the support of a friend who has encouraged me without rushing me to do it in her time. Talk to your friends, explain your need of support and encouragement instead of pressure. I'm hoping you'll become Hopeful in Central Texas . . .

Maggie stared at her answer. How she longed to be brave enough to trust her heart to a man. She prayed that one day soon she'd meet the man that she could feel comfortable trusting. Despite everything she knew to be wrong about him, her thoughts shifted instantly to Tru. Why she continued to torture herself with thoughts of him, she did not understand. She was an advice columnist for crying out loud. And her advice to herself was that he was all wrong for her. Wrong with a capital *W*.

Pushing those thoughts away, she picked up the next letter. It was five before she knew it. She realized she was supposed to be back at the barn for another lesson. She had a long night ahead of her if she was going to get through the rest of the emails. And she still had to write her columns. Taking a deep breath, she headed out the door. Going to see Jenna had taken some of her time, but it had been worth it.

She arrived at the barn and there was no one there, but she spotted Tru's truck up at Pops's house. She wanted to check on Pops, so she left her car and walked up the long lane.

The walk felt good. Back in Houston she'd jogged some and walked some. It cleared her mind and helped her work through answers to her letters as she walked and thought and prayed.

When she knocked on the back door, Solomon barked frantically and scratched at the floor of the doorway.

Maggie wasn't sure if this was a good idea after all. Getting bitten on her second day was not in the plan.

She was seriously contemplating walking

away when the door opened and Pops peered at her through the screen.

His eyes widened and he smiled. "Did you bring my pizza?"

Maggie blinked, and her heart clutched. He looked confused again. Then suddenly his brows dipped and he took a breath.

"No, you were here yesterday. You saved my puppy."

Relief shot through her. "*Yes.* I was here yesterday."

"You crawled under the bed."

She laughed. "Yes. I did."

"What'd you do a gall-dern thing like that for?" he asked. "A gal can get stuck doing that."

His memory was good. She laughed. "Yes, she can."

Solomon had stopped barking the moment he'd opened the door and sat on his haunches staring up at her. He trembled all over with excitement or fear while he assessed her. She figured he was trying to decide "bite her" or "don't bite her."

Taking a chance, Maggie bent down and held out her hand. She cringed and hoped she wasn't about to make a return trip to the vet.

Solomon sniffed, his long nose crinkling and his dark eyes wary.

"You're pretty brave, I'll give you that," Tru said, walking from somewhere behind Pops. Maggie jumped and yanked her hand back. Solomon jumped too. Startled by her movement, he tucked his tail and ran.

"Thanks a lot," she said, keeping her voice even, not wanting to scare Pops like she had the dog.

"Didn't mean to scare you. But you are brave."

"Or dense."

He chuckled. "Your words, not mine. But since Solomon hasn't ever been known to bite before, you might be pushing your luck. I'd be cautious, if I were you."

She crossed her arms and bit her tongue, deciding to move the conversation on. "I came for my lesson. But if you're busy —"

"I'm ready. Pops, I'm teaching Maggie to ride."

Pops flashed her Tru's crooked smile and in that brief moment, she wondered how much like Tru he'd been when he'd been a young man.

"You have the look," he observed, his momentarily keen eyes studying her, sharp and true before clouding.

"Maybe tomorrow you'll come down and watch her," said Tru.

Pops grinned bigger and motioned her

inside. "I'll show you."

She glanced at Tru and he nodded, so she followed Pops into the den of the house. She stopped in the doorway, and her breath caught. Everywhere she looked, bronze trophies filled the space. They were beautiful — of man and horse hunkered down with a dodging calf in front of them. Walking over, she read a couple of the engraved plates on the trophies. They were from the American Quarter Horse Association.

"He's very well respected in the AQHA," Tru said.

"I see that. These are amazing."

On the wall were large portraits of beautiful horses. Among them was an extraordinary pencil portrait of a man and a horse. She knew before she walked over and looked at it that this was Pops in his forties. He was strong and fit and just as she'd thought, he resembled Tru and Bo in a combined sort of way. She looked over at Pops, and he quirked a brow, his eyes mischievous. It gave him a rakish look, and she knew he'd been a flirt in his day.

She glanced over at Tru. He was watching her interact with his grandfather. What he was thinking?

He quirked a brow, mimicking Pops and she chuckled. They were one and the same.

That look reminded her that Tru Monahan had a reputation as a ladies' man. She could see how. Her toes curled and tingled just looking at him.

She turned back to Pops. "These are amazing."

"Me," Pops said, and she could almost see his mind churning as he searched for the next words. In the end he gave a sheepish smile.

"Like I told you, Pops was a major player in his day."

"I can see that. These were his horses?"

Pops walked over to one of three portraits and placed his hand on the chestnut horse in the picture. "Pep."

He looked up adoringly at the horse, then at her. "He's beautiful," she said.

"Stardust's grandfather. Stardust's registered name is Stardust Peppy."

She turned to Tru. "Really?"

He nodded. "Isn't that right, Pops?" He glanced at Pops, who had come to stand beside him. Maggie saw amazing love in Tru's eyes when he looked at his grandfather. And there was incredible grief there too. She'd seen it when he'd asked her to protect his grandfather's dignity. What would it be like to have someone care for her like that?

She'd have loved to have had grandparents to love and dote on, but they'd been gone years, and even when they'd been alive, she hadn't known them. Her mother was estranged from the family.

Pops looked thoughtful. "Yup. That's right. Best horse ever. Smart."

It was amazing to compare him yesterday with today, spouting coherent sentences. Her expression must have shown her surprise, because Tru gave her a sad half smile that seemed to say, "Yeah, he's still with us sometimes."

"You ready to go meet your destiny?" Tru asked, looking restless.

"That sounds kind of ominous."

"Naw. It's a good destiny."

"Long as you're still promising no broken bones."

She told Pops good-bye. Then with Tru's help, she managed to get Solomon to let her scratch him between the ears.

Outside, he took a deep breath, then climbed into his truck. She did the same and they drove in silence to the barn. She studied the horizon — safer than letting her gaze wander to Tru, especially since the inside of the truck suddenly felt as tight as a matchbox.

Finally Tru offered, "He has good days

and bad days. Good weeks and bad weeks. You've met him on a bad week. The doc — not Doc Hallaway," he clarified, like she might think he was taking his grandfather to see the town vet. That was obviously reserved for her. "His doctor is trying him on new medicine and it's got him swinging from one end of the spectrum to the other. But he seemed better while we were in the den."

"I thought so," she agreed. "It must be hard for you, watching him."

His jaw tensed. The edges of his eyes pinched. "You have no idea."

They reached the barn. "I'm sorry."

"Me too. But we move forward. It is what it is."

She reached for the door handle. "There's a saying . . . not every day is good, but every day has something good in it. Today is one of those days for Pops."

He gave her a quick smile. "Yeah. It is."

She opened her door and got out. He did the same.

"Am I going to brush Stardust again?" Maggie asked.

They were walking into the barn and he let her go past him at the wide entrance. The scents of hay and oats and horse filled the air, but of course her nose keyed into the totally male scent of Tru, woodsy and spicy and appealing as anything.

He was more relaxed this afternoon than he'd been that morning. Maybe he just wasn't a morning person. "Nope that's all done. Now you're going to learn to saddle him."

11

On Wednesday, as a much-needed bit of rain drizzled outside, Tru had the country station cranked up as he sanded the slender branch of a redbud tree that would become an armrest for the new chair he was working on. The knotty wood was beautiful and the golden tone showed the irregularities of the wood to perfection. It wasn't the strongest wood, but it held a beauty that always drew him. Right now he wasn't thinking much about the wood.

He was going to have to come to terms with what he was doing, and with how Maggie was affecting him. He would have to head toward the barn soon for their evening lesson, but right now, he just needed to unwind and try to get his head on right.

She was all he could think about.

All she had to do was walk into the barn and his pulse would race like he'd just started competing in a championship Quarter Horse event. The accidental brush of her hand, the look in her eyes . . . he sanded harder. Picking the wood up, he blew the dust particles off of it and then ran his fingers over it to check the smoothness. Instantly he thought of how soft Maggie's skin was. He'd been trying to avoid touching her, but sometimes there just wasn't a way around it.

"You sure are looking frazzled."

Tru glanced over his shoulder and found Jarrod standing in the doorway of his shop. "Nope, just —"

"Frustrated," Jarrod supplied.

Tru's gaze narrowed. "Did you need something?"

Jarrod chuckled. "I must have hit a nerve. You're wound up tighter than I've seen in a very long time. I got in around two this morning coming back from Amarillo. When I dropped the trailer off, I saw your lights were on. You having trouble sleeping?"

"What is with the twenty questions?"

"I'm just curious how this bet is affecting you, is all."

"It's driving me loco. How's that for the truth?"

Jarrod came into the shop and propped a boot on the lower shelf of Tru's workbench. "That disturbing."

Tru didn't want to talk about it. He hadn't slept since Maggie arrived. Bo had asked him earlier if he'd been burning the midnight oil reading or something.

Tru snorted at that. Reading. Yeah, right.

Thinking about long blonde hair, translucent pale green eyes that sparkled like raindrops . . . and then there was the rest of her — Tru glanced at Jarrod. That was a good way to stop thinking about Maggie. His brother studied him with open speculation.

"Pops is pretty good today. He showed Maggie his trophies yesterday." He decided to change the focus off of him. She'd come to see Pops. Pops liked her. He'd been in a fog before she'd arrived and then like magic, the fog cleared and there was his old Pops. The big flirt had shown off his trophy room. Tru smiled thinking about it.

"What did she think about his room?"

"She loved it." Tru loved that room too. It made him proud just to enter it. Tru had always had a lot to live up to. Not that he ever felt that from Pops, but from the cutting world, yeah. And he'd wanted to. He wanted to make his Pops proud of him. Wanted to be the one to carry the torch down the path his grandfather had blazed.

"Do you think she'll keep Pops out of the

limelight like you asked her to?"

"I think so. Watching her interacting with him, I felt reassured. There was genuine interest on her face. She wasn't just humoring him."

She'd glanced at him as she studied the pencil portrait and he knew she was making the comparison. He and Bo resembled Pops in many ways, but he knew it was Jarrod who resembled Pops the most. Not only in looks but in nature.

She hadn't seen his older brother yet, but when she did, she'd know exactly what Pops had been like as a younger man. There was a steeliness to Jarrod that Pops shared, a keenness in the eyes that even translated to that picture. Looking at his brother now, Tru's heart ached for the way his grandfather had been. And all the more the determination to carry on his legacy burned hot inside of him.

"Did you need me for something?" he asked, as he went to turn off the radio.

"Nope, I was just coming to see Pops, and thought I'd check and see how you were holding up since I've been gone."

Tru shrugged. "Let's just say we're making it."

Fifteen minutes later, after Jarrod had left and he was waiting for Maggie in the stable, he knew it was far worse than "making it." Instead of just getting through this deal, he'd started looking forward to seeing her and he was thinking that was a bad idea.

There was a liveliness in her step as she came toward him — as if she were floating. By the smile on her face, he knew she was in a good mood.

That was a good thing, seeing as he was planning on putting her on a horse today, he'd worried that she'd be a nervous wreck. This was really good for the riding aspect of the day — but seeing her smiling like that was a setback of major proportions.

"So, cowboy," she said, her voice as perky as that of a kid in a candy store. "What's in store for me tonight?"

"Tonight?" he asked numbly, as his gaze locked on the tantalizing smile on her full pink lips. Kissing came instantly to mind.

"Tru —" the sudden uncertainty in her tone was like a shot of cold water from an ice bucket.

He slammed his brows down in anger at his lack of self-control. He grunted, "You're going to get in the saddle, that's what."

Her mouth fell open and then snapped shut. Finally, her brow crinkled cutely and she asked, "You're sure I'm ready for that?"

"You're ready." His voice reflected the

strain he was under. "You just don't know it, yet. It's time. We probably won't start cutting lessons for a couple of weeks. Right now you just need to relax about getting your body snapped into pieces and try to enjoy getting the feel for the horse. You're going to love it." He focused on teaching. Not on Maggie.

"If you say so, but I'm really not athleti—"

"Stop putting yourself down, Maggie, and do this. Anyone can ride a horse. You may not become a world champion, but you can get enjoyment from being in the saddle. Trust me." He'd stepped closer to her, realizing he wanted to boost her confidence even if she still didn't trust him and he knew it.

He reached for her hand. Danger signals went ballistic in his head. "Come on, Maggie. I know you don't, but I promise you can trust me on this, even if you don't trust me on anything else." She met his gaze as he squeezed her stiff hand.

"I'm trying. I really am. I-it isn't as though I don't want to trust you."

That got his attention. Her fear was real, no doubt about it whatsoever now. Her pupils dilated in wide eyes as she took a shaky breath; those things couldn't be faked. "What can I do to help you trust me?"

She looked away, but let her hand stay limply in his. He squeezed gently. "Is this just about you being mad at me about the interview? I thought at Pops's yesterday you might have started to let that slide some."

She pulled her hand away and gave him a a stiff smile. "I'll try. I can't promise I'll be graceful or successful, but I will trust you on this and give it a try."

Her answer didn't satisfy him, but he figured if that was the best she could give him right now, that was what he'd have to take. But he wasn't done with this.

He smiled and pushed a wayward strand of hair from her forehead. "I'm holding you to that. Now, come on, let's saddle up."

She turned to Stardust and froze.

"Just do like I taught you yesterday," he urged her with patience.

"Okay. I will do this," she said, practically gritting the words.

He didn't say anything, just let her push herself.

He could see that though she was hesitant when she touched Stardust, as if still worried the horse would bolt or kick, she seemed to relax when he didn't.

He grinned like a fool when she was done

saddling her horse. "Good job." He squeezed her shoulder and she turned to smile at him. Beamed, actually, and it kicked him in the head. He wasn't so sure he had any brains left at the moment.

"That wasn't so hard." She spun back to Stardust and surveyed her handiwork. She tugged on the cinch, and then the saddle, making sure it was tight just like he'd taught her. "I really did it."

The awe in her voice was unmistakable.

"Okay, now we're ready to ride." He needed to ride. To do something other than stand here looking at her.

She nodded. "I'll try but again, I'm not making promises. So what do I do?"

With some effort, he forced his mind to think about the lesson. He showed her how to grab the saddle and where to place her foot in the stirrup. To demonstrate he took hold of the saddle horn, reins in his hands, placed his boot in the stirrup, and stood into the stirrup, pulling with his hands. For him it was second nature, requiring no thought, but a novice like Maggie watched every move he made with an intensity that had him smiling.

"See there, five seconds and you're in." He looked down at her from his seat in Stardust's saddle. "You can do this."

"Easy peasy," she said, that brow crinkling with her frown. "For you."

"Yup. And you too." He swung his leg over the horse and stepped down beside her. Their arms brushed. "Your turn."

She took a deep breath, hesitated, then grabbed the reins. He was standing close to her, to make sure she was okay, he told himself. But he sure was enjoying it more than he should have, especially when she reached for the saddle horn.

She was tall enough that it wasn't a stretch for her to grab it. He held on to the reins to control Stardust if something should go wrong. Not that he expected it to, but he wasn't taking any chances since unexpected things seemed to happen to Maggie all the time.

She placed her running shoe in the stirrup, and then, sucking in a breath, she lifted herself up and threw her leg over Stardust — or at least that was her intention. Somehow, he wasn't exactly sure how, but she swung too hard and her foot that was already in the stirrup slipped and went through the stirrup up to her knee and she fell. Tru grabbed for her and caught her in his arms, as Stardust moved sideways — not sure what his rider was signaling him to do. Tru gripped Maggie with one arm while reaching for the reins with his other hand. Stardust was good, but Tru was taking no chances. If the horse decided to bolt with Maggie tangled up like she was she could be hurt — her leg could be broken . . . or worse.

"Whoa, fella," Tru said, relieved when he had his grip firmly on the reins. Now to focus on Maggie.

She was hung over his arm like a sack of potatoes, helpless since one foot still rested on the saddle and one knee was hooked inside the stirrup. He looked down at her and caught her looking up at him with narrow eyes.

"So, I don't know much, but I'm guessing this isn't exactly good."

By the time Tru got her disengaged from the stirrup, Maggie had started to feel like a complete disaster. How had she done that? Tru said she'd gotten overzealous with her leg swing, and on the next go-round, maybe a little more caution was in order. Of course she was trying to focus on helping herself get untangled, but she kept getting distracted by the feel of his arms wrapped securely around her. Oddly, she realized she wasn't scared or worried that Stardust was going to run away with her. It had absolutely nothing to do with trusting the horse. She simply knew that while Tru held her, she was okay. That probably had something to do with watching him with his Pops the day before.

When her feet were finally planted on the ground again, she felt a little weak in the knees and had a hard time disengaging her fingers from their death grip on his shoulders — his very broad, firm shoulders.

"Are you okay?" he asked. He studied her with his hands planted on his hips — probably wondering how a woman her age could possibly have two left feet like she did. It was perplexing for Maggie herself, let alone anyone else.

"Oh, I'm fine. Just fine." She waved off his question. "Thanks to you."

"Good, then let's try it again."

She shot him a glare. "No way. Not after that. I think I'll head home and answer some emails. Get my sea legs back under me."

He chuckled. "We're about a hundred and fifty miles from salt water."

She scowled. "You know exactly what I'm saying."

"And I think you should get back in the saddle."

"I was never *in* the saddle."

"Maggie, it was an easy mistake." He reached to take her hand and she stepped back.

"Nope. Not tonight. See you in the morning." She didn't wait to argue, but headed for the exit instead. The cowboy had no clue that this was as much about getting away from him and catching her breath as it was about not getting on Stardust.

At the moment the horse was the least of her worries.

12

Maggie was in serious jeopardy of letting Tru past her guard.

"Wait up."

His voice brought her to a halt before she reached her car. "You are not getting out of this that easy. We have a deadline, and if you quit that easy, then we are in trouble."

She glared at him. He might be right, but at the moment she didn't care. All she could think about right now was throwing her arms around his neck and kissing him.

Her face burned hot thinking about it, and she knew she was probably the color of an overripe plum. This cowboy loved-'em and left-'em faster than she could blink, and at the moment she didn't care. "I don't want to get on the horse right now."

He crossed his arms and planted his boots wide and just studied her. "Why are you getting red?"

"I'm embarrassed. Wouldn't you be?"

True, but stretching it.

"Look, I get that you're a little clumsy sometimes. But I've got to say that I'm a little surprised how easy you give up. Especially after I read your column."

"You read my column?"

"Last week's. It was my first, I have to admit. But, Maggie, you gave sound advice to that woman who asked whether to settle for the deadbeat dude she was dating or to move on. How did you put it? To 'open your horizons in the hope of finding another man who will appreciate you.' " He grinned and Maggie's insides turned all gooey.

"Thanks."

"You're welcome. I was smiling when I finished reading what you said. I also noted that you didn't tell her to leave the deadbeat, but I'm pretty certain that after reading your words of encouragement, she and any other women out there who were settling would totally know that you were advocating moving."

"I can't believe you read it." She really couldn't.

"I was curious. Wanted to see what all of this is about."

Maggie thought about the woman he was speaking of. "I hope she moved on," she said, wistfully. "She deserved so much better."

"Yes, she did. Now, let me ask you what you would tell someone who wrote in about how to handle being clumsy. Would you tell them it was okay to just give up?"

Maggie sighed. She had walked right into his trap. "No, I wouldn't."

He stepped back and waved toward the barn. "After you."

Her nails dug into her palms and her feet resisted, but no matter how much she didn't need to be around him at the moment, she didn't have a choice. "Fine." She hiked her chin and marched past him. He chuckled and fell into step behind her.

This bet was getting harder by the instant. Two months. She had to make it two months and not fall under the spell of the man she knew was a female magnet. The tabloids had said it was true. Why at the National Finals Rodeo last year there were reports that two women actually got into a catfight over him. There was a picture on the front page of the thing that showed them fighting and him walking away.

And there were other stories floating around out there too. Maybe not so wild, but they were out there about him churning through a slew of women. The man was movie star good-looking, and it was reported that he'd been asked to star in some romantic western movie too. And she completely understood why.

But that was all the more reason for her to stay back. She had had her share of heartache where men were concerned. Maybe it was because of her mixed-up childhood, who knew why, but the few times she'd dated — despite how careful she was — she'd picked real jerks. But she still held out hope that she was going to find a good man one day. Someday she wanted to fall in love. She wanted kids and lots of them and the man she planned to let father her babies would not come from a background with even a *hint* of womanizing.

Nope, her man, and he would be *her* man, would be everything a real man was supposed to be. He would not be on the cover of a national gossip rag next to two women fighting over him.

Or any of the other things she'd heard.

No matter how much that man's touch or smile sent her insides to rioting and pulse to galloping.

"Okay, this time, easy with the leg. Nice and smooth, okay?"

Maggie gave him a where-would-you-like-

191

me-to-kick-you look and then took a deep breath and reached for the saddle horn. She did as he'd shown her, but this time she was very careful with her long leg. He hid a smile as she gently swung it over Stardust's back and she eased just as gently down into the saddle.

Her shoulders sagged in visible relief, but she shot him a scathing look that only made him want to chuckle more. She was a hardheaded woman and that was for certain. She was determined not to let him forget that he'd basically goaded her into getting back in the saddle.

So be it. He was a big boy. He could take it.

What he couldn't have taken was if she'd fallen out of the saddle again and into his arms.

Nope, this was much better.

"That's real good. Now, you just hang onto the saddle horn, hold your back straight, shoulders back, and settle into that seat. I'm going to lead you around the round pen."

"Go for it. I'll just hang around up here until you say I can go home."

"Fine." He shot her a don't-push-your-luck glare and led Stardust toward the round pen. What, did she think she was the only one all of this was affecting?

He looked over his shoulder. Maggie moved in the seat well. She might not realize what she was doing, but she'd adapted to the feel of the horse and was riding pretty smoothly. Some folks would have been bouncing all over the place. She might not be as hard to teach as she believed.

"You're sitting the horse good. You will do fine in the competition when we get to that point." He'd almost let her wonder if she was doing good or not but decided telling her was the best thing. There was no need to stretch out this afternoon feud any longer if at all possible.

"I just got on the horse and I'm terrified. How can you possibly tell that?"

"Hey, give me some credit here. I can just tell."

She gave a nervous laugh and he glanced over his shoulder to see the death grip she had on the horn.

"Relax, Maggie. Stop tensing up. I've got Stardust and he's not going to go anywhere except in this circle I'm leading him in."

He led the way around the circle pen, letting her get more comfortable with the feel of the horse. She struggled to relax and he knew she just needed time.

"So, how did you get the gig as the 'Gotta

Have Hope' gal?" He wanted to ease her nerves, but he was curious too. She was riding like he'd told her — stiff, but following instructions. "Not everyone would give sound advice. You answered four questions last week and you gave great advice of the heart."

"I try. I worry over each answer. I don't want to take a decision of the heart for granted. There are too many factors to evaluate. I believe we all hold the key to our happiness in our own hands. I try to figure out ways to empower my readers in my answers. I try to take the power out of the other person's hands and put it into my reader's hands."

He looked up and she smiled at him. A jolt rocked him like an earthquake. He realized keeping her mad at him might have been the best choice.

"So, how did you get this gig as the writer of this column?" he asked again, unable to stop himself.

"Amanda." She shifted in the seat and pushed her shoulders back a little as she looked off into the distance. He concentrated on walking Stardust in an easy pace around the round pen. There was something about the rhythmic movement of a horse's gait that could a lull a person — maybe that was why Maggie was opening up some.

"I met Amanda when I was at a very hard spot in my life. She invited me to move into the extra bedroom of her apartment." She paused and he glanced at her to see a lost look in her eyes. She gave a tiny shrug. "I really don't know why I'm telling you this, but I needed her help."

"I promise this won't be going anywhere else. I'm glad she helped you. Then what?" He couldn't believe she was opening up to him either. But he was glad.

"I ended up being her roommate for a few years while I went to school. Long story short, the paper was looking for some kind of advice column and she got a wild brainstorm about my name and pitched 'Gotta Have Hope' to them without my knowledge. After they liked it, she came to me with the job offer. She said my attitude of always trying to find some hope in everything inspired her. And that's how I got this."

He was trying to read between the lines. There were a lot of blank spots in her story that had him wanting to know more. Did the low spot she was talking about have anything to do with why she didn't trust easily?

Clara Lyn stared at Pebble Hanover. Pebble

owned the Sweet Dreams Motel, and had since she and her husband, God rest his soul, had bought it twenty years ago. She'd run that motel for the last ten years all by herself after Cecil fell off the roof during a thunderstorm.

Pebble was nice and sweet as they came — a bit too prim for her own good as far as Clara Lyn was concerned, but to each his own. Clara wasn't going to rain on her parade just because they had a different set of priorities.

But Clara figured she was having a whole, *whole* lot more fun than Pebble. She told Pebble that at least once every week, and right now was that time.

"Pebble, you need to loosen up. You've got knots the size of bowling balls between those shoulder blades of yours."

The thing was, she hadn't always been such a stickler. Oh, she hadn't ever been relaxed-relaxed, per se. But after Cecil had his accident, she'd gotten worse. Like a bolt tightened by a power tool. It wasn't healthy.

Still, she was the prettiest sixty-five-year-old woman Clara Lyn knew. And every single older man in town had tried his hand at asking her out — not a lot of good it did them. Pebble refused to date. Eventually, they all gave up and left her to her widowhood, though it was surely with great regret.

Everyone, that is, except that handsome scoundrel Rand Radcliff. Back in the day when they'd all been in school, Rand, the rebel of the group, had had a thing for Pebble. Much like Danny and Sandy from the movie *Grease* . . . Clara just loved that movie, but Danny got the girl in the end of the movie, while Rand did not. No, though Pebble and Rand had had their good-girl/bad-boy fling, Pebble had walked away and married the class president and lived happily ever after. Until he fell off the roof. Pebble had always seemed as happy as could be over the years.

Rand, on the other hand, had gone to college and come back to Wishing Springs and lived his life never quite settled. Though he'd changed and even eventually taken his seat on the city council, he had never married, and after Cecil's death he'd begun to change in many ways as it became apparent he was still sweet on Pebble after all those years.

The city councilman was nice-looking himself, he'd aged well and everyone knew that he had a crush as big as the Pacific on Pebble. It had become a weekly thing for her to turn down his offer of a date. Why, the moonstruck man sent flowers repeatedly over the years and he was dedicated to her — whether she wanted him to be or not.

Pebble, being the sweet person that she was, remained kind to him, but she continually insisted she was not interested in a relationship this late in her life.

But when there were events and festivals and such, he was always near, watching out for her. Everyone knew that Rand still loved Pebble.

The town bad boy was caught in a web of unrequited love.

And it was not good for him.

Clara Lyn knew this, as did everyone else. They'd been watching him deteriorate because of it with more and more drinking. It was causing him all kinds of misery and Pebble was at her wit's end. But Clara Lyn wasn't sure what to tell her friend. A person couldn't just jump off into someone else's personal business — not something like this. A drinking problem was not something to take lightly. And a relationship with a drinker was like waiting for dynamite to explode.

"What do you mean he had to be escorted home from the grocery store?" Pebble was looking at Clara Lyn with dismay. "Not again."

"I'm afraid so. That is what I heard from

Dorothy Simpson. She heard it from her grandson, you know, the cute teenager who works there. He said Rand came in staggering and ran right into the green beans on lane two. Said they went everywhere."

"No," Pebble gasped, the blood draining from her face as she fidgeted with the baby blanket she'd been knitting for one of the Over the Rainbow residents.

"It's true," Reba joined in, worry lighting her eyes as she studied Pebble. "He's been in a bad way ever since —" she paused. "Well, you know. Since he got drunk at Sadie and Malcom's fiftieth wedding anniversary and embarrassed you so much."

Pebble stiffened, her dainty mouth quivered, and her cheeks blushed pink gaining back a little cotton-candy coloring. "He had no right to do that. No right to embarrass me like that."

Clara Lyn slapped a hand to her hip. "He didn't have a right, but he sure enough did it. Taking over that mike and singing — or trying to sing — you a love song was a little over the top. What was that song?"

"How in the world could you forget something like that?" Reba declared, horror written on her face. "When a drunk man tries to sing a Whitney Houston version of a Dolly Parton song, *no one* forgets. I have never, and I mean never, recovered from hearing 'I Will Always Love You' sung *that* way."

Clara Lyn shot Reba a warning. Yes, she too, still suffered from nightmares because of that night but . . . "I'm *tryin'* to be encouragin' here, *Reba.*"

Reba huffed. "Well, excuse me for livin'. I only speak the truth. Sorry, Pebble."

Clara Lyn just could not help herself any longer. "Pebble, the truth is you need to move on. Cecil's been gone a long time. He'd want you to be happy. And I, for one, think you harbor some deep feelings toward Rand. There, I said it."

Pebble looked horrified now.

"Clara Lyn," Reba gasped. "I can't believe you just said that."

"What just happened to you speaking the truth? You know you believe the same thing."

Pebble started tossing her baby blanket in the bag. "And why would you think that? I've never been drunk a day in my life. What would I do with a man who gets drunk on a regular basis?"

Clara Lyn and Reba exchanged glances. Pebble had a point, but still, that didn't change what they both believed. Clara sighed. "Now, don't go getting all upset.

You did have that thing for him in high school. Back before you married Cecil. Everyone knows it."

Her cheeks went from cotton-candy pink to Maraschino-cherry red. Pebble didn't say anything, just kept scooting her baby blanket into the knitting bag along with the needles.

"Maybe you could help him," Clara Lyn said.

Pebble snapped her bag shut and stood. "I have told him that I will never welcome the affections of a man who drinks. And that did not help the situation. It is obvious that he feels stronger about his bottle than he does about anything, including me. You are mistaken, Clara Lyn Conway. Why, stumbling around in the grocery store — it's, it's a disgrace."

Before Clara Lyn or Reba could say anything, Pebble marched to the shop door, bag in hand and with a decisive tug, the door swooshed shut behind her leaving the Cut Up and Roll in silence.

"Oh, my," Reba said, her voice hushed.

"I've never seen Pebble that mad before." Clara Lyn's eyes narrowed. "It's a good sign."

"A good sign? If she'd been a rocket she'd be to the moon by now."

"Reba, think about it. Yes, she is embarrassed. Yes, he's fond of the bottle and she's
a teetotaler — wouldn't touch a drop if it
was all there was to drink and she was lost
in the desert. But I don't think she would
be that mad if she didn't care a little. Do
you?"

"You know," Reba drummed her finger-
nails on her manicure table, looking
thoughtful. "You just might be right."

Clara Lyn grinned. "I think it bears some
thought. And Rand does need to get his act
together. What kind of example is he setting? This is gettin' out of control."

"Maybe we need to speak to someone —"

"Doonie's his best friend," Reba said.
"He's also the mayor and Rand is on the
city council. As citizens we need to voice
our opinion. We could complain to the
preacher too. You know, for Rand's own
good."

"Reba, I'm sure that Doonie and Doobie
and the preacher all know. The problem is,
I think we all need to get together on this
and do one of those interventions. I was
watching one of them on a TV reality show
the other night. This guy's friends and family got together and planned a hijacking of
him. They just all got together and confronted him. What do you think? It never

hurts to be the one to squirt the first grease on a wheel and get it to squeakin'."

Reba stared at her. "That does not make a lick of sense but I know what you're saying. And I agree."

Clara Lyn felt better. "Then let's get to greasin'."

Maggie got her first column about Wishing Springs in by the Friday noon deadline. She pressed send at exactly 11:49 a.m. She actually loved the piece. It was a get-to-know-the-town article and it made her smile. She celebrated with a cup of green tea.

The fact that Tru had an exhibition on Friday and left early Thursday morning had worked for her. She needed a break from him.

Every day she was around him was a day of more conflicting emotions.

She had some letters to answer and then she was heading out to Over the Rainbow. When she'd been there earlier in the week, she'd been invited to come eat spaghetti and hang out this afternoon. She'd promised to come if she could. At the time, she hadn't been sure of her riding schedule. Or whether she would meet her deadline. She also hadn't known Tru was going to be out of town and that she'd get caught up because of it.

And she hadn't known just how much she was going to want to go back and see everyone. Especially Jenna. The girl was about as brave as they got as far as Maggie was concerned.

When she arrived, there were several cars parked in the driveway. Almost like they were having a party.

Turned out they were.

"Hey, Maggie, you came," Jenna called from the deck as Maggie rounded the corner of the house. She'd learned that most people used the back door.

"I sure did. I got my columns written and Tru is out of town, so no riding this evening. What's going on?"

"It's game day. There are a group of older ladies in there from town. They come out and teach us things, like cooking or knitting and then we play a bunch of board games. Today, Ms. Hanover is teaching a couple of the gals how to knit. I'm all thumbs where that's concerned."

"I would be too. That's really cool, though."

Looking at the cars, she recognized one of them as Clara Lyn's. She had a feeling if the hairstylist was in there, they surely were having a party.

Sitting down in the chair beside Jenna, Maggie saw she had a photo book of some kind in her lap. "What are you doing?"

Jenna gave a big sigh. "I'm looking for a family for my baby."

Her words hit Maggie hard. "You are —" she paused, "— giving your baby up for adoption?" Maggie hadn't expected this. Not after all Jenna had gone through to take care of her child.

Jenna's hand went protectively to her stomach. "Yes."

The word was soft, and for a girl as worldly and in-your-face as Jenna, it spoke volumes. Maggie ached for her. It was a terrible situation.

"It's for the best," she said, stronger. "I'm barely sixteen, a kid myself."

Maggie's heart clutched hard at Jenna's still-uncertain words. She sounded as if she were trying to convince herself it was true she couldn't take care of her baby.

What was Maggie supposed to say to that? Maggie thought of herself and what she'd have done if she'd been in that situation.

"I'm sure you've thought this out. And Lana and Peg have helped you a lot. Right?"

Jenna nodded, her expression grim. "It's my choice. It's why I worked so hard to get here." Her voice trembled slightly, but determination won out. Though resignation hung thickly in the air.

Jenna was out here making an obviously heart-wrenching decision and it was game night. The irony of it was not lost on Maggie. These girls made choices like this every day here at the home. They'd made the choice for their babies to live, now they had to make the choice to live without their babies.

It cut Maggie straight to the heart. Instantly she said a prayer for Jenna and all the girls in the home.

What did she say to Jenna, though? It wasn't as if it was any of her business. Or as if she could possibly help her make such a choice.

"Those . . . are they pictures of families?" She leaned over slightly and glanced at the page. Pictures of a couple and what looked like their home.

Jenna toyed with the edge of the page. "Yes. They each have a book they make and submit to the agency. It tells me about them and it tells me why they want my baby. And," she paused, "it tells me of the life they can give my Hope. The love."

Hope.

Maggie fought tears, Jenna naming her

child Hope hit her on so many levels. "It's a wonderful thing you're doing," Maggie said. "You love your baby enough to think of her before yourself. I'm sure those couples want a baby as much as . . . as much as you love little Hope. And there are so many babies out there that don't get the chance you're giving her."

Jenna nodded, her hand rubbing gentle circles on her stomach. "I —" she paused. "I love her. This is best way to show my love." She inhaled sharply and sat up straighter. "Let me show you the ones I'm interviewing over the next week. I'm having to kind of rush this process more than most girls because I had such a late start. But these couples really seem like people I'd like."

Maggie felt so sad. Really sad. Jenna was being extremely brave, but Maggie saw through it. The girl was putting on a face. She wanted her baby. Maggie could tell.

Maggie basically had no one growing up. She'd have had to do the same thing as Jenna had she become pregnant. And for a girl like Maggie, who ached to have a brood of babies and toddlers surrounding her, it would have been almost an impossible thing to do.

Did Jenna long for a family she could love

and be surrounded by as much as Maggie did?

Maggie knew not every runaway had had the same experiences she'd had. Still, looking at Jenna as she tucked her sable hair behind her ear and turned the page, Maggie got the feeling they thought alike.

But what could be done? If Jenna couldn't take care of a baby at her young age then this was the best way. Right?

A prayer welled up inside of Maggie and formed on its own. *Please give Jenna strength and guidance . . . and the courage to make it through.*

13

Tru drove into the town on Saturday afternoon. He was glad to be home. He'd left a day early to head to the cutting because as planned, he had a test to do.

Thursday had been the day he was supposed to show up at MD Anderson. As usual, the cancer center in Houston had been a busy place — it was so huge and there was no quick trip ever, but it hadn't taken all day and for that he'd been thankful. He'd just been glad to get the test over with. Now he waited. He'd told no one what he was doing, not even Bo or Jarrod. He should have. But he hadn't.

He'd agreed to the testing, because lately the idea of fathering children had been on his mind. Whether he could was a question that had haunted him over the last few years, but only this year had it suddenly grown to where he couldn't ignore it. All the road time was wearing on him, and he'd started thinking more and more about settling down. And maybe Pops's illness had put a burr under his saddle too. Life was short. He'd been sent a notice about a group study of the effects of cancer treatments on young boys that his oncologist was involved in, and so he'd made the call and waited for Dr. Jenson to call him.

He didn't plan on dwelling on it over the next little while until he heard the results of the study. But it hovered firmly in the corner of his mind like a shadow.

Driving through town on his way to the ranch, he stopped by the feed store for supplies.

When he finally made it home to the ranch, it was almost five. He was startled to see Maggie standing at the arena fence holding her hand out to Stardust.

So, she'd been keeping up her friendship while he was gone. He smiled at the thought. And immediately thoughts of lifting her from Stardust and holding her close swept over him.

When she turned, the breeze lifted a wisp of her hair from her face and ruffled her filmy shirt, molding it to her gentle curves. His pulse quickened at her beauty.

His stomach clenched looking at her.

"Looks like you have a friend there," he

said, walking over to her. She'd grown darker having spent time in the arena, and the cream-colored shorts she wore showed off her long, tanned legs. "Stardust is eating your attention up."

"He's a friendly one, that's for sure." She studied him as he stopped only a foot away.

He was crowding her more than he should, but he was unable to help himself. He'd been thinking of her for the last three days — how good she'd smelled when he'd held her. He breathed in and smiled as the sweet scents of her filled his senses in living color. Thinking of her had meant not thinking about the test so he hadn't really tried not to.

His stomach clenched tighter and he fought a battle, wanting to pull her close and bury his face in her soft hair and kiss those lips that had been driving him crazy since Wednesday night in the barn.

He was suddenly hot. That it was Texas in midsummer explained some of it — not all of it.

"You look relaxed." Not exactly what he'd meant to say. But certainly safer than telling her how beautiful she was and how glad he was to see her legs again.

She'd been wearing jeans every day for riding lessons which was safest. Still . . .

"I got my first column written about Wishing Springs and also met my deadline for my 'Gotta Have Hope' column. It was a little tough this time. My email submissions have doubled. I've got a new batch waiting on me right now."

The news stung like ice water reminding him that she was benefiting from this venture.

"That's good. I assume."

She leaned her hip on the arena fence. "It is — my boss will like it. For me it means late nights reading all of them and answering them and picking out which one will be in the paper."

"You answer all of them? You read all of them?"

"Sure I do. It's overwhelming sometimes, but that's what I'm committed to."

He thought about that. "So that's why you looked so tired on Tuesday and Wednesday."

"Oh, yeah. That's why. Your early mornings were killing me after my late nights."

He laughed and she did too. He liked her laugh. It had a husky edge to it and a kind of musical lilt.

She turned back to Stardust and scratched him between the ears — lucky horse.

Tru stepped away at that thought. He was toying with fire and he knew it. "I need to unload Cinder." He strode away from her, back toward the trailer.

"So how did your exhibition go?" she asked, following him.

He focused on work. "Good. One of my main sponsors is the producer of horse feed and special care products for horses. Periodically, I have these exhibitions at arenas and it actually draws a good-size crowd. Most of the time. I've done a few that were flops. This one had nearly two hundred people at it."

"Wow, and you showed them how to cut?"

"Yes, but mostly I showed them things I'm going to be showing you in a couple of weeks."

"So you were practicing."

He smiled, feeling better suddenly than he had when he'd first driven into the yard. "Oh, yeah, I've got to win this thing after all," he teased, and it felt good. He pulled the lever and opened the trailer gate, swinging it wide.

She laughed. "Oh, like you think I'm competition or something."

"Hey, you never know."

He walked Cinder off the trailer, having left Crimson home for this go-round and taken the younger horse out for some experience. He was glad to have a job to do or otherwise he might have snatched Maggie up and kissed those teasing lips.

"Now that I know you better I don't believe it."

Her smile blossomed full as she fell into step beside him. "Good."

"Hey, I need to check on Pops, but we could ride in about forty-five minutes. If you want?"

"That sounds good to me. I've been trying to make myself not be so skittish. I stopped in to pet Stardust at least once a day while you were gone."

"Great."

"I'll go change and read a few emails," she said and headed for her car. He went into the barn and realized after a moment that he was whistling.

Maggie had missed Tru and she wasn't quite sure how to handle it. It went against everything she wanted, and yet when he'd walked into the barn, it was as if the day got suddenly brighter. Her spirits had lifted.

She'd been happy to see him.

Wanting to give herself some time to clear her head, she changed quickly and sat down to read a few emails. But instead, she picked up the bag full of mail and reached for a letter. Using her mail opener, she split open

214

the end and tugged out the typed letter. She started to read it, then halted. Her mouth went dry and her hands began to tremble, causing the paper in her hand to shake violently.

Maggie stared at the letter.

I know who you are and what you did — what would happen if I exposed the truth about you?

There was nothing else in the letter and no return address on the envelope. Icy fingers of her past wrapped around her heart — reached in and gripped around her windpipe cutting off her breath.

Was it her dad? Of course, that would be her first thought. He was the only person alive she thought would ever recognize her from the girl she'd once been. But was he out of prison? And if so, how had he found her?

Her hand went to her throat and she sucked in a shallow bit of air.

Closing her eyes, she willed her pulse to calm down, but it didn't pay any attention to her, speeding up instead, as thoughts of her past reared from the shadows . . . and threatened everything she'd worked so hard for.

She glanced at the clock and knew she had to go. Tru would be waiting on her.

Five minutes ago she wasn't sure what to do with Tru Monahan. Now, that was the least of her worries.

"Is something on your mind?"

Maggie glanced over at Tru, still shocked that they were riding across open pasture and not in the round pen. She'd been so numb with worry about the threatening letter that she hadn't even questioned him about why. He'd told her anyway as if thinking she was worried about the horse.

She wished.

He'd explained that this was what she needed. That she would learn to relax and get used to the feel of the horse beneath her as they rode a casual pace across country.

At the moment Maggie wanted to bend low over Stardust's neck and ride like the wind. Ride far away and out of reach of whoever knew she was here and knew the secrets of her past.

She couldn't do either. She'd probably fall out of the saddle and break her neck if she tried galloping Stardust, but the plus of that was it wouldn't matter then whether anyone knew that Maggie Hope wasn't her real name. Or that she'd been a con-artist and a thief from the age of four — until right before she'd met Amanda.

She closed her eyes and swayed.

"Maggie, what's wrong?"

She focused, meeting Tru's concerned gaze. "Nothing. Just enjoying the ride."

He didn't look convinced. Her stomach was feeling as uneasy as he looked. "You don't look all right," he said. "You look pale."

She studied the scenery and tried to think of an honest reply. "I went to see a friend today — Jenna. She's a teen out at the home for pregnant girls." It was the truth and while it didn't explain her lack of color, it did give her something to talk about. And right now she needed that for more than a cover.

The sun was brilliant and she was glad she'd put her shades on before they'd headed out so at least he couldn't see her eyes.

"How did you meet her?"

"Well, it's a unique story, actually." She smiled in relief that she had something else to focus on. She patted Stardust's neck and told him about finding her on the side of the road and taking her to Peg and Lana's. He took his shades off and gaped at her in disbelief.

"She *hitchhiked* in the back of a truck under a tarp and she was seven months pregnant."

"I know it's unbelievable." Maggie felt sudden tears well in her eyes.

"She must have been very desperate." He pulled Cinder to a halt and she pulled on the reins and Stardust stopped too. "You're crying."

She sniffed and brushed a tear from her cheek with the back of her hand. "It's just . . . you're right. She told me the other night that she was running from her abusive father and doing whatever it took to get her baby to safety." Maggie's thoughts veered to her own father and the emotional abuse he'd put her through all of her life. She was at least thankful she'd not had to endure the physical abuse that Jenna had endured for so long.

Tru's eyes hardened and his jaw stiffened. "Unbelievable. What a jerk."

Maggie nodded. "Thankfully, she is safe. But now she's making the choice to give her baby up for adoption. And it's breaking my heart." Sighing and feeling restless, she urged Stardust to start walking again and Tru did the same with his horse.

"So how's she doing with it?"

"Being as brave as she was to take out on

218

her own. She's going to do it. But I don't think she wants to. It's for her baby." Maggie couldn't imagine — the idea was becoming a little too tough to linger on. Time to change the subject. "Thank you for bringing me out here today. It's beautiful."

He touched the edge of his Stetson. "Glad to be of service."

She studied her surroundings. There was a small pond to the left and several black cows grazed. One even stood in the pond. "I really didn't believe I would enjoy riding. But I am." And she'd needed it. The whole experience was like some kind of deep therapy. Thinking about the letter in the cabin waiting on her, she felt a little better prepared to face it now.

"I'm glad you're liking it. I love it. And I can promise you," he cocked his head to the side and shot her a dazzling white smile, "it's only going to get better."

Maggie swallowed hard, despite the emotions tearing at her, and her pulse ricocheted at his smile. Tru Monahan had a way of making her feel things she'd longed to feel all of her life.

And she had no idea what to do about that. It was such a deep longing that even now, it had the ability to override everything.

14

Tru led them down the grassy path that weaved its way through the pastures. She was quieter than she'd been earlier, and he chalked it up to her concentrating on not messing up. Or she was worrying about her friend. Poor kid.

Maggie had a good heart. It became more and more evident how good with every day that he knew her. Trying to rescue Pops's pooch the first day, and then on her next visit being so sweet when Pops showed her his trophies. And then to find out that she'd picked up this poor, pregnant runaway and taken her to safety . . . Maggie Hope was the real deal.

They rode in more relaxed silence for a few minutes. He actually hadn't ridden for the enjoyment of it in a while. He'd missed it. These days, he had so much on his plate with the duties of sponsorship and his training business and the ranch. Then there was

Pops and now this thing with the media. Sometimes he wasn't sure he'd ever get his life down to a simpler form. Maggie made him acutely aware of how badly he wanted that. He couldn't even think about a family until things settled down.

"So, you being here for so long isn't upsetting your boyfriend?" The question came out of nowhere. He'd been wondering about her, but he hadn't planned on asking. A woman like Maggie had to have someone anxious for her to be around.

He saw her shoulders stiffen immediately. "No boyfriend."

"Really, how's that?" Now what was he doing?

A couple of scissor-tailed birds swooped past them in a game of chase, their long, split-tail feathers giving them a playful air.

"I'm selective," she said, hesitantly.

"As in picky?" He was crazy. Why was he pushing?

"No, there's nothing wrong with being careful who you date and trying to choose well. Much better than dating anyone and everyone." Her last words sounded accusing.

His spirits sank. "So, you read tabloids." Why that hurt, he didn't know.

"Hardly. But it's kind of difficult not to

notice headlines and front pages when I'm in line at the grocery store. Especially if it's a similar headline on all of the different rags at the same time."

"Point taken." He grimaced. They'd reached a shallow ravine with about a twenty-foot slope down to the dry streambed. He stopped on the edge, and she pulled up beside him. Doing good.

"It's actually none of my business," she said. "I shouldn't have said anything."

"But you did." His hand tightened on the rein, understanding now some of the lack of trust that had been directed at him. Or at least he thought this could be it. He'd done this to himself.

She colored and he realized he was staring at her. He yanked his gaze off of her, feeling the sting of her judgment all the way through him.

Urging his horse forward, he began to maneuver down the uneven slope.

"Wait. I can't do that," Maggie called, panic in her voice.

"You're not going to. Stardust is. You just sit back in the seat and move with him. He knows what he's doing. Trust him." He stared at her over his shoulder. "You can do this."

She glared at him. Did he care? Not at

the moment. Not at all.

Well, that was a lie and he knew it. Stardust knew what he was doing and whether she realized it or not, she wouldn't fall out of the saddle.

At least he hoped not.

He'd learned if there was a way, Maggie would figure out how to accomplish it. Good or bad.

Maggie should not have brought up the tabloids. Really, what had she been thinking? She hadn't been.

And what was he thinking? Obviously he wasn't thinking either. The cowboy had ridden down into the ravine and expected her to follow him.

She'd just barely started getting comfortable in the saddle. She'd just told him she was enjoying learning to ride and now he wanted her to ride Stardust down that rocky, uneven — not to mention steep — path. He had lost his mind.

"I can't do that," she called as he reached the bottom. Instead of answering, he rode Cinder through the middle of the ravine bottom, heading away from her. Just leaving her sitting there.

Maggie's eyes narrowed to slits and she felt the steam rush from her ears — saving her from blowing a gasket or something. How dare he be so mean. This was all too much.

The man was a — a jerk. Just like every other man who'd ever entered her life.

She wanted to turn Stardust around and gallop back to the barn. That would show him. She envisioned him watching her lean over Stardust's back riding like the wind away from him. That would show him she wasn't to be toyed with.

But that was just her mad imagination. For one, from where he was, he wouldn't be able to see her flying across the pasture. And two, she knew she'd fly right out of the saddle and land in a heap on the ground. Nothing good about that. Except to give him something to be smug about.

She glared down the slope in front of her. *Trust Stardust.*

Tru's words echoed through the flames of her anger as she watched him heading away from her. Heading around a bend, he would soon disappear behind if he didn't halt Cinder.

She was suddenly so sick of everything. Her dad, her past, everything that wanted to work at defeating her. She at least needed to try this.

"Go, Stardust," she ordered in a husky

whisper, nudging the horse forward with her knees. That was all it took for the horse to take the first step down. Maggie's left hip dipped with the downward movement of the horse's step and then her right hip dipped with the next step. She automatically leaned back in the seat to compensate for the new angle, gripping the saddle horn and the reins at the same time for extra insurance.

She glanced toward Tru. He was gone.

Her heart pounded and she gritted her teeth as the incline grew steeper. Yes, it wasn't a huge incline, but as Maggie's first, it seemed like a straight drop-off to nowhere.

But she was doing it.

Halfway down, her heart leveled off some, and Maggie realized her death grip on the saddle horn had turned into just a firm hold. She was doing it.

By the time Stardust leveled off, Maggie's grin overpowered her face, straining to reach from ear to ear.

"We did it," she breathed, still in disbelief as she leaned forward and patted Stardust's neck. "We did it."

The urge to tell Tru what she'd done swamped her and she looked again, but he was long gone around the bend. The disappointment weighed heavy on her.

She'd never really had anyone to share things with, no accomplishments — until Amanda had come into her life. Before that, she'd been so alone that her life seemed silent. It would have been nice to see Tru watching her and know that he'd helped her accomplish this even if he'd made her mad in the process.

But, he wasn't there. Why had he just left her like this?

She'd goaded him with the stupid crack about the tabloids. Up until that time they'd been fine. But then he was getting too close and she knew it. That tabloid jibe had been more to remind her of why she couldn't fall for the cowboy than it had been for him.

She'd needed something to remind her that this was a working relationship. *Working.*

Purely a working relationship and nothing more.

The pride she'd felt slipped away, and she followed Tru's path down the trail and around the bend. He was there, up ahead waiting in the shadows of an overhanging tree. He'd gotten off his horse and was letting it drink from a section of the stream that intersected from another ravine.

In a flood, this would be a dangerous

226

place to be, but for now, it was a peaceful, secluded hideaway.

"You made it," he said. His voice sounded neutral, distant.

"Yes, we did." Deflated by his attitude, she went to dismount from Stardust, but she swung her leg over his rump too fast and lost her balance. Her foot hung in the stirrup *again.*

Tru must have moved like a superhero, because he was there and she fell straight into his arms. Foot still in stirrup. Stardust jumped and for one terrifying moment she thought the horse was going to take off and she was going to be torn from Tru's arms and dragged through the gully.

"Whoa, Stardust," Tru said soothingly as he snagged the reins and held the startled horse. "Hold on there," he urged, calming the animal. Stardust stabilized and Maggie relaxed a little. She was clutching Tru's shirt with both hands and realized if she'd been torn from his arms, his shirt would have gone with her.

"Tug your boot out, easy. There you go." Tru helped her ease her foot out of the stirrup while he continued to hold her close. When her foot dropped free, his arm tightened around her, holding her so she didn't fall.

Immediately, he dropped the reins and used both his arms to shift Maggie so she was standing.

Well, she could have been, except somehow with his arms tightly around her waist, her feet didn't quite touch the ground. Her heart pounded in rhythm with his and he stared into her eyes with longing that took her breath away. Longing that mirrored the longing she was feeling for him. How could this be? He'd made her so mad and now she wanted him to kiss her.

When his gaze dropped to her lips Maggie's blood hurtled through her veins. Yes, she wanted Tru Monahan to kiss her and that feeling was stronger than anything she'd ever experienced in all of her life.

His golden eyes were warm with what? Wanting?

He wanted to kiss her too.

Somewhere in the back of her mind, alarms were clanging, but Maggie had honestly never felt this before. He shifted slightly, his hand coming to her hair, wrapping around the nape of her neck. The sensation sent shivers racing through her, causing her stomach to tremble. Their hearts beat together. At least his was pounding as hard as hers, and then the endless moments passed and with shadows crossing his beautiful eyes, he dipped his head and his lips moved to hers.

Maggie wilted at the contact. His hand dug into her hair, and his lips, warm and firm, moved across hers, sending more shivers of emotions rioting through her. It was like a starburst exploding over a calm lake, and there was no denying that she'd never experienced anything remotely like this before.

She slanted her mouth, wanting more, needing more. Her arms tightened around his shoulders and her fingers tangled in the short thickness of his hair.

This, was . . . *wrong.*

She ignored the warning.

Then Tru pulled back, looking as dazed as she felt. Her lips felt swollen and lovely. He kissed her again, slow and gentle this time.

Then he pulled back, set her on her feet, and moved away from her.

"That," he raked a hand through his hair, "was a mistake."

Maggie couldn't move. Could barely think.

"That shouldn't have happened," he repeated. Reaching down, he swept his hat from the ground, raked his wavy dark locks off his forehead, and settled the hat back in place. Just like he did his emotions.

Maggie was breathing hard as she stared at him. Still stunned by everything that had just happened. It wasn't as though she had a lot of experience in a situation like this. She'd only been kissed a handful of times in her life. Maggie was innocent where emotions and experience collided. He, on the other hand, was not.

"You're right." The words came out as weak as she felt. She gave herself a hard mental shake and said stronger, "Thank you for stepping in just now. I always have had my klutzy moments. Maybe we should go back now." She would not cry. She would hold up her head and she would not let him see how deeply that kiss had affected her.

"Yeah, you're right."

He didn't look at her as he took the reins of his horse and handed her Stardust's.

"That won't happen again," he said and anger flared deep inside her. As much at her foolheartedness as his callousness.

She kept her temper intact and said nothing.

What was there to say?

15

"What's got you all stirred up?" Bo asked on Sunday afternoon.

"I'm not stirred up," Tru grunted. *Nothing except that I'm an idiot.* That was about it.

Bo looked slightly bored with his brevity. "Yeah, so I'm supposed to believe that you're not mad about something. I was at church this morning. I saw you. You did more grunting than talking, like you're doing now. And you didn't stay for 'Happy Trails.' You love that song, and don't think I don't know it. You sing along with the kids every Sunday."

Crazy brother. They went to the Cowboy Church of Wishing Springs, and the kids singing "Happy Trails" at the front of the sanctuary was the last thing they did before they broke for lunch. And Bo was absolutely right, Tru enjoyed watching the little toddlers and kids singing the song, but today he hadn't stuck around.

His conscience had been bothering him plenty. Tru had failed and failed miserably where Maggie was concerned.

Why had he kissed her? They'd barely gotten this two-month gig going and he was already kissing her. What happened to not acting on the attraction? What happened to not being tabloid fodder again?

What had come over him? He'd acted like a real jerk leaving her to ride down that ravine alone when he knew she didn't trust herself. He'd known she could do it. He'd trusted Stardust to get her down safe. But still that was no excuse.

And then to haul off and kiss her like there was no tomorrow.

He was a real class act. Yeah, a real dirtbag was more like it.

And then the look in her eyes when he'd pulled back from the kiss. She'd been as stunned and dazed as he'd been. What was going on between them was powerful, but now was not the time to explore it.

Not if he wanted to keep Maggie from starring on the front cover of tabloids across America. Hopefully he was wrong, but he worried that after the TV special, there would be at least a few people with cameras snooping, hoping for some cheap shots that could make them some money. And if they had any kind of relationship it would only make the chances of that happening more certain.

Nope, this wasn't happening.

Truth was, he'd seen the pride in her eyes when she'd rounded that bend in the creek bottom and known she'd made it down that slope on her own. He'd been so proud of her, but more *for* her.

And, yes, he'd been mad that she'd believed that junk about him — despite the fact that he deserved her scorn.

If she'd just gotten off the blamed horse without mishap, things would have been fine.

But she hadn't. And once he had her in his arms, well, it hadn't been his brain that took over. It had been his emotions and the purely male drive inside of him that sidestepped everything he knew was right and took over.

The fact that she'd kissed him back had only thrown fuel to the fire.

Her eagerness had undone him for a minute — the warm, sweet response of her mouth on his. Thinking about it now had his hands shaking as he reached for a sack of feed.

It was as if their lips had been made to fit perfectly and the — he shook his head and forced the sweet memory away.

"Is this about Maggie?"

Tru yanked up the sack of feed to his shoulder and carried it from the feed room to the back of his truck. "Why would you say that?"

Bo walked over to the tailgate and tossed his load into the back of the truck, staring at him. "Because you've been acting different ever since this bet thing started up. And she was there. Clara Lyn and Reba were introducing her to everyone. I saw you sidestepping to miss her. That is not like you."

"Look, Bo. I've got my reasons."

"That just doesn't make sense. You're giving her riding lessons every day but Sunday, and she's living about a half a mile down the road. So why you're avoiding her at church is a little suspicious. I mean, I know I'm just your brother, and I've only known you all my life, so this kinda throws up the red flags. You know what I'm sayin'."

Tru shifted his weight from one boot to the other and studied the horizon hard. Finally he said, "You want to know? Here it is — I hauled off and kissed the woman yesterday."

Bo grinned. "So what's wrong with that? She's a beaut, and I'm not talking about a car. Sure there's that whole I'm-gonna-put-you-in-the-funny-papers thing going on here, but, hey," he said, hiking a dark brow. "She's single. You're single — and getting older by the minute, I might point out. We've got kids to produce, and big brother is kinda failin' us on that end. I'm trailing y'all by a couple of years, so I've got leeway. But you, my man, have got no excuses. Go for it."

Tru scowled. "Would you cut it out?"

Bo laughed. "What is wrong with kissing a beautiful woman? And since when did you ever have a problem with that?" Bo suddenly stopped smiling. "You really have feelings for her." It wasn't a question.

Tru stared at his brother as the truth hit him hard — since he'd met Maggie he'd realized that he could very easily lose his heart to her. And knowing that meant there was no way he was doing anything right now to mess up her life. Him being in her life right now wouldn't be a good thing. It was the math, and she knew it.

On Sunday night Maggie stared at her computer trying to concentrate on her job. The letter jumping out at her tonight was from a woman who had just broken up with her boyfriend — who had repeatedly

dropped her — and now after finally walking away from the guy, the letter writer
wasn't sure if she could live without him.
She was asking Maggie if she should try and
get him back. It was signed Second
Thoughts and Confused.

"Isn't that a fine kettle of fish? Confused
— excuse me!" Maggie frowned at the
computer. *It wasn't fine at all.* What was it
with women who thought that their happiness depended on some guy who could treat
them badly then just drop them whenever
the moment struck? Where was the hope in
that? It was an endless loop that didn't favor
the female at all.

Maggie stood and walked to the window
of the cabin. Men. She didn't understand
them. At all.

She'd spent most of her life avoiding
relationships with them, and yet she gave
advice — and *hope* — on the subject.

The disturbing idea that she was a fraud
rattled through her. A fraud.

And someone out there knew it.

She pushed the thought away. The person
who'd written that threatening letter had
given her nothing to go on. All she could do
was wait and see when the next letter
showed up. What did they want?

The weight on her shoulders felt too heavy

to bear. Maggie felt weary suddenly. Rubbing her temple, she closed her eyes and knew right now she couldn't answer Second Thoughts's letter. She didn't really know anything about what she was trying to give hope to women about. Nothing. And yesterday with Tru proved it unequivocally.

What was she supposed to really tell that woman? Could she give that poor woman hope when she didn't know what to do with her own life?

Like what was she supposed to do about Tru?

Stay away from him, that's what.

That wasn't an option though. That kiss had happened over twenty-four hours ago and she could still feel it.

How could something that had sent her heart soaring have been a mistake?

She'd seen him at church and he'd been careful not to be on the same side of the church with her. And he'd left early. Obviously it remained a big mistake to him.

It was truly aggravating, but why hadn't she expected him to act that way? He hadn't spoken the whole ride home after the kiss, so why did she expect more today?

Nope, the man had led the way out of the ravine and straight to the stable with her trailing him.

But once there, she'd dismounted before he had — this time without incident — and led Stardust to her stall. They'd each taken the saddles off their horses and brushed them down, and that done, she'd left the stable and not looked back. He had tried to say something, but she'd told him to save his breath. That he'd been right — the kiss should never have happened.

The tension had been unbelievably thick.

The lonesome cry of the pack of coyotes echoed outside the window. On first arrival she would have been frightened by the sound. Tonight she empathized with the soul-wrenching sound. She still didn't like it though.

It was time to try to go to bed. She double checked that the doors were all locked — as if the coyotes were going to come and open the doors with their teeth. Feeling ridiculously low, she went to her bedroom hoping sleep would help her see things in a better light tomorrow.

Wearing her oversize pajama bottoms and her pink tank top, she crawled into bed and cuddled up with her pillow. At the rate she was going, it was probably all she'd ever have to cuddle up with.

Oh, how she wished she was back home in Houston working in her cozy apartment where the wildest animal noises were the occasional bark from her neighbor's Toy Poodle. Where she didn't get bit by oversize Basset Hounds. Where she went to see regular doctors and not vets. Where her face wasn't plastered across the morning show, making it possible for her past to creep up and kick her in the back.

And where the men, well, they kept their distance. That was a whole lot more appealing than a man who kissed her till her head spun and her heart turned over. Only to have him declare what a mistake it was.

Hope. What did she know about hope? Other than it was a name she'd applied for to cover up her bad history.

16

Maggie would not be mortified, or even the least bit embarrassed. She got out of her car the next morning and pulled her shoulders back while giving herself the pep talk. What was behind was behind and today was a new day.

She stalked into the barn with her head held high. She was here for the riding.

Actually, she was here to keep her job.

And Tru was here to teach her to ride.

There would be no more kissing. Not that he would want to, but she didn't want to either. She was no wimpy little woman to be toyed with. She gave good, strong advice that helped other women who were feeling both wimpy and walked over. She had plenty of letters from women who told her how much her column helped them.

Yes, it had taken her a long, sleepless night to pull on her big girl pants and stop feeling sorry for herself, but she had done it. No more kissing. It just messed up a girl's head. Blocked her good sense and wreaked havoc on an otherwise workable plan.

Whether he won or she won the bet wasn't really the issue. The issue was that she keep her job.

That she keep "Gotta Have Hope" alive. And that meant she had to keep her readership happy and interested. And she had to figure out who sent the letter. Could it have been Shane? Later, after her lesson, she was going to make some phone calls. It was time to find out if certain people had gotten out of prison.

Today, she planned to make it clear to Tru that this was strictly a business deal for both of them and that there would be no more kissing.

It was the only way to get the elephant out of the barn.

He wasn't in the barn waiting on her like usual. She stalked to the end of the run where all the different round pens were. And there he was in the larger of the two riding. Her heart stumbled seeing him and that made her all the more determined to hold to her guns. She wasn't a wimp. She'd told that girl in the letter last night to hold to her course, that she could live without that wishy-washy guy, and to not think she couldn't. It had been her most decisive letter to date. And that meant Maggie couldn't wimp out either.

She watched as he and the horse moved in unison. The horse's front feet planted hard to the left then moved swiftly to the right and then back again in a fast back and forth dance that churned up the dirt. This was cutting at its best and though he made it look easy she knew staying in the saddle during this rigorous change-up took talent.

He and the horse were one. He was mesmerizing.

Maggie gave herself a mental kick in the shins and gritted her teeth. *This was a business deal.*

This was a business deal.

Easier said than done when, as she watched him, the kiss that had shaken her world came back in vivid color.

When he looked her way and pulled up the horse, whose name she didn't know, her heart began pumping — it was really, *really* aggravating. How was she supposed to stay in control of her life if she couldn't control the way he seemed to lure her in?

"Good morning," he said, riding over to the fence in front of Maggie.

"Good morning. You look good out there." Okay, not the thing to say, but at least she'd said something. "You and the horse, I mean," she added quickly.

"Thanks. Hazy Rey's the best. I just have a few more paces to take him through and then we'll get started. I've already saddled Stardust for you. You can take him into the small pen and just start riding circles, warming him up till I get there."

"Sure. Sounds good." So he was all business too.

Great.

No problem.

Fine with her.

Tension strained between them for the entirety of the lesson, but there was nothing Tru could do about it. Spin back time and take the kiss back? He was hard out of luck on that front. Though, selfish as it was, he didn't want to take it back.

Tru worked with Maggie on stops and turns with Stardust, and her hand positions and control.

She was different today, in that there was a concentration that hadn't been there before — a determined glint in her eye and a tension in her pretty jaw as she worked tirelessly to get everything he told her right.

They didn't talk about the day of the kiss. They didn't talk about the kiss. It was as if it had never happened . . . that is, if you ignored the strain between them and the fact that they both worked extremely hard to not have contact. And they spoke only about the instructions.

"When she gets down low in the dirt and cuts back and forth to keep the calf separated, am I supposed to lean forward?"

"You'll learn to move with your horse. You'll flow with her and that's part of it."

"Okay." She concentrated on backing Stardust up and holding her reins up like he'd taught her.

"You're really giving it your all today," he said when the lesson was almost over.

She stared over at him, her expression blank. "I've decided that the best way to get and keep the interest of my readers is for you to win this bet. That means I've got to be able to do this, and in order to help my readers know that there's always hope, I need to do this well."

Yeah, of course, it was about getting and retaining her readership.

His phone started ringing as they were leading their horses back into the barn. He saw that it was the doctor's office.

"You know the routine," he told Maggie. "I need to take this call."

Walking back out into the arena he pressed

accept and was surprised to find Dr. Jenson on the other end of the line instead of the nurse.

He was a no-beating-around-the-bush kind of doctor and Tru respected that, though the blow was hard when it came within moments of his greeting.

Tru was sterile.

"You're sure?" It was a reflex question. This was not something the doc would tell him if he weren't sure.

"Chemo in childhood can have the effect of making a man infertile, though not always. So I'd hoped . . ." The doctor's normally brisk tone softened. "I'm sorry, Tru."

"Me too." Tru's shoulders sagged and he hung his elbows over the round pen rails and stared out into the pasture, seeing nothing after he'd hung up. He'd been cancer-free for over twenty years. *I'm a strong, healthy twenty-nine-year-old male.*

He seldom even had to sneeze.

Sterile . . .

The cold word reverberated through him like a gunshot. Every muscle in his body clenched. His head throbbed, and his throat felt like he'd just poured scalding water down it.

He couldn't father children.

245

When he'd been six, it had been a three-year battle. He could still remember how sick he'd been. He could still remember the pain his illness had caused his mother and the way she'd rallied around him. His whole family had, though his mother was the most vivid in his memory.

Tru hung his head and rubbed the bridge of his nose. He didn't move further, just stood there feeling the sun on his face, but he was as cold as ice on the inside.

He couldn't father a child.

He wouldn't be able to give the woman he fell in love with children.

Not even one . . . it was a knife through his heart.

How was a man supposed to deal with that?

17

"Maggie, come on, sister. I know you are holding back. I can hear it in your voice. *What* is going on out there with that cowboy?"

Maggie frowned into the phone. Amanda was being Amanda, the persistent interviewer who always got her story. Not that this was on the record. This was a conversation between friends, and Maggie knew it. Still, she was struggling with what to say.

Over the last few days she and Tru had worked hard together on her riding skills. They didn't talk about kissing. They didn't talk about much at all. Other than him giving her instructions and her following through with them. But there was tension as strong as heated steel bands between them. They weren't touching . . . but they were.

And then there was yesterday at the end of the lesson — after he'd taken a call, he'd seemed almost solemn when he'd returned. And hard.

He had told her she'd done well, to cool Stardust down, and that he'd see her at the next lesson. And then he'd gotten in his truck and left. At the lesson last night and this morning he'd been distant like before the call, but something was different. She didn't know what, but she sensed it.

And then there was Maggie's fear each time she opened letters, either email or handwritten, that she was going to have another letter from her past. She didn't mention that. Not yet.

"Okay, Amanda, I'm telling you this, but it goes nowhere else. No. Where."

"Ooh, sounds fun. You know my lips are sealed. The PTB's don't have to know everything — as long as you give them something."

Maggie nodded to the phone. She really did need to talk to someone, and her best friend was the only one she would even dare to talk to about it. She raked a hand through her hair. "The man is driving me crazy, Manda. And I mean crazy with a capital *C*."

"Now, we're really talking interesting. I mean the man is gorgeous. That alone would drive most people crazy. And that's one reason this deal works in the first place.

So what's he doing? Any kissing going on?"

Maggie held her breath trying to figure out how to answer that question. "Yes." It came out as a squeak.

Total silence greeted her on the other end of the line. After a few beats, "Seriously? Wow."

That was so not like her friend to be speechless. "Yes. He kissed me." *And it was amazing.*

"And what do you think about that, Maggie? I was teasing you, but I knew by the sound of your voice that something had happened. Was it amazing?"

Maggie sighed, remembering though she was trying so hard to forget it. "It was. So amazing. But Manda, you and I know he's not what I want."

"How can you not want him? Look, my friend, don't judge him without really knowing him. The challenge just started. You may deny it all you want, but there was something that passed between the two of you in that interview. The camera came alive when he touched you. Maybe he is the playboy the tabloids have portrayed, but my gut tells me that he's a really nice guy. And you're a really nice girl who deserves a really nice guy so much."

Maggie's stomach trembled.

"But it's barely been two weeks and already he kissed me. That supports the playboy —"

"It could also mean that there is something incredible between you two that is undeniable."

Maggie propped her elbow on the table, dropped her head to her hand, and gripped the phone to her ear with the other. "I'm so miffed about the whole kissing incident. But at the same time I'm flip-flopping back and forth on my emotions when he's around. But . . . I can't make a mistake. I can't."

"Oh, Maggie, you can't always gauge your life by your past."

She took a deep breath. "Look, Manda, I can't think about this right now. I need to finish my column."

They talked for a few more minutes before saying good-bye. Maggie was relieved to hang up the phone. She was struggling with angles to take with the column that would sustain the new interest that was being generated by the TV promo spots advertising her column and the special with Tru Monahan.

After a pot of coffee and a lot of pacing the floor and with the deadline quickly approaching, Maggie finally plopped her rear into the chair and wrote.

Sometimes free writing was what it took to get the juices flowing. In the end, what appeared on the page was a piece about the gorgeous day of riding that she and Tru had shared. She focused on how she'd not trusted her abilities to ride Stardust down that incline, the fear that gripped her, and how Tru encouraged her to go for it. She omitted his scowl and the fact that he'd ridden off — that still baffled her, but after the kiss, she wasn't about to ask him why he'd done it. She'd written instead about how he told her to trust Stardust, not herself. She finished the article with the positive twist about being able to let go of her fear and ride down that incline and the sense of accomplishment that she'd felt. It was a good article.

She ended the piece with a few thoughts about how this experience was stretching her as a person. Sometimes it was trying her patience, but it was also making her reach deep. And that, she told her readers, was a good thing. It was something everyone should try.

As she hit send and watched the article wing its way to her editor, Maggie began to feel the grit of weariness in her eyes. Crawling into bed, she knew that all she needed to do now was believe her own words . . .

and hope no more letters came that threatened to destroy everything she'd worked so hard for.

The doc's call had knocked the legs from beneath Tru.

Add to that the feelings he'd begun to have for Maggie — that had only been complicated by his boneheaded move the day he'd kissed her.

She'd withdrawn from him after that and he'd stepped back too. They had enough issues in the pot without tossing in the attraction that linked them like a rope around their necks.

He'd really overstepped his sanity on this one. And to top it off, Maggie had no use for a man with the ridiculous dating baggage he dragged behind him like a ball on a chain. And he didn't blame her.

The longing for children had been clear and undeniable when she'd talked about the young, pregnant girl. He'd heard it, seen the longing in her eyes, and known instinctively that she had plans to have lots of babies.

She'd be a fantastic mother. The care she took with her advice and the heartfelt way she talked about Jenna and about those who wrote her spoke of a heart that was made to nurture and cherish others. It was one of the many beauties about her that drew him.

Maggie was out of his league.

Did that stop him from wanting her?

Nothing could do that. But knowing what was good for her was another story and he knew he wasn't it.

A few days later he was working with a new colt when Maggie drove up to the barn. His gut tightened up. *Strictly business, cowboy.* He was no good for Maggie and he couldn't let himself forget that.

The passenger side door opened and a petite, obviously very pregnant, young girl stepped out, startling Tru. This must be the girl Maggie had helped. She was a tiny little thing, almost as round as she was tall.

Riding over to the rail, he reined in his colt, who fought him a little before settling down. Not before the girl stepped back, a protective hand on her stomach and an expression that dared the colt to come closer.

Tru liked the kid instantly. She was small but she was tough.

"It's okay, he's just fresh and not used to me riding him too much. He's not coming over the rail."

"That's good to know." She looked up at him, more wariness in her eyes toward him than the colt.

"I'm Tru Monahan," he said, hoping to ease the girl's apprehension.

"I'm Jenna," she said simply, not supplying a last name, he noticed.

"We're on our way to lunch at the Bull Barn, but I wanted to show Jenna the horses, if you don't mind," said Maggie. "Like me, she's never had the opportunity to be around them before."

"That's great." He wondered if Maggie realized the growth she'd made since she'd arrived. Less than three weeks and she was showing horses to a pregnant girl when she would hardly go near the horse on her own on day one.

If nothing else came of her time here he was glad of that.

"Take your time. And if you want to see some young colts, drive down the lane." He nodded, indicating the road behind him. "They're down that way. I've been meaning to take you down there, Maggie, but just haven't made it yet. You'll both enjoy seeing them."

Maggie smiled and it nearly knocked his boots out of the stirrups. His heart clenched.

"Thanks, I'll do that."

"He's beautiful," Jenna said, stepping up

to the rail and holding her hand through it. Obviously, she'd decided to trust the colt.

"Yeah, he's going to be as good as he is beautiful. He has a great bloodline."

"And that matters a lot, doesn't it? In horses," Jenna said, looking up at him her expression bland.

"Yeah, it does." Tru saw a flicker of pain — something — cross through the kid's eyes and then she blinked it away and it was gone behind that bland façade.

"We're going to go visit Stardust, then we'll go see the colts," Maggie said, barely looking at him before heading into the barn.

He watched them go, wanting more than anything to fix the rift gaping wide between them.

Instead he went back to working with the colt.

Soon, he heard laughter and that made him wonder what was so funny. They were having a good time. He realized he hadn't heard Maggie laugh in a while. The kiss, the stupid toe-curling kiss had been the cause of that. And he realized suddenly that he missed her laugher.

"Great, Tru," he muttered. *Just great.*

They waved after a little while, getting into Maggie's little sky-blue car and headed down the lane in a puff of dust. Intent on pacing his colt, he couldn't spare his hands, so he just jerked his head in acknowledgment.

And almost got tossed when he lost his concentration to watch them drive away.

They'd enjoy the colts.

He'd found himself wishing he'd already taken Maggie down there. He'd have liked to see her reaction the first time she saw all of them. Fifty colts of varying ages all together in one beautiful pasture was a sight to see.

Then again, that was one of the reasons he'd probably, subconsciously, chosen not to take her down there. Seeing the way her eyes would light up right now would just make his life a little harder. He was having trouble enough keeping his distance.

When they finally came back down the lane and headed toward town, he was sorry they hadn't stopped.

Then again, he'd see Maggie that evening. Maybe they'd go see the colts.

Then again, maybe they wouldn't.

18

"You're sure you're feeling okay?" Maggie asked, glancing over at Jenna when she stopped at the end of the lane to the Four of Hearts Ranch. The poor girl looked like she could give birth any second and Maggie was a little nervous. "I can go ahead and take you to the hospital."

Jenna laughed. "I wish. Believe it or not I'm still two weeks away from my due date. Peg says she thinks I'll go right up to the date or maybe past it."

"Okay, then, hang on, little mamma, let's ride." Maggie teased her, turning the car in the direction of Wishing Springs. It felt good changing up her routine. Doing something for Jenna while putting *everything* else out of her thoughts. She was sick of worrying about Tru or fearing when the next letter would arrive that might expose her.

Jenna laughed. "You're in a good mood."

"Hey, I have you in the car with me again,

and we're not rushing to the hospital. I feel great."

Maggie's heart was so heavy for the teenager; she was determined to make this a fun outing for her. She was not going to think about how strained the atmosphere was between her and Tru. Today was about Jenna and she planned to do everything she could to make the kid feel less alone.

Sure, Lana and Peg were there for Jenna, but what would happen to her once the baby was born? Where would she go?

These were questions that plagued Maggie when she'd walked out of her own mother's apartment as a teenage runaway. It had been such a terrible feeling, leaving with only a small duffle bag of clothes, her toothbrush, and her small red Bible that she'd gotten at school from some men who'd visited. *I wish you'd never been born.* Her mother's slurred words clung to her as she'd roamed the streets looking for her way. All the things her mother had said over the years echoed in her mind during the nights she'd lived on the street alone. She empathized with Jenna more than anyone could know.

A couple of minutes later she parked in front of the Bull Barn, and Jenna looked slightly uncomfortable as they stopped.

"It's a great place," Maggie assured her. "This is where I did the interview with Tru."

They'd talked a little about that interview and why she was here the day they'd first met on the side of the road. Of course, Jenna had heard about it like everyone else.

"There are just a lot of people here."

Maggie heard the hesitancy in her voice. "Yes, there are, but it's okay. You've met some of them on game night. Come on, you can help me remember names. Not that I'm writing names other than Tru's in my column, but I need to know them. And if you're going to stay in Wishing Springs after you have the baby, these will be your friends and neighbors too."

Jenna took a deep breath. But "Yeah," was all she said as she followed Maggie inside.

The place was packed. People called out to her. Doobie and Doonie were sitting with Doc over in the corner and they all waved her over.

"How's the hand?" Doc asked. "Have you been taking your medicine like I told you?"

From the corner booth someone grunted. "Doc, you old coot, you've been at it again I hear."

Maggie looked at the woman. She was a large woman with the look of a marine sergeant unhappy with his troops. Her severe bun on the top of her head stretched her features tight and broad shoulders stretched even tighter inside the medical scrubs she wore.

"Now Bertha, don't get all riled up," Doc snapped. "You were off that day. This girl needed medical attention for her dog bite and I provided it."

Bertha tilted her head to the side and surveyed Maggie. "Hope you don't get rabies. Or swine flu," she grunted.

Maggie wasn't sure if the drill-sergeant-like lady was joking or serious. Her expression was dour.

"Stick that arm out here and let us look," Doobie *or* Doonie said.

She did. Why not? She'd stopped wearing the bandage on her hand after the third day. It was fine. "See, no blood or guts hanging out. I'm fine."

Bertha harrumphed.

Doc shot Bertha a scowl, punched his glasses higher on the bridge of his nose and studied her hand. "Looks good. You're officially released from my care."

The nurse snorted and shot him a dour look over the rims of her glasses.

"Thanks," Maggie said and hoped Doc didn't think she was going to be coming to him on a regular basis.

"Did that pig climb up into your lap while you were in there?" Nurse Bertha looked over the top of her glasses.

"Pig?" Jenna asked.

Maggie chuckled. "Yes, I'll tell you all about it. Y'all, this is Jenna."

Bertha looked at her. "Are you at Peg's place?"

Jenna nodded. "Yes, ma'am."

"You're in good hands, more than I can say for some," she drawled, shooting one more glare at Maggie. "Peg knows how to take care of a woman. And I'm quite certain you aren't going to have no pig climb up on the birthing table with you. Just be sure Doc's not near you at delivery time. You are not a cow."

Maggie wanted to chuckle. Yes, the pig had been annoying and unexpected, but it did make for some funny copy.

"Clover didn't do any harm," Doc defended. "She's just curious, that's all. And at least *I* wasn't eating lunch for three hours on end like you're known to do or taking a day off like you do every other day."

Bertha shifted her considerable shoulders back and glared at Doc. "I eat lunch for one hour and my days in the clinic are dictated by the county, and you good and well know it."

Whoa, time for a subject change.

"Doonie and Doobie, y'all are dressed identically today. What happened? Makes it really hard to figure out who is who."

That got laughs from everyone sitting around the café.

"Some days we're just on the same wavelength," said one of them.

"That's right," said the other.

"Yeah," Big Shorty snorted from across the room where he was filling a coffee cup. "Just *happened* to be on the day of the town council meeting."

"Yup," a cowboy from the table beside Maggie agreed. "For some reason they always tend to have those moments on a day of mayoral duties." He hiked a brow.

Jenna looked as confused as Maggie felt. "So who is who?"

"I'm Doobie, the good lookin' one. That's my brother, see, he's the ugly one with the big nose. Did you ever see a honker like that?"

Laughter erupted through the room. Maggie sighed. Jenna was grinning, but the look in her eyes said she thought she might have entered the funny farm.

"Okay, that was rude. So, back to my question. Did you go to the meeting?" she asked Doobie, really wanting to know what the deal was.

"Me, nah, I'm not much on the meetings." He grinned. "Hey, you coming to the Thanksgiving in July festival this weekend?"

"I am. I wouldn't miss it. I need fodder for my column. Are you going to give me something good to write about?"

"We'll do our best," Doonie answered, instead of Doobie. "As the mayor, I'd like to thank you for mentioning it in your column last week. We've had a lot of calls down at the city office."

"Very glad to be of service." Maggie winked and then smiling, led Jenna to the table Big Shorty had indicated for them to take.

"They're funny," Jenna said, leaning slightly toward Maggie.

"They're mischievous." Maggie thought they were a hoot.

A few others around the room called out to her and she waved and answered their questions. She was surprised to remember most of their names, but there were others whose faces were only familiar. It would come. That was one thing about small town life — eventually she would learn their names, because there weren't really all that many of them.

She was pleased when Clara Lyn, Reba,

and their friend Pebble walked in. The ladies worked the room like they'd just walked into a family reunion, stopping at each table along their way. When they reached Maggie and Jenna, they pulled up an extra chair and squeezed around the four-top.

"Well, hi there, Jenna," Clara Lyn said as she took the chair beside the teen. She gave Jenna a quick hug as Reba and Pebble greeted her.

"So have you picked the parents of your baby yet?" Reba asked with kindness.

Jenna toyed with her napkin and shook her head. "It's a hard thing to decide. I met with six couples this week. And they all seem like nice people. Any kid would feel lucky to have any of them for parents." Her eyes were sad. "A kid deserves to have good parents."

The wistfulness in her voice tore at Maggie and she was certain from the looks that passed between the others that they'd had the same reaction.

The hurt grew in Maggie's heart for Jenna.

The teen pushed her shoulders back. "It was okay. I've narrowed it down to three of them. I'm gonna have more meetings with them next week. I don't want to get their hopes up, but this is the most important decision I'm gonna ever make and it's for my baby. So they'll have to come back. And they know in the end I might not pick any of them." She took a drink of her iced tea and her gaze shifted to the table. "I might decide to look for a different couple."

Or raise your baby yourself. Maggie wished, but with Jenna having no family support, it was impossible for the poor girl to even think it was a possibility. And Maggie knew it. Hated it with all her heart, but knew that was the reality.

Tru felt his pride swell for Maggie as she rode into the arena behind him. Morning mist hung in the air after an overnight heavy rain, making the humidity as thick as butter. And the tension even thicker.

Maggie had progressed a long way from where she'd been when she'd walked into the barn that first day.

He admired her, and yet he was struggling to maintain his distance.

He'd never experienced anything like that kiss.

It had scorched through him like a page on fire, burning up every memory of every kiss he'd ever had before it.

The fact that his respect for her grew with every moment only made it harder to keep his distance. He was drawn to the way she dedicated herself to becoming a good rider so that her readers could see that goals could be achieved. Even if that meant he would win the bet. He loved it. Loved knowing in the long run she wanted her readers to be the winner in this deal.

How could he not respect that? How could he not find that attractive?

Maggie Hope had heart. And he wanted a part of it.

But that was impossible.

It had been five days since he'd learned he was sterile. Five days since he'd learned that he had nothing to offer Maggie. If he pursued the overpowering emotions he could have for her, it would only be out of selfishness on his part. While she, on the other hand, was being selfless. She deserved more than he could offer her.

But that didn't stop him from wanting her. And it was about to drive him crazy.

His life had become a wreck of a mess and it was killing him.

"So what is this?" Maggie asked as she rode Stardust into the covered arena and pulled up alongside him.

It was going to be a hard morning.

"This is a mechanical flag system." A cable stretched across the arena with a small flag attached to it. "The flag represents a calf. It will move from one side to the other, mimicking a calf that wants to dodge you and Stardust and get back to the herd. It will move casually at first. I control the speed with my remote. And as you progress, I'll increase its movement, allowing you to learn to adjust to the seat while Stardust pivots and cuts. I'll show you."

He took his position, the flag started moving, and Hazy Rey played cat and mouse with the flag, doing a back and forth that required the horse to dig its front feet low and stir up dust.

"It's fun when you get the hang of it. Now it's your turn."

"So now is the time that I start getting tossed out of the saddle?"

He frowned at his inability to not get distracted by everything about Maggie. "Hey, I thought we'd made it past all of that. Think positive. Do what we've been working on and let Stardust do his thing. He's experienced."

She inhaled deeply, making the big pink rose printed on her white tank top rise and fall — Tru forced himself not to get distracted by that flower.

Maggie stared at the flag. "Okay, then let's do this."

He agreed, needing something to do other than stand there looking at her.

He got the flag going and she and Stardust started working. Maggie started out looking good. Tru realized he was holding his breath — when Stardust planted his feet then switched the other direction, the switch-up caught Maggie by surprise. When the horse dove one way, she went the other.

Fear surged through him as he watched Maggie sail from the saddle. She hit the dirt with a thud. He was out of his saddle and kneeling beside her almost instantly. He'd done it now. She was never going to trust him. Every fear she'd had from the beginning of this bad idea had just come true.

"Are you hurt?" he asked, taking her arm.

She looked at him, brows scrunched together and determination in her eyes, but no pain. Relief overtook panic.

"I'm fine." She stood up. He assisted her, but she didn't need him. Not even dusting off her rear, she strode to Stardust and grabbed the reins. "I'll do better next time."

Tru watched in disbelief as she climbed back into the saddle without hesitating. "Who are you and where did you put the woman who was terrified of getting thrown out of the saddle?"

Mild amusement lit her face. "I lost her

somewhere between the saddle and the ground. Let's do this, cowboy."

He shook his head, trying to knock the disbelief out of the way. "Now, that is the attitude of a winner right there. When you get knocked down, you come up fighting."

And that is exactly what she did over the next hour. She rode — not fast, not spectacular, but she held on and started getting the feel of the horse. Determination etched her features as she managed to keep her feet in the stirrups. She remained rooted to the saddle and stayed out of the dirt.

By the time they called it quits, her smile was huge.

And he was again fighting an internal battle of wills with himself over wanting to pull her into his arms and congratulate her with another kiss.

They both led their horses into their separate stalls and Tru was glad to have a few minutes to get his frustration under control. He was still yanking at the straps of his saddle when Maggie came into his stall and leaned against the rail.

"We need to talk."

He glanced at her from beneath his hat and kept on working.

She hiked a shoulder. "I'll admit I've been pretty mad at you this week. But I've finally calmed down a little, and it hit me that something is different about you. If it's the kiss, then I think we need to get this talked out and over with, so we can move forward."

His gut twisted, but he remained silent.

"Look, we have a little less than five weeks to go. We can't continue with this tension straining between us like this."

He scowled. He could tell her that, yes, the kiss was a big part of it. He could not tell her his problem.

He couldn't tell anyone.

He carried the saddle past her and out into the stable run. She followed, hurrying to keep up with him as he went into the tack room and placed the saddle on its rack. The room wasn't very large and when he turned to her she was closer than he'd expected. Her mint-green eyes dug into him. The frame of long lashes surrounding her beautiful eyes blinked slowly before she met and held his gaze.

Every muscle in his body tensed with wanting to pull her to him.

His heart thudded in his ears.

She moistened her lips and his insides curled with longing. Watching her attack the challenge of riding had only made him want her more. He stepped toward her — yanked himself to a halt and backed up. She backed up too, bumping into the door frame and stopped, her back pressed hard against it.

"What should we talk about, Maggie?"

She inhaled a shuddering breath and held her chin up. "Why did you kiss me in the first place?" Her words were breathy, enticing when he knew she hadn't meant for them to be.

"Because you drive me crazy." Honesty won as he stepped off a moving train into thin air.

"Oh." Her gaze dropped to his lips, then she frowned.

"I'm no good for you, Maggie. You know it and I know it."

Maggie knew what he said was true. But her knees went weak realizing that he'd admitted that she drove him crazy.

She told herself to remember that she wasn't the first woman to drive him crazy. The cowboy had made a regular habit of it if the tabloids were to be believed. And he'd just said he was no good for her.

That made it pretty obvious that there was truth mixed in with the trash.

Lifting his hand, he took a strand of her hair and rubbed it between his fingers. The air in the room vanished.

"This can't happen." He looked tortured for a moment, then he seemed to get control

271

of his emotions and shields fell into place. He turned and strode from the tack room, down the alley, and out into the back of the barn.

Maggie couldn't move. Maybe she should have followed him and asked him to explain what had just happened. But she didn't. It was a question that had gotten all of this started. No, she pushed away from the wall and walked unsteadily to her car.

It was best to process her own emotions before pushing his again.

19

On Saturday morning Tru found himself standing beside a fryer in the overhang outside Doonie's office. They had orders for thirty-five fried turkeys. These turkeys would be eaten sometime during the year and some of them maybe that night.

There were ice chests full of turkeys lined up around them. The eight gas burners with tall pots of oil heating up for the frying were lined up along the wall — Doobie had placed them there to be out of the slight wind that was blowing like hot breath.

"Thanks for coming to help us," Doonie said, a whimsical grin cracking across his face. "We needed another turkey around here."

Tru laughed. "Yeah, believe me, I've been called that ever since I accepted this invitation to cook with you three."

"Hey, we're glad you're here," Doobie said. He was wearing an apron with a slogan

273

that read, "I'm not the turkey. That's my brother."

"Yes, I'm not exactly certain how I got entangled with this motley crew. I for one have never fried a turkey." Rand rubbed his freshly shaven face and looked at Tru with clear eyes, which was a good sign. And a much better way to write any articles for the *Gazette.*

Tru knew how Rand had gotten pulled into it. Local folks were getting increasingly worried about Rand's drinking. The consensus was it was time to step in, and this was part of the plan.

"After we fry thirty-five, you'll be a pro," Tru said. "*And* you'll have done a civic duty, Councilman." He grinned at the distinguished-looking man.

He gave Tru a speculative look. "Maybe since you're here, that little Maggie and her friend will give us some good promo for Thanksgiving in July. It's not a bad drive from the Houston area. A nice day trip for folks to support a good cause."

Tru grimaced. He wouldn't count on it after yesterday. "Only because I'm with you turkeys."

That got him chuckles. "We work hard at it."

And they did. The mayor might be a funny

man, but he — and/or his brother — had come up with this idea last year and it was turning out to be a huge success.

"We have more ordered this year and if it keeps up we might have to rope more turkeys into helping us fry."

"That'd be great." Tru watched Doonie start the flame under each fryer.

Folks were gathering at the booths that were set up along Main Street. There had been several vendors setting up with home-made food. Peg and Lana had the girls who were able help out at a pie table. There were five of them all together and he could see Jenna there, too, getting ready for the people that would soon start showing up.

He looked around for Maggie. She'd said she was coming and he knew she wouldn't miss it. There was going to be a lot to put into a column for this and the town was already talking about trying more things to include in her column. They wanted to advertise the town while they could. He wasn't sure how he felt about that, but then again, it didn't matter. Once this was over, he'd get on back to his ranch and his work and it wouldn't matter to him how many people came to town looking for their dreams. His were right there on his ranch.

Grief, sharp and caustic, cut through him

for the family he would never know. He knew he was going to have to learn to deal with the loss —

Someone yelled, and he spun to see flames bursting from one of the fryers reaching for the overhang of the house.

It was the burner at the far end of the cookers from where Tru stood. Doonie was reaching to try and turn it off. Tru yelled.

Maggie had her pen and paper out for notes on the Thanksgiving in July Day. She was very aware of Tru down the street where the turkey frying was getting under way. After yesterday's encounter in the barn she was hyperaware. He'd said he was no good for her, and she believed it, but the look in his eyes said he didn't want to believe his words. Why had he looked so troubled and gruff as he'd walked away from her?

Tru Monahan was not easy to understand. And she'd begun to think he wasn't at all the man she'd thought him to be.

He intrigued her, attracted her and by all accounts should be off-limits to her, but she could not stop thinking about him. And in order to concentrate on her column she needed to desperately. Her editor had called the day before. Helen Davenport had not been happy. Yes, the column had garnered

276

some interest, but there was no real meat to what she was writing about. There needed to be something more to hook and sustain the readership of the project. Maggie had to come up with something. It was time to give the column life and focus, but what?

Spotting Peg standing beside a booth that had all manner of handmade items and cookies for sale, Maggie headed that way.

"Hi, Peg," she said, "How is it going?"

Peg broke into a huge smile when she saw Maggie. "Oh, Maggie, come here and let me give you a hug." She did exactly that, engulfing Maggie, squeezing her hard then patting her arm as she released her.

"You did good yesterday. So good. Jenna needed that outing more than you'll ever know. Most of our girls come to us looking for a way out, a way to get back to their lives and start fresh, knowing that they gave their child a future with loving adoptive parents. But there are a few of our older young women who just need help and come here to have their babies while they get their lives sorted out for themselves and their newborns. But Jenna, poor kid, is struggling. Your involvement with her is a blessing. The kid is so alone. You're being a great friend to her and it means the world."

"I'm just trying to help. I really like her

and I . . . I know where she comes from when it comes to a bad family situation. Not that I talk about it much, but I've been there."

Peg's eyes filled with compassion. "Then it is wonderful for her to be able to look at you and see the success you've become and know she can achieve great things as she moves forward with her life."

Maggie wasn't so sure "great things" could really be tagged on to what she'd achieved. But if she could give Jenna something positive to grasp hold of, she was glad to do it.

"I haven't really spoken to her about any of it. Like I said, it's not something I talk about much. But I think I will."

Peg studied her, thoughtfully. "Maybe you should. Opening up can be a freeing experience."

Maybe. She glanced down the road and saw Tru working. Longing filled her. She focused on the table Peg was working on setting up with all kinds of homemade goodies. "So what do y'all have here?"

About that time Lana came walking up carrying more boxes. "Candles and pot holders. They're all handmade. Check out this soap. It has the most wonderful ingredients in it, rosemary and thyme. You'll love it if you buy some."

"I plan to. Maybe I could include an address in the column this week for folks who want to purchase some of your products."

Lana and Peg beamed. "That would be amazing," Lana said as Jenna came up pulling a little red wagon with boxes in it.

She greeted Maggie with a hug and the gesture nearly brought tears to Maggie's eyes.

"So show me what you made." She peered into the box of sensational smelling candles.

Jenna grinned. "I made some, but most of these candles were already made when I arrived. Still, the cherry bomb ones are mine. I love the color." A slight blush came to the tough girl's cheeks. "Hey, even a tough girl likes girly stuff." She laughed, as if reading Maggie's mind.

"Totally," Maggie agreed. She moved on after that, giving them time to set everything up. She wove her way through the crowd toward the turkey frying.

Publicity from her article and Amanda's show might cause Thanksgiving in July to get some national exposure, and they could have a great turnout next year. That would raise them thousands.

It was a good feeling to know what she and Tru had thought of as a disaster could possibly turn out to be good for the town. She had come to care about Wishing Springs and her heart tugged. What would it be like to call a place like Wishing Springs home?

She *could* call the town home if she wanted to. The thought hit her hard. After all, her physical presence wasn't required all that often. The town was only an hour and a half from the office anyway. It made a perfect scenario for her to be able to commute from Wishing Springs if she chose.

But it was small — she thought of the threatening letter she'd gotten. She'd made the calls and both Shane and her dad had been out of prison for over a year. So she felt certain the letter was coming from one of them. They could find her easier in a small town.

Especially with all the advertising that was going on about the bet and upcoming special. It wasn't a reassuring thought.

She'd almost made it to the guys frying the turkeys when she heard yells and saw Tru running. A turkey fryer had caught fire!

Obviously, it had just happened. Doonie or Doobie — whichever — had eyes as round as tractor tires. The flames were reaching for the roof. One of them ran toward the fire and a scream lodged in Maggie's throat just as Tru reached the twin and grabbed him, pulling him out of the way before he got himself hurt.

The roof had started to burn now.

Maggie's heart thundered and she started to run forward, but someone grabbed her in turn.

"No, Maggie," Clara Lyn said, holding tight. "You'll only be in the way."

"But Tru needs help," she cried.

"He'll be fine. You'll only give him more to worry about."

Maggie saw that it was true and clutched Clara Lyn. Fear gripped her as Tru waved the twins and Rand out of the way as they tried to help turn off the other fryers. It was chaos. The out-of-control fire and canisters of gas were not a good combination.

The sound of a siren rang out suddenly. Relief filled Maggie. Maybe the firemen could help Tru. Fear for him was almost more than Maggie could stand.

People parted as the fire truck moved down the street. Maggie wanted to scream for them to hurry. The building was on fire and Tru was in the middle of the trouble, turning off the gas flames on the fryers that weren't out of control.

The four firemen jumped from the truck and started hauling hoses instantly. One of them was Bo — a *cowboy fireman*. With dimples. Maggie was startled and relieved at the same time as he waved Tru out of the way and then he and his fellow firemen took over.

Within several moments the fire was out and Maggie breathed a sigh of relief.

Clara Lyn started clapping and the entire town joined in. Tru looked serious, but Bo and the other firemen grinned at the crowd. Bo, a teasing light in his eyes, took a bow, then he and his buddies went about rolling up the fire hoses.

"Isn't that the best-looking fire department you've ever seen?" Reba sighed, coming out of the crowd to stand beside her. "Our cowboys know how to get rid of fires. Kind of like that old George Strait song, 'The Fireman.' Mmm-hmmm."

Clara Lyn agreed. "And that Tru, he was a real hero. Why that crazy Doonie would have let the whole town burn down if Tru hadn't been there."

Maggie doubted that that would have been true, but there was no denying that if Tru hadn't been close, someone might have been hurt. It certainly would have been far worse. As it was, the damage had been contained. Of course, it was still a disaster.

One of the firemen pulled off his helmet and Maggie gasped. She'd thought Bo and

Tru looked like the younger version of Pops, but this guy looked *exactly* like Pops. It was as if Pops had walked right off that pencil portrait and donned a fireman's uniform. "Who *is* that?" she asked.

Reba chuckled at her reaction. "That's Jarrod, Tru and Bo's older brother. He's the volunteer fire chief. You haven't met him yet? He's a real dreamboat. And just as single as his little brothers."

"No, no, I haven't." Maggie's mind started whirling with sudden ideas. "Cowboy firemen. It's like John Wayne and George Strait to the rescue."

Both of the older women chuckled.

"Yeah," Clara Lyn said. "We tease them that fires are set in the county just to see all them handsome cowboys roll to the rescue."

Maggie looked through the crowd, and even if they didn't realize they were doing it, every woman's gaze tracked Jarrod as he walked over to speak with Tru. Women had crowded as close to the brothers as possible and hovered as if ready to run in and administer CPR.

Maggie's gaze narrowed as one of them called Tru's name and he spoke to her before he turned back to his brother. Both men looked serious as Tru, judging by his hand movements, was explaining to Jarrod

what had happened. Despite the serious-
ness of the situation, excitement sprang to
life inside Maggie.

Her heart dropped, though, when she saw
the cute female who had called out to Tru
move his way as soon as Jarrod left him.
The woman stood entirely too close, and
though she couldn't see his expression,
Maggie was well aware of the fact that Tru
didn't seem to be in any hurry to get away
from his admirer.

Maggie's ears felt hot as she forced her
gaze away and got back to work thinking
about her new idea.

Everyone was talking and the crowd had
converged on Rand, Tru, and the twins.
Within minutes they were dragging the
freezers of turkeys from under the overhang
into the open air. Maggie moved to help,
but there were so many men in the mix, the
women just hung close. It didn't take long
with a group pitching in to help. Tru's
admirers had grown to a small entourage
who seemed intent on making every move
he made. Maggie hung back, feeling an
overwhelming sense of humiliation as it
became very evident that she had somehow
become one of the many who'd succumbed
to the undeniable appeal of Tru Monahan.

As everyone was intent on getting the fryers that had survived the fire spray ready to start up again, Maggie gave herself a good talking-to. And then she shut off her aching heart and got back to work.

She made a note that it took more than a little fire to stop the town from their goal of raising money for Over the Rainbow. As she kept writing, Tru came over to stand beside her.

"So, I guess that gave you something to write about." He had soot on his cheek and on his clothes. He looked as good as a roasted marshmallow.

Maggie's voice stuck in her throat — she *loved* roasted marshmallows. And she was obviously not alone. "Yes, I've got ideas." She looked away from him toward where the firemen were. They had opened their hot fire suits and those hung around their hips so their sweaty T-shirts could dry out.

Those T-shirts exposed muscled arms and broad chests that made her almost certain the town had a fire hazard on their hands just from spontaneous combustion in the female population.

Bo, with his dark fun-loving vibe and that build . . . yeah, he was a hazard.

And Jarrod — rugged and tough — would surely snag women's attention.

And the other two whom she didn't know

— she wondered if they were single too.

While none of these capable, appealing men made her heart race like the heart-stoppingly handsome cowboy standing beside her, she frowned at that thought and focused. "I believe I have finally found what will make my editor happy."

Tru looked perplexed by that. Of course, he was a man and completely clueless about what the turkey frying disaster had stirred up in her mind.

"How many of those firemen are single?" she asked out loud. How many other single men were there in town? But she didn't voice that. If she combined this amazing small town with amazing cowboys and fire-men heroes, the hunk appeal alone would make a column. This wasn't just a town — it was a dating destination.

"All of our firemen happen to be single."

She groaned and jotted a note to herself.

"Are you all right" Tru asked.

She felt the sting of pink burning her cheeks. "Oh, yes, I have finally gotten the most fantastic idea."

"Really, just like that?"

She nodded and looked back around at the townspeople milling around and smiling and laughing despite the near disaster. They were continuing. What a great place.

"Oh, that's how the best ideas come to me. And your sponsors and my sponsors are going to be very happy."

He cocked a brow. "Oh, really?"

"Yes, really. Talk to you later, cowboy. I've got to go find a quiet spot for a few minutes and write my thoughts down."

With that she hurried off and forced herself not to think about the shrink wrap that was squeezing tight around her heart.

She'd almost lost sight of the fact that this was about saving her column. But thankfully, she'd just had a hard reminder of why she was here in the first place.

Not to get tangled up with a cowboy who drew women like a magnet.

20

Maggie wrote like the wind. She was so excited about her idea. It had been here all this time and she hadn't seen it. It wasn't just about the lovely town and the good things going on — that was the easy part. But the whole idea of Wishing Springs being the place where a girl's dreams could come true had hit her hard the instant she saw those cowboy firemen. This lovely town could fulfill the small town dreams of anyone, and it could fulfill a need to belong if someone had that — like her. That she'd already found out. But only now had she realized how happily-ever-afters could come true here.

Would it grab readers' imaginations?

She refused to let her thoughts go to Tru. She was so angry with herself for falling under his spell. It had happened during the interview and simply grown worse once she'd arrived.

It was over, though. This was strictly about upping her ratings.

And she had a feeling that after her article came out this week, Wishing Springs would probably be really happy about it.

Yes, indeed. This was not a day to get down in the dumps about anything.

It was a great day for her job.

Because today, she'd just saved that job and she knew it.

She could feel it, *this* was going to work. And with every negative problem she was facing it felt good to know something was working out well.

Maggie had disappeared after they'd talked and Tru hadn't seen her until she walked into the barn on Monday morning. He'd missed seeing her. It wasn't good. He was not good for Maggie, but he couldn't help responding to her. He grinned and the tension in his chest eased. "Good morning. How's it going this morning?" he asked, telling himself this was strictly business.

"My column comes out today. This one is going to be a huge hit. And, like I said, your sponsors are going to love you."

He chuckled at her exuberance. "So tell me what you've done."

"Oh, no. You'll know as soon as the newspaper is delivered. A girl's got to keep the suspense up. What are we doing today?"

"Boy, you don't play fair."

She met his gaze and her smile wavered. Was that sadness he saw?

"What's on the agenda today?" she asked, moving past his teasing and straight to business.

"Practicing with the flags. If you keep improving, we'll work with real calves soon."

"The sooner the better. Did y'all finally get all your turkeys cooked on Saturday?"

He couldn't take his eyes off of her. He might not have anything to offer her, but that didn't stop him from thinking about her.

He was finding that he couldn't.

Bo's truck suddenly skidded on the gravel at the entrance to the stable. Tru knew something was wrong from the reckless way his brother was driving. Tru swung out of the saddle as Bo slammed out of his truck and came stalking toward them waving a folded up newspaper.

"Did you see this?"

"The paper?" Tru said. "Can't say that I have. What's got you riled up?"

"Your girlfriend —"

"I don't have a girlfriend."

"Yeah, well then, Maggie. She's gone and

done it now. *Read this.*"

He slapped the paper to the workbench and pointed at Maggie's column. "Read it and you'll see exactly what I mean." He started pacing.

Tru looked at Maggie, who looked shocked. Her eyes were wide. He glanced down at the headlines and his own eyes nearly jumped out of his head. Wishing Springs: The Place a Girl's Wishes Really Can Come True. Driven by his curiosity, he read on quickly. He pulled the paper closer with both hands. "No, way," he said. His head shot up and he met Maggie's alarmed gaze. "Are you serious?"

"Ah, *yea-ah,* it says *exactly* what you think it says, big brother," Bo drawled as he paused to glare at Maggie again. "She's telling women to come to Wishing Springs to find a really great small town life, *then* pointing out the *hunky firemen and cowboys.*" He scowled, more upset than Tru had seen him in a very long time. "But wait, there's more. Oh, yes. She's promoting the idea that there's a bunch of needy single men here. It sounds suspiciously like that crazy newspaper column that had all those women converging on that other poor ol' Texas town. You know, the one on the other side of Hill Country."

"Mule Hollow," Tru supplied, looking from Bo to a suddenly silent Maggie.

Bo snapped his fingers. "That one. Didn't you have a buddy who got hitched over there last month down in Corpus?"

Tru hadn't thought much about his friend Steven, but yeah, he'd been his groomsman a month ago in a Corpus Christi destination beach wedding. This was crazy. What had Maggie been thinking? His mind flew over all the facts. Maggie stood there, about as shocked by the turn of events as Bo was.

"Why'd you do this?" Bo asked, accusation in his words. "You're selling us out for your column." There was no doubt that she hadn't expected this kind of reaction.

"I'm not selling you out. I'm helping you out."

"Helping? Lady, I'm not exactly thrilled to be a hook for your readership."

"Hey, Bo, back up. You're way out of line."

"Me?" he tapped his fingers on the page Tru was still scanning. "Read that."

"She's not saying outright come and marry the cowboys like that other reporter did. At least this is promoting the town and the people."

"*And* the cowboy-firemen-heroes," Bo added, not differentiating the two. "She is tossing the firemen under the wagon too."

"I am not," Maggie protested.

Tru had to admit that Bo had a point. This was off the deep end. But then, Maggie was right — his sponsors were going to eat this up with happiness.

"Well, what are you going to do about it?" Bo demanded. "I don't want my love life fiddled with like this."

"You're making a bigger deal out of this than it is," Maggie said.

"She's right, Bo." Tru shot him a skewered look. "You'll be fine."

"Yeah, right, 'said the farmer to the turkey.' " Bo drew a finger across his throat.

Tru choked out a laugh. "Right. So go careful little brother." Tru couldn't get as riled up as Bo. Heck, nobody could.

Bo glowered at Maggie. "Oh, believe me, I will."

Tru started laughing, he couldn't help it. Bo acted like he was going to be forced to marry someone just because of Maggie's stunt. Oddly, he understood what she was doing. Or at least he thought he did. "Look, Bo, man, dial it down, okay? No one can force you to do anything in your love life that you don't want to do. It's not like some woman is going to come to town and you're going to *have* to marry her because it's your turn."

"Well, I know that. That's a ridiculous thing in the first place. I just don't understand this whole concept. I mean, Wishing Springs is fine the way it is. Sure, some new faces would be good, but I'm just not liking the whole expectation thing. This wishes-come-true stuff is getting on my nerves."

Again, Tru told his brother to relax.

Pops walked into the barn, causing them all to refocus. Tru was thankful for the distraction. Bo needed it badly. And poor Maggie had paled. From her happy enthusiasm this morning, she obviously hadn't been expecting backlash like Bo's for the column.

"Hey, Pops," Bo said, waving him over. Then he asked Tru in a lowered voice, "Is he having a good day?"

"Yeah, it's a clear day," Tru said and instantly Bo brightened. They would take every good day they were granted with Pops. He glanced at Maggie and gave her a small, hopefully reassuring smile. She looked a little like she'd been blindsided by a linebacker.

She responded with a softening of her eyes, then turned to say hello to Pops. Tru and Bo were going to have to have a little man-to-man when they were alone. And his little brother was going to give Maggie an apology . . . he just didn't know it yet.

"I came to see my horses," Pops told them, pausing at one of the stalls to pet the horse before coming to stand beside them.

Tru gave him a pat on the shoulder and his heart tugged. "They're doing good, Pops. Check them all out and let me know what you think."

"I'll do that." He looked around, surveying everything like he'd been coming down every day and riding, just like the good old days. He walked to each stall and held out his hand. Looked over each horse and they talked about what was good and bad about each one. He had trouble finding his words sometimes, but Tru or Bo took turns filling in the spaces for him. They'd become pros at pretending like there was nothing amiss. Today Pops was in his element.

Raking a hand through his still-thick hair, Pops took a deep breath, then nodded toward the saddle. "I have a cuttin' to go to in the morning. Championship." He raised a brow and looked cockily at his grandsons just like he had so many times when they were growing up. "I've got a feeling it's gonna be a good day. I'm feeling lucky."

Tru's throat clogged with emotion as Pops spoke the words they'd all grown up with him saying before he headed off to compete.

Most of the time his feeling would be right and he'd come home a winner.

"Sounds good, Pops. You go show them how it's done," Tru said, hating everything about the disease that had stolen the man his grandfather used to be.

"My ranch looks good," he added, looking at Bo. "You're doing a good job," he said, then turned and headed toward the house.

Bo sighed and looked at Tru, the strain etched on his expression. It was hard on all of them, but Bo took it harder than any of them. It ate at him. As the youngest, he hadn't gotten as much time with his grand-dad as a vibrant man like Tru and Jarrod had experienced. Tru understood completely, because he cherished every moment spent with his Pops and every grain of wisdom that Pops had shared with him. Bo was only a year younger than he was, but even a year was precious.

"I'll go back with him," Bo said, all the wind gone out of him. "It's my turn to cook his supper tonight too."

Tru nodded. "Hey, Bo, the good news is he knew you were responsible for the ranch. He got that right."

Bo looked down then swallowed hard when he raised his head. "Yeah, today."

"We take what we can get. I'll be up later. And don't worry, Bo, Wishing Springs will survive this marketing stunt. That's all it is."

"Yeah, we'll see." He shot Maggie a glance then went to catch up to Pops.

Tru called after him. "Is Jarrod coming to dinner?"

"I'm supposed to call him. I'll tell him it's a good night to come."

"Yeah, do that. He'll want to know."

Tru watched Bo and Pops walk together up the lane, his heart heavy, then he glanced at Maggie. "You okay?"

Just looking at her lifted his spirits . . . a fact that didn't go unnoticed by him.

"I'm fine." Maggie was still reeling from Bo's reaction as she met Tru's searching look. "I never anticipated such a strong negative response to my idea. Bo was really, really mad. Will others feel the same way?"

"He'll get over it. He was probably just in shock is all."

"Maybe, but still, I'm worried about everyone else's reaction now."

She'd been so happy and relieved that she'd come up with the right hook that she hadn't thought everything through. Now, she would just have to wait and see what happened. It wasn't as if she could take it back.

Helen had loved it, just as she'd expected her to. She'd thought it was brilliant. *Brilliant* — not really, but Maggie had to acknowledge that she personally liked the idea.

She couldn't explain how good she felt about the piece. Saturday at the festival she'd felt connected to the small town in a way that she'd never felt connected to any place. She'd looked around and it had felt like . . . like home. Even now, thinking about it gave her an odd, wonderful tremor inside. The people were nosy and funny and caring. And she absolutely loved it.

And then there was watching how they embraced Jenna and the other gals who were at the unwed home. Lana and Peg had placed the home in the perfect place.

Anyway, she was feeling suddenly enthusiastic about the challenge before her. The horse riding and her warm and cold relationship with Tru remained confusing, but the column was truly taking shape for her. She'd had the column to think about over the weekend and had tried to keep her mind from how easy it had been for him to let his attention be seized by his admirers on Saturday.

"Okay," Tru said. "Enough with the excitement. We have a lesson to get to this morning. I've got you signed up to compete in less than two weeks."

Ready — *she wasn't ready. Two weeks.* "That soon? There is so much for me to learn. I-I'm barely hanging on."

"You'll be ready. We're going to bump up practice and I want you here riding even when I'm working my other horses. You're going to show all those readers and television viewers what you're made of."

Butterflies winged their way through her at his words. Tru believed in her.

And that could very well be her downfall. Because he'd taken up for her with Bo and now he was standing by her. And she'd never, ever had that before — not from a man.

They were just riding out into the arena when Tru's phone rang.

"Jarrod needs me in the field. One of the calves has had an accident."

"Oh," she gasped. "Can I help?" She had no idea how she could help, but she would do what she could.

"Sure." He grabbed a tackle box off the shelf near the exit as they headed to his truck. "Medical supplies," he said.

They climbed in and he headed out of the yard and down the dirt road into the interior of the ranch at a fast speed for pasture terrain.

Jarrod watched them drive up, as tough and handsome a cowboy as she'd ever seen in any movie or on a book cover — grim expression, chaps, spurs, the whole bit. He was on his knees holding down a calf. Suddenly it hit Maggie that she might not want to see what he was looking so grim about.

She could hear a calf bawling and her stomach felt a little ill.

"Doc's tied up on the other side of the county and can't get here," Jarrod called.

They got out of the truck and Tru grabbed the tackle box. Maggie followed him to the fence, dreading what she was going to see up close.

Oh. A poor little black calf was tangled in the broken barbed wire from the fence.

Jarrod held the calf down, keeping it as still as possible, because it was bleeding and every time it moved it got worse. Wire cutters lay on the ground beside him. Tru bent down and picked them up. "Maggie, could you help Jarrod hold him down?"

Maggie swallowed any need to toss her cookies and dropped to her knees beside them. She put her hands on the poor baby's neck and felt it trembling beneath her touch.

Tru started clipping the wire from around

300

the calf. It looked weak.

It was tedious work. The poor calf struggled despite the pain it was in as she and Jarrod held it down. It stared up at her with one terror-filled eye and Maggie willed Tru to hurry setting it free.

"How did it get like this?" she asked.

"Something spooked it," Jarrod offered since Tru was concentrating hard on what he was doing. "And I was planning on bringing some of my ranch hands out here to repair the fence this week so something like this wouldn't happen. Thanks for coming to help." He gave her a Monahan grin. Maggie decided if she could bottle the grin these brothers sported, she'd be a millionaire — and they'd have to hide from all the women.

"I'm glad I can help."

Tru finished up about that time and let out a breath as he rocked back on his heels. "You've been a big help too. That was intense there for a few minutes. Let's get him cleaned up."

Maggie was completely startled when Tru pulled out a needle and thread from that tackle box and began to stitch cuts on his side of the animal. She was fascinated. And when he'd finished, he held the calf while Jarrod stitched the wounds on his side of the calf.

"I can't believe y'all are doing that," she said at last. "And it looks good."

Tru shrugged it off. "You have to be prepared for anything."

"Doc's not always sitting around his office drinking coffee and playing with Clover while yacking with Doobie and Doonie," Jarrod said, as he continued to work.

"Most of the time," Tru amended. "But then other times, he's swamped. When it rains, it pours. So that leaves us out here in the pasture to fend for ourselves."

One more interesting tidbit to highlight in her column.

When the calf was all doctored up, Jarrod tied its legs together, then scooped it up into his arms and carried it to his truck.

"Why did he do that?"

Tru gave her a patient smile, understanding she was clueless. "So it won't be able to get up between here and Jarrod's house."

"Oh, that makes sense."

"Come on, let's get you back to your car so you can do your thing."

"Will the calf live?" she asked.

"Yes, Jarrod found it soon enough. But if it had been later in the day, probably not. Thanks for coming."

"I wasn't any help other than holding the

poor thing. But you and Jarrod were astounding. Did Doc teach y'all that?"

He laughed. "Some. You'd be amazed what a cowboy has to know how to do. Stitching up things is just one of them."

"Amazing. This has nothing to do with my learning to ride, but it's going into the column anyway. You fellas rock." She laughed with relief for the hurt calf.

She grimaced. "Of course Bo might not like it too much, but this is going to up all y'all to hero status."

Tru rolled his eyes. "Right."

"No, really. That was so wonderful you pulling out that needle and going to work. Everyone can't do that."

Tru started laughing. "Well, Bo sure can't. The man isn't too good with blood. But we won't tell anyone that. Still, why don't you take my name out of the story and put his in."

"Oh, no. This is payback for your part of getting this whole bet going in the first place. Your name is definitely going into this story."

21

Letters flooded in.

By the time she got back to the computer after her riding lesson, Maggie found her inbox wasn't just full, it was busting at the seams.

And she'd been so anxious to read what was coming in. There were a lot of lonely people out there. But there were also a lot of women who dreamed of relocating to a town that sounded just like the town she'd described.

Of course if everyone could actually do that, the town would be taken over. Realistically, Maggie had no worries that that was going to happen. But who knew? Someone, a few perhaps, might come. And that, she thought, would be cool.

She fixed herself a sandwich and a glass of lemon water and curled up on the sofa with her computer to read. As always, the time flew when she was doing this. She opened one of the hard copy letters, and just as she sliced it open, she realized there was no return address on it.

Her mouth went dry and the room swam as she read. It had been over two weeks — a knock at her door made her jump.

She stuffed the letter into the pocket of her jeans and stowed her emotions as she opened the door. "Tru, hi. What's up?"

Her already shaky nerves jangled more at seeing Tru. She hadn't expected to see him until morning since she'd told him she was expecting a lot of mail and would need to work instead of having their evening ride. He'd said that was fine, so she wasn't sure what he was doing here.

"I hope I'm not bothering you."

"No, actually, I've been hunched over the computer screen and needed a break." She rubbed her shoulder. "Is something wrong?"

He was still standing on the porch and he'd gotten this expression on his face, like he didn't know what to think about her or something.

"Well, I'm just curious about what's going to happen after all these women and their dreams start rolling into town. I'm not panicked like poor ol' Bo. But I am curious."

She grimaced. "You read the whole article?" She knew that he'd only had time to scan the headline and a few paragraphs that morning when Bo had confronted her.

He laughed. "Yeah, I finally had a chance a little while ago. After Bo reacted like the sky was falling, I had to read the whole thing. I have a feeling a few of the other confirmed bachelor cowboys are going to have the same reaction."

"But it's not like they're going to be forced." She was glad to have something to take her mind off the letter burning a hole in her pants pocket.

He shrugged. "A confirmed bachelor can't help but feel this is going to cramp his style."

"So, are you one of those?"

"No, I'm not actually. I see this for what it is. You figured out a way to get more readers to your column. TV uses romance all the time to sell products. Even my deodorant's ad is of a guy putting on his antiperspirant so women start falling at his feet."

She laughed, despite the fear she was trying to control. "So does it work for you?"

"You mean my deodorant?"

She nodded.

"Well, you're still standing, so I guess not."

Oh, if he only knew. Maggie guessed he wasn't counting all the women drooling over him at the turkey fry.

She crossed her arms. "That is, after all, my whole purpose in being here."

"Right," Tru said, as he studied her.

A shiver of attraction raced down her spine and Maggie tried not to hold his past against him. It wasn't as if her past was a beauty.

The note in her pocket was proof of that.

The note had been written to Trixie. And it clearly stated that whoever sent it knew her real name wasn't Maggie Hope, but Trixie Pierce. A pickpocket juvenile delinquent.

But did the sender know about Shane?

Could it be Shane?

Maggie's gaze shifted away from Tru. She seemed distracted. "I came to see if you had time to take a break and come to dinner. At Pops's. I know you need to work, but I thought you might want to come. He's having another good day and Jarrod and Bo are going to be there too, and we just thought, since Pops enjoyed visiting with you the other day, it would be nice if you joined us. If you had time."

Her expression softened. "You love your Pops so much."

"Yeah, I do."

She blinked suddenly and glanced off to stare out across the pasture. Was she near tears? When she looked back at him there was the unmistakable glisten of dampness in her eyes.

"I would love to join all of you for dinner."

He stepped close and couldn't help touching her. He slid his hand to the back of her neck. Felt the throb of her pulse beneath his fingers. "Why are you crying?"

She shook her head. "No." She stepped away from his touch.

"Look, if you're upset because of Bo this morning, don't be." He searched her eyes and felt like there was more. "He'll get over it. I've already told him you aren't going to force him to make some woman's dream come true."

"Of course not, and I'll tell him that as soon as I see him."

"Good, reassurance is all he needs."

Tru held her door for her and she climbed into his truck. As he walked around to his side, it felt oddly like a date. Foolish heart. He'd simply asked her to a family dinner.

Nothing more . . . but a guy could wish.

A few hours later he was still wishing. Tru had enjoyed the meal with his family and Maggie and he knew he had fallen completely for Maggie Hope.

There was a sweetness about her that tugged at him. And it was apparent in the way she cared about Jenna, the kid who needed someone to lean on. It was evident in how she reacted to Pops. That had been one of the reasons he'd wanted her at dinner tonight, so she could see Pops more like his old self.

When they arrived back at the cabin, he knew he was in serious trouble on so many fronts. He'd been preoccupied all evening as his thoughts ran wild. He needed to fall in love with a woman who already had children.

He would have to let his dreams of having a child of his own blood go. But he knew marrying someone with young children was his best plan. At least with this plan she would have experienced the whole motherhood package and then she might not grow to resent that he couldn't give her babies of her own.

Maggie needed the entire experience. He'd seen how much it bothered her that Jenna was going to give up her baby to adoption.

She would never be okay with not carrying her own children. And he couldn't live with himself if the woman he fell in love with came to resent him.

It was hard, and looking at Maggie, fresh-faced and lovely, with the whole world ahead of her, he knew he had no business feeling anything toward her.

But he did.

And that was going to make getting through the next month the hardest thing he'd ever done.

But he had to make it through the end of this charade and then Maggie would go on to her life. And he would go on with his.

"You sure are quiet. I loved dinner. I think Bo is going to be okay. He seemed fine after he calmed down."

"Yup, he'll live." He wasn't worrying about Bo right now. Bo could take care of himself. "I'll walk you to your door," he said, not ready for the night to end even knowing it wasn't what he needed to be doing.

"Thanks. I hate to admit it, but I get a little spooked out here at night by myself. I like to be inside with the doors and windows closed before dark."

"For real?"

She nodded sheepishly. "Yeah, I'm a big baby. I'm a city girl, remember. I haven't spent any time in the woods with the hoot owls hooting and the coyotes doing their weird, eerie thing."

"Just wait right there, I'll walk you."

She waited for him to open her door and then she hopped to the ground. A coyote wailed, sounding like the war song of a Native American tribe. She shivered and stepped close. Instinctively he wrapped an arm over her shoulders and looked down at her.

"I won't let anything happen to you. If I'd known it spooked you, I wouldn't have put you out here. I'm sure the powers that be would have put you in town at the Sweet Dreams Motel. If not, then I would have. They're clean and neat, and right in town."

She was staring up at him and her eyes turned luminous in the moonlight. His Adam's apple bobbed as he gulped and lost his voice. She was beautiful.

"I've gotten better. And I wish I could get comfortable. I tried walking out on the deck one night, but I didn't last long."

He wanted to kiss her again. He knew he could want that every day for the rest of his life. Looking down at her, a deep wave of yearning drowned him. He started walking toward the cabin, keeping a firm arm around her shoulders. At least if they were moving he couldn't kiss her. He needed to get her inside with the door firmly locked between them.

Once they reached the porch, he let his arm drop away from her. "There you go, safe and sound. I'll wait while you go inside and lock up. And if you need anything, just call me and I'll come down."

She was still staring at him, biting her bottom lip and looking as if . . . as if she was wishing he'd kiss her.

He held himself in place with an iron will and tipped his hat.

"Goodnight, Tru," she said, then went inside the cabin.

He turned to go — flee was a better term. He was almost to the truck, almost home free, when her sweet voice halted him.

"Tru."

He spun on one boot heel.

"Would you like some coffee?"

No. "Sounds good. We could sit back there on the deck and enjoy it."

She smiled. "Yes. And enjoy the peace and tranquility."

He groaned inwardly, knowing it was a dangerous idea. "Exactly. We wouldn't want you going back to the city without having learned to enjoy one of the best things about living in the country."

She opened the door wide and the warm light spilled out on the porch, lighting his way inside.

He was just being a friend.

Had they become friends?

Truth was, he wasn't sure what they were. But tonight, he was going to ignore the warning bells and he was going to enjoy her company sitting on the porch, watching the stars, and listening to the coyotes and the crickets.

And that was that.

She would be gone soon enough and he would still be here. Tonight he would help her enjoy country life.

That was what he told himself. He knew his reasons for staying were purely one-sided. He just wasn't ready to walk away.

22

She was flirting with fire.

Yes, she was, but she didn't want the night to end. She wanted . . . enjoyed talking to Tru. She loved the way that he loved his Pops. And she wondered at the deeper things that she could see moving behind his eyes. Tru Monahan had only shown her that he was a good and decent man. But there was something going on with him.

Something was driving Tru and she could feel it. What made the man so elusive, as if, other than his brothers, there were things he held inside that no one was allowed to see?

She walked straight to the coffeemaker and went to work getting a pot brewing. Time to do something other than obsess about the man standing in the cabin with her. He was such a puzzle to her. He wasn't good for her, not at all what she needed in a man . . . and yet he drew her. Watching him with his Pops warmed her heart and stirred a deep longing in her. And then there was the memory of his kiss . . .

She scooped the coffee from the container and then filled the carafe with water. She glanced over her shoulder to see Tru stuff his fingers in his jeans pockets and look around the space.

"Has this been comfortable enough? Other than having you scared and spooked out?"

She chuckled at that. "It's been perfect. And I've done pretty good after that first night. Once I'm locked in, I'm fine. But coming back after dark is when I get my wimpy girl on."

His lips parted into a heart-tugging smile. Goodness, that smile caused dancing to break out in the pit of her stomach. This might have been a bad idea. *Might have been? Ha.* Of course it was.

She crossed to the back door and opened it. Tru stepped beside her immediately and the scent of his aftershave, spicy but subtle, taunted her as it had been doing all evening. He led the way out onto the deck instead of waiting for her to go first.

She realized belatedly that the only chair was a love seat rocker sitting in the corner. There was plenty of room on the rustic wooden rocking bench, but still . . . the image of them snuggling on the swing burned into her mind and she suddenly wanted to bang her head against her palm. What had she been thinking?

She sat down, making sure to sit as far to one side as she could get as she studied the darkness, her nerves a jumbled mess.

Tru sat down beside her as if it was no big deal.

"I love this spot." He studied the darkness. "The bubbling brook makes a very peaceful refuge. You're missing that when all you can concentrate on is the sound of the coyotes."

She glanced at him, unable to stop herself. He smiled.

"Let the other sounds seep in around you. There's peace there. Feel it?"

She was only aware of the man beside her.

For a few seconds they stared at each other and she felt that unbelievable tug on her heart. Maggie had always, deep down, felt so alone in the world.

"Maggie, why don't you ever talk about your family?"

Her breath caught at his question and Maggie shot a startled gaze at him. "I. I, um," she stumbled over her words. "Because, there's nothing good to talk about."

It sounded so stark when voiced.

"I've never had what you and your grand-father and your brothers have." She sighed. "I've wished for it."

"It's a nice thing to wish for." His words were low, his gaze searching, his question tense. "What was your family like?"

Maggie's nerves balled tightly. "Different." She couldn't tell him about her past. What would he think? She had a mother who was . . . she couldn't tell him about her mother. And she had a father who was in prison. Her name wasn't even what she said it was.

She looked up at the sky. "It is beautiful out here," she said, then stood. "I'll get that coffee. How do you like yours?"

He stood. "I'll fix it."

"Is there some secret to the way you fix it?" She hurried inside, needing something to do.

"No. So why do you never talk about your family?" he cornered her at the coffee pot.

She stiffened. "There's really nothing to share." She poured coffee into the two mugs she'd set on the counter earlier. Her hand trembled as she passed one to him. "The cream and sugar are there. I'm sorry I don't have a lot of different flavors."

He took the coffee and set it on the

counter. "So, what about your family?"

She faced the counter as she stirred a teaspoon of sugar into her coffee. He stepped close and reached around her to cover her hand with his. "I want to know about you, Maggie." His words were a soft whisper against her ear.

It was suddenly hard to breathe. He was so close, and his hand so gentle as his thumb caressed hers. Slowly pulling her fingers away from the cup, he drew her around to face him. "There is something so sad in your eyes. And today, when you teared up, what were you thinking about?"

Maggie fought for composure. She really wished Amanda's thing for red would work, because she was wearing a red shirt and she needed fortification. Right then and there, she wanted to wrap her arms around Tru and never let him go. He looked genuinely concerned for her.

"Let's just say not everyone could have a great family like yours."

"Oh, believe me, mine wasn't that great. Everyone has family problems. I had a doozy if you're worried about some kind of family skeleton."

She couldn't believe he came that close. What would he think of her? She'd never been a chicken. "You know why I am so drawn to Jenna? Besides that she's a great kid."

He shook his head.

"I was a runaway when I was around her age. My dad left when I was in seventh grade and my mom, well, home life had always been a struggle even with Dad home. He wasn't the most reliable guy, my dad." *A real loser, nothing more than a crook who involved his young daughter in his cons.* She didn't say anything about that. She couldn't. The letter in her pocket weighed heavy on her soul. "He actually went to prison for all sorts of crimes. Theft being the main one." She finally admitted it, giving him a satirical smile. "He was a real winner."

His gaze was unwavering and kind. "I'm sorry. You deserved more than that."

She didn't really know what to say, but now that the floodgates had opened, Maggie kept talking. "My mom, she kind of spiraled out of control. It was hard. She drank, and we moved from apartments pretty often. It was very . . ." What was the word? "Hard. Let's just say Mom loved her drugs and her revolving door of boyfriends. I was —" she broke off on that note, not certain she could tell Tru, but she saw his fear for her there in his gaze. "It was bad. I never knew from day to day if I was going to have a place to sleep and if I was going to be safe if I went to sleep." That had been the worst. She looked away on that note.

Then added, "I spent a lot of nights curled up in the corner of the maintenance room of the apartment house or some other corner I could find." Tru's eyes had hardened.

"So you ran away? Was it because someone finally hurt you?" She could hear the struggle for control in his voice.

She shook her head. "I knew it was a possibility, that it was only a matter of time before something happened. I knew it was up to me. No one else was looking out for me and so I had to have the courage to leave. I stuffed a backpack full and walked out and never looked back."

He just stared at her for the longest time, his fist curled up on the counter beside the coffee cup. His eyes glittered. "How did you make it?"

"I was just barely seventeen when I left. A little older than Jenna. I'd been creative and lucky and had managed to live unharmed until then. So I was able to get a job at a coffeehouse. No one was looking for me. I didn't matter and so I was able to get odd jobs . . . but I lived on the street, hiding out in bathrooms and a few other places." She didn't mention Shane. Couldn't tell him that she'd gotten mixed up with a bad guy who'd ended up robbing a convenience store. Shame ate at her. Had followed her all these years. She'd run away from him and changed her name after that. But she'd never forgotten it. Shane had been caught and had gone to jail.

His expression hardened. "You had to live on the *streets*? What happened?"

She smiled. "Like I said, I got a job in a coffee shop. The owner, a very nice woman, let me have all the hours I wanted so I worked most of the time for a few weeks. If I was there, I wasn't on the street. I went to church, too, and met Amanda there. She happened to be sitting in the pew when I sat down beside her. Which was a God thing." Maggie would never forget that moment. Amanda had smiled at her, offered her name and asked Maggie's. For some unexplainable reason, she'd felt amazing hope in that moment. Without even blinking an eye, she'd told Amanda that her name was Maggie Hope — she'd been using that name ever since she'd run from Shane. It had just come out of thin air the day she'd started using it. She didn't tell Tru any of that.

"When the service was over, I was walking down the road, my backpack on my shoulder with everything I owned inside. Amanda saw me and pulled over and asked me if I'd like to go eat lunch with her. And from her act of kindness, I found a roommate and best friend."

Tru traced the line of her face. "I'll have to thank her sometime. I'm glad you were safe."

Maggie had never told anyone her story. Amanda knew she was a runaway and that her home life held threats that made not being there her safest bet. But other than that, no one knew she was a runaway. And no one knew Maggie Hope wasn't her original name.

And she'd told Tru almost everything. Why?

Because she'd come to trust him.

She laughed shakily, grabbed her lukewarm coffee, and moved past him. Needing space between them desperately.

Needing to think.

She walked back outside and Tru followed. This time she bypassed the swing and walked to the edge of the deck to lean against the railing. The stars glistened down on her and the air felt so clean, much better than the stifling memories.

"I hate that you went through that."

She shrugged. "I lived. And it could have been worse. I'm one of the lucky ones. I worked, got my GED, and managed to get through community college." In order to do all of that she'd first officially changed her name to Maggie Hope.

"That's amazing."

"Yeah. My mom died that year. Overdosed." She didn't say how deeply guilty that had made her feel. How sad and guilty. If she'd stayed, could she have helped her?

The very thought haunted her.

"I'm sorry."

"Yeah." Maggie knew she'd done what she had to do. She stared out at the night. The turmoil conjured up by thoughts of her past eased a little as she stared into the still darkness. The cry of the coyote seemed more of a lonely cry to her now rather than spooky.

Tru stepped up behind her, and all of her senses came alive. He touched her hair, his fingers tracing gently down it as if soothing her. "I'm glad you were strong. You did what you had to do. You have nothing to feel guilty about."

He understood. She turned and found herself surrounded by his presence. Her heart raced. He was all she wanted to think about in that moment.

None of her past mattered right then.

None of it.

She got lost in his eyes. Drank in the way the porch light silhouetted him as she touched his chiseled jaw. Her gaze dropped to his generous mouth. "God always has a plan," she said softly, lifting her gaze to his. Wanting his kiss, and his arms around her.

He gently pushed the hair at her temples away from her face. "Your attitude is amazing. You're amazing."

He was going to kiss her. She wanted him to so badly.

"You deserve so much. You deserve to have everything your heart desires. All of your wishes." The words were earnest, his eyes fierce, when he looked at her again and with a barely there brush of his lips against hers, he backed up. "I have to go. Are you okay here?"

She felt breathless and suddenly confused. Had she shared too much?

"I'm fine." She wasn't, but he wouldn't know that. She followed him through the house to the front door. He didn't pause until he was in the yard.

"I'll see you in the morning."

Maggie felt the ground shifting unsteadily beneath her. "Sure. I'll be there." *Sure . . .* boy, did that sound easy and uncomplicated.

Especially since she wasn't sure about anything.

And he was gone. In his truck and gone, leaving her feeling more alone than she'd ever felt in her life.

23

Tru's heart pounded relentlessly as he drove away from Maggie.

He ached for her and the desperate situation she'd faced as a defenseless girl growing into a young woman. If he could have found her father in that moment, he'd have broken every bone in the man's face. Tru wasn't a violent man, but he had his limits. His anger dissipated only because there was nothing he could do about her past. Looking at her now, he knew that she was okay. She'd landed on her feet — her spirit of survival and belief gave her an indisputable hope. And that made her resilient.

She'd even landed a job that enabled her to help other people look past bad situations and find the hope in them.

She was remarkable.

His life had hard times, but nothing like this. Nothing. He was grateful that he and his brothers had things under control even in the worst of times — which didn't compare to Maggie's life. The ranch would be solid and on its feet for good if they all kept up the hard work they were doing.

And his cancer when he was six had been found in an early stage. They'd treated him aggressively and he'd handled it by focusing on following in Pops's footsteps. He'd not been thinking about children or the possibility of not being able to have them. But the difference had been that he'd had family supporting him. Maggie had faced everything alone.

His respect for her compounded. Only adding to the fact that he was falling hard for Maggie Hope, and there was no good that could come of that.

Maggie deserved the house full of kids like she mentioned. He could already see the amazing mother she would be. Her children would never suffer — feeling unloved and worthless as she'd felt. Her children would know that they were wanted and adored every day of their lives.

But not if he were in the picture. There would be no children.

Unless they adopted . . . how would she feel about that?

And what right did he have to even be thinking these thoughts?

He had to get through the rest of this challenge. Help Maggie be a competent rider so that she looked good when that camera caught her cutting and showed it to the world.

And then he'd watch her leave and wish her life every happiness. God had dealt him a hard card. But, looking at Maggie and seeing how she was so optimistic, it gave him the determination to move forward and handle it better himself.

It just wasn't going to be with her.

The next couple of days just got plain weird.

In the following days, Maggie realized even more than she had that night that in opening up to Tru she'd put a wall up between them that she couldn't quite figure out. She hadn't ever opened up to anyone. Except in omitting Shane, the convenience store robbery, and that she'd changed her name, she'd told him everything. And now he was distant.

He was kind. He was patient in showing her what she needed to do with her horse but he was oh, so far away.

He was very careful not to touch her. This she noticed the most because she wanted him to so badly.

She tried not to let it bother her and spent

the time in between lessons holed up in her cabin working on her columns. Despite his behavior and the way it worried her, she felt a keen excitement about the column.

It was a cool feeling.

The second day's lessons felt hard physically and emotionally. She pushed herself to improve on her riding, while at the same time trying to not wear her heart on her sleeve. When they were done with the lesson, she headed to see Jenna. Thinking back on her past as she'd done had really put the girl on her mind. She needed to talk to her. And she needed the distraction.

Peg was the first person she saw as she walked around the corner of the house. She and one of the other girls, Anna, were pruning a rosebush. When Peg saw her, she came her way.

"I'm so glad you're here. I was going to call you. Jenna hasn't been doing well over the last few days. She's going to give birth soon and she's not ready mentally. Maybe you can talk to her as her friend. Maybe you can help her make the decision that's right for her."

Maggie had known in her heart this was coming. Jenna's heart was so torn. She had confided that she was giving the baby up even if it hurt her because she knew that was the right thing to do. But Maggie worried that it was killing her more than she wanted to admit.

She found her sitting in her room. The tough kid looked as alone as Maggie had felt when she was that age. Maggie couldn't stand it.

"Hey," she said, after giving a light rap on the doorframe.

Jenna had her hands resting on her stomach protectively as she did most of the time. And on the table beside her the book was open to the smiling couple she'd chosen to be the parents of her baby.

The expression in Jenna's eyes was as grieved as Maggie had ever seen.

Maggie closed the door of the room and went to kneel on the floor at Jenna's feet. She placed a hand over Jenna's and felt little Hope move. Bittersweet sadness filled Maggie. The horrible spot this girl was in . . . Maggie could hardly stand it. Jenna would make a wonderful, loving mother. Every child deserved to be loved desperately by their mother. Maggie knew what not being wanted or loved felt like, and it hurt beyond words.

Jenna's eyes filled with tears that she blinked furiously to get rid of. "I'm never going to know my baby girl. It's hard."

"Then don't do this." Maggie had never said words she meant more. For weeks she'd said nothing, torn about whether to voice what her heart was thinking and what was best for Jenna and Hope. It wasn't up to her to encourage this young woman to decide to raise her child when she wasn't much more than one herself. But now, Maggie couldn't hold back. Couldn't look into the pain in Jenna's eyes and not speak what was on her heart. "Jenna, you love your child more than life itself and your child deserves to know that."

Jenna brushed the tears away. "That's true. But I have nothing to offer her and keeping her would be selfish of me. No, I made myself promise to give her the best I can give her, and that's a good family." She closed her eyes and a tear slipped out. It rolled slowly down her cheek, breaking Maggie's heart all the more.

Words that spoke of the maturity of this girl, but . . . "You have yourself, Jenna. Do not underestimate that. Your fierce love of your child means so much. I won't lie. It would be hard. But you have grit. Look where you are. No one but you can make this decision. Do you know that I chose to run away when I was about a year older than you?" Jenna's chin came up and her eyes brightened with interest.

"Really."

Maggie settled on the floor, crossing her legs and cupping her hands together. She told her about the reasons she left, about not feeling like her mother would protect her. Jenna nodded knowingly.

"I'm sorry, Maggie. I mean your mother should have protected you."

"Yes, but we both know sometimes that's just not the way life works out. I know now that I shouldn't have hit the streets alone, but I should have sought out help at a local child protective agency or a women's shelter. Someone would have helped me. Running and living on the streets like I did only put me in further danger, and there are so many places where girls like us could have gotten help. But it worked out for me. And your choice worked out for you. No matter what, taking that step to find safety takes bravery and courage to carry through."

Jenna's brows dipped, and her expression hardened. "That's why I'm going to do this. I am. No matter how hard it hurts. I'm giving my baby a better shot at the things she deserves."

Maggie had heard it before from Jenna. And no matter how much she tried to convince her differently, Jenna wasn't budging. "You love your child, though, Jenna."

"And that's why I'll do this. Because it's best."

Maggie tried not to let her emotions take over. This was ultimately Jenna's choice. She had no right to push. No right.

As she left a few minutes later, promising to be at the birth and support her, Maggie was torn beyond belief.

She went straight to the barn and saddled Stardust. She needed something to take her mind off of the emotions spilling through her.

She did not need to see Tru. Thankfully he hadn't been around when she'd decided to come to the barn. But as luck would have it, he drove up before she got Stardust saddled.

At that morning's lesson she'd forced herself to take his lead and pull back as he obviously had. Opening her heart to him had caused this and she really didn't understand, and right now she had no patience for it.

"Hey, what's up?" he asked, as she led Stardust from the stall.

She walked past him, toward the exit. "I'm riding."

He fell into step beside her. "Okay. Are you okay?"

"No. But that's not your concern, so don't worry," she lashed out at him and kept on walking. He'd run so fast from her his boots were still smoking. She realized she couldn't do that to Jenna and that was one reason she'd gone to see the girl. Not that it had done any good.

He reached for her arm. "Hey, hold on. What is going on?"

She glared at him, uncontrollably angry. "Everything. Jenna is going to give up her child for adoption and she's going to regret it for the rest of her life. And I don't know how to stop her from doing it."

"It's not your call to make."

She glared at him. "Don't you think I get that? She loves that baby. She'll be a great mother."

"She'll have a really hard time as a sixteen-year-old mother with no family. You know what that is like. What would you have done if you'd had a baby when you went out on your own? How would you have held a job?"

"I wouldn't have given it up. I'd have found a way."

He stared at her, compassion softening his expression. "It's Jenna's decision to live with, Maggie."

"You are not helping me." He was actually making the situation worse. Tension that she'd bottled up while talking to Jenna welled forth and the best scenario would have been for him not to have shown up.

"Maggie, you're used to giving out advice through a newspaper. This kid is actually here in front of you. You can't make a decision for her based on what you're feeling. You're too close to it. You're making an emotional decision."

Maggie glared at him. "I'm not. She's making a mistake and I can feel it. She's strong enough to do this, but she has a messed-up vision of what is best for her baby."

Tru looked suddenly stricken, but he ran a hand over his face, then confronted her again. "Maggie, that's not true. She came here to Over the Rainbow and she's showing amazing care and strength. Sometimes pieces don't always fall into place like we want them to. Life is not fair. You know that. Some decisions require you to detach from your emotions no matter how hard it is, in order to make the right choice. And it's usually the choice that goes against what your heart wants to do."

Maggie knew in her heart of hearts that what he said was true. Jenna had, at high risk sought out excellent care. Still, she didn't like it. The baby needed to know how desperately its mother loved her. Tears threatened to overtake Maggie. She needed to ride. She needed to get rid of this pressure in her heart. Looking at Tru was only making it worse. And he wasn't understanding at all.

"Look, I don't have anything against those couples who want Jenna's baby. They're wonderful people, I'm sure. And they'll make great parents for someone's baby. But not Hope. Why am I the only one who sees this as a mistake?"

"Maggie, this kid knows she would have a hard time. She's alone. She's not even seventeen. She'd have to work, and provide day care. Plus deal with the stress of being a new mother. Not to mention healing from the birth. If she had a parent to help her, or a boyfriend or a husband, it might be a different story."

Okay, so he was reading her mind. He had the uncanny ability to anticipate what she was thinking sometimes. "She doesn't have to give up hope."

"It's heartbreaking, but it's not hopeless. Jenna is going to give her baby a chance to be loved and nurtured by a couple she handpicked. And she's going to give herself a shot at a new life. It's only hopeless to you."

Letting out a frustrated groan, she stalked from the stable, stuck her foot in the stirrup, and pulled herself into the saddle. She knew she was being unreasonable. She could feel it, but she couldn't make herself listen to reason.

"This is a mistake," was all she could say and then she rode Stardust toward open pasture. *This* was *a mistake.*

Peg had told her the legal papers were all being signed and arrangements were being made . . .

Maggie knew there was nothing more she could do. Except pray.

Tru grabbed the stall with both hands and bit back saying something he really didn't want to say. He wanted to tell Maggie that he loved her and that he wanted to marry her and keep her safe for the rest of his life. He wanted to give her those babies she wanted and the life of happiness she dreamed of. But this conversation confirmed that telling her he loved her would be a mistake. Her view on adoption said everything — proved he'd never be the man she'd need.

If she hated the thought of Jenna letting her baby be adopted by a loving couple, then Maggie would hardly want to be the one forced to be in their shoes.

It wasn't anything to hold against her or anyone who felt that way. It just left him with no options.

Maggie had no idea how much he and Jenna had in common right now.

24

"What if we assure her that here in Wishing Springs she'd have a support group?" Clara Lyn said that evening to Maggie, hunched in a booth at the Bull Barn. They happened to be in the booth where Maggie had done her interview with Tru. He stared down from his many pictures and she turned slightly so she didn't have to look at him.

After her fight with him, Maggie had ridden for an hour and then decided to try and see if there was anyone else who could help her come up with a solution for Jenna. She'd immediately turned to Clara Lyn and Reba.

"The problem . . ." Reba toyed with her glass of soda, stirring the straw as she thought, ". . . lies in the fact that it would be hard for her."

Maggie's shoulders slumped along with her spirit. She thought of Amanda and how her friend had lent her moral support and even helped her financially by letting her live rent free in her apartment until Maggie could contribute.

"With all of us around here, she would have an unending stream of babysitters when she needed us," Maggie said.

Both ladies met her with curious looks. "Are you moving here?"

"I've been toying with the idea. I love Wishing Springs." She wasn't sure how that would work with Tru, but she could manage. "If I could help Jenna, then, yes." Maggie felt a little panic at what she was doing.

Clara Lyn studied her. "We would love to have you, Maggie. I can't help but wonder if you're getting in too deep with Jenna. There is only so much you can do. And didn't you say the papers were being signed? Honey, why is this so important to you?"

Why was everyone so intent on telling her she was getting too personal? "I'm just trying to help. I am the one who found Jenna on the side of the road that day. I guess I feel responsible for her in some ways." With a sigh she told them about her past. To the same extent that she'd told Jenna. It wasn't as if she was going to go around telling everyone she met about her past. And certainly not about her father or Shane.

"I don't think the papers were going to be

signed 'til later. I just feel like I need to try one more time. I really needed someone to tell me I wasn't crazy." She turned her back a little more to Tru's picture.

Men, what did they know anyway?

"I pledge to do what I can to help Jenna and Hope." Reba clasped her hand over Maggie's.

Clara Lyn laid hers on top of Reba's. "Count me in, too, and I'm sure we can get several more to help. Including Pebble. But Maggie, I still have reservations. You are a young, single woman. This is something that will change your life forever."

Maggie's heart squeezed tight. "Thank you."

"Now, don't you have someplace to get to?" Reba asked. "That girl needs to know she has options."

Maggie got up and was so thankful the restaurant was slow for three in the afternoon. She walked out into the bright sunlight and found her past waiting beside her car . . .

Even though it had been almost ten years since she'd seen him, she knew her father instantly. Tall, lanky, and with hollow cheeks, he looked ridden hard.

"Hello, Trixie, how's tricks? Or should I call you Maggie?"

The moment she saw him a chill rolled through her. Maggie glanced around. "What are you doing here?"

"What, no hug for dear old Dad?"

"No." She wrapped a hand around the back of her neck while her stomach continued to roll. Her dad had always been a schemer. She saw it in his eyes. Maybe there was something wrong with her, but instead of feeling any kind of good emotion at seeing him after all these years, she only felt apprehension. What was he here for?

"That's kind of harsh, don't you think? Especially since you're doing so well for yourself. What — don't you think your poor old dad could use some help getting on his feet?"

"Money." She should have known. It didn't take her a split second to decide. "If you'll leave, I'll give you something to get you on your way." It was all she could come up with. She didn't want him around ruining everything she'd worked so hard for.

A slow, slick, con-man smile slipped across his face and his eyes shuttered. "I thought you'd want to help me. I think ten thousand would be a good number to start with. What do you say?"

A chill raced over Maggie. Giving him a little cash out of her purse to get him on his way was one thing. But this — she snapped her attitude into place. "No way. I'm not going to do that."

He stood and stepped close to her just about the time Clara Lyn and Reba came outside. Maggie's pulse grew sketchy and her mouth went dry.

"Who's your friend?" Reba asked, from the porch. Their car was on the other side of the parking lot.

"Drew Danner," her father said, giving a false name, adding to the knowledge that she had just become the target of one of her father's scams.

"I was asking this nice lady how the food was inside the diner."

"You can't beat it." Clara Lyn looked from him to Maggie. "Maggie, you better hurry if you're going to make that appointment you were going to. It was nice to meet you," she said to Maggie's dad. "But we have to hurry or we're going to hold up our appointment."

Maggie turned back to the man who'd fathered her. "Leave."

His eyes narrowed. "I need a stake, and with my daughter being famous now and all, I deserve it. That was a lot of years to spend in the pen."

"You're going to go back there if you start

this all over again."

"I figure if you changed your name there was a reason. So you'll need dear Dad to stay in the background, and you'll give him what he wants. I'll be around. But I need my money by tomorrow noon. I'll be parked right over there waiting. If you don't give me what I want, I'm going to have to sell my story to one of those tabloids. I hear they pay well."

"They won't care about me."

"I beg to differ, you being involved in this show with Tru Monahan. I think your newspaper would care too. You giving out advice to folks when you ain't nothing more than a con-artist."

The ground shifted beneath Maggie's feet. What was she supposed to do now?

"I'll be waiting," he said and sauntered toward the diner, then stopped. "You tell anyone and I'll ruin you. Right now I'm just Drew Danner, passing through. But — that can change whenever I want it to. Understand?"

Maggie was still shaking when she got far enough down the road to pull over without him seeing her. She gripped the steering wheel and dropped her forehead to rest on her knuckles. What was she supposed to do now?

Everything she'd worked for was at risk. She felt like her life was falling apart. Unraveling stitch by stitch. *Think, Maggie. Think.*

Go see Jenna.

She needed to see Jenna. Not think about her dad. Her life. She looked up and focused down the road, steadying her emotions. None of this mattered right now. The baby was what mattered.

"Go see Jenna," she said out loud, her voice weak.

Hands shaking, she put the car into drive and headed toward Over the Rainbow. Her mind reeled as the realization surfaced — her father had been sending the notes.

As she pulled onto the road again and pressed the accelerator, the blast of a siren sounded. Glancing in her rearview she saw a fast-approaching ambulance with lights flashing.

She yanked the wheel and drove her car to the shoulder again, letting the emergency vehicle have the road.

She hadn't thought her emotions could take another hit in a single day but she knew . . . pressing the gas she followed the ambulance. And just as she feared it turned at the road and headed straight up the lane to Peg and Lana's.

And Maggie's gut told her it was Jenna.

Tru burst through the doors of the Kerr-ville Hospital and stalked down the hall into the waiting room of the maternity wing. His spurs sang as he went, but he wasn't singing along as he scanned the crowd in the waiting room. His gaze found Maggie almost immediately.

"Maggie." He spoke her name and she turned from the window. Her expression lined with strain but when she saw him relief transformed her face. Automatically he opened his arms and she launched herself into them.

"Tru, she's in surgery. She hemorrhaged. Peg was able to stabilize them both until the ambulance arrived."

"Are they doing ok?"

She looked up at him and he pulled her close. "We don't know yet."

Tru hated this. "Jenna's tough and baby Hope is going to be her mother's child. After all she did to get that child to safety, it's going to be good. God's got this, Maggie."

He held her for a moment, then they walked over to everyone else. They all said a prayer together and then they waited.

"Peg, did this happen after they got the

papers signed?" Maggie asked.

Tru hadn't figured she'd let up on this. Not after how mad she'd been that morning.

"Yes. She signed." Peg looked worried. "I have to say I'm worried about this whole situation. Normally, the girls who come to us are happy about the decision they've made. It's hard on them, but they aren't prepared to be mothers on their own. Jenna is different."

"She's grieving," Lana added.

"Maggie." Tru stroked her arm with his thumb.

"I think it's because she wants someone to love so badly. I know for me, I can't wait to have a houseful of children to love."

Tru's gut soured again.

"Where is the couple who are wanting to adopt the baby?"

Peg looked serious. "They're on their way."

"I just feel like this is a mistake."

"Maggie, it's not for you to decide." Tru had to say it. And wasn't surprised by the glare she shot him.

"That's true," Peg agreed. "We can only encourage her, but she has to make the choice in the end. You might help, but you also might make this harder on her. Have

347

you thought about that?"

"You asked me to talk to her before."

"Yes, but she's made her choice now. I'm not telling you what to do. Just letting you know. It's a hard decision for her."

"But, she needs to know she has options. I could help her."

A pretty lady in scrubs and a surgical cap came into the waiting room and conversation halted as she walked over to them.

"Peg," she said, as if they knew each other, "Jenna is fine. A little weak and tired, but she gave birth to a healthy baby girl. She wants to see someone named Maggie, if she's here."

Maggie's eyes grew wide and she nodded. "Go," Tru said, giving her a little nudge toward the doctor.

Lana gave her an encouraging smile. "Go on. She thinks you hung the moon, you know."

"Give her a hug," Peg said. "We'll see her soon."

"I'll tell her." Maggie's eyes sparkled as she looked at him, then followed the doctor.

And Tru wished . . .

But wishes didn't always come true, and he knew that with every day that passed the time grew near that she would get in her car and drive back the way she'd come, leaving him and Wishing Springs in her rearview.

And he would let her.

Maggie pushed the door open and found Jenna holding baby Hope in her arms and staring down into her child's tiny pink face. It was one of the most beautiful sights Maggie had ever seen.

"Come meet Hope," she said. Her big, weary eyes flickered to Maggie then returned to her child.

Maggie crossed the room on a flying carpet, ignoring the worry that Jenna was going to hand Hope over to the nurse and her new parents at any moment.

"Isn't she beautiful?" Her awe shone clear.

Maggie's heart thundered. Since Jenna was holding her baby, did this mean she'd decided to keep her? "She's perfect. Oh, Jenna, congratulations from all of us. Peg and Lana and Tru are out there and I'm sure before the evening is over there will be more."

Jenna held sleeping Hope's tiny hand, caressing her fingers. "Maggie, I know you want me to keep her. But I'm looking at her and I know that I would give my life for my baby."

Maggie sat down in the chair beside the bed, so conflicted about what she should do.

Jenna looked from Hope to Maggie. "And I almost decided to keep her. But once I held her, and looked into this sweet face, I knew for me to do that wouldn't be the right choice for Hope. I know she's going to be in better hands than mine with the Hansons. They're going to love her, and send me pictures and let me be a part of her life if I choose to be."

Searing pain burned a way down Maggie's windpipe. Air evaporated. She'd thought there was a chance to change Jenna's mind and now she wasn't sure if it was right for her to say anything. Tru's and Peg's warnings rang in her mind and she didn't know what to say.

"Oh, Jenna —"

"If you're going to try and talk me out of it, please don't. I just wanted you to get to see my little girl before the nurse comes to take her to her new parents." A tear crept from her eye and she swiped it away, her nostrils flaring as she breathed in deeply, as if to calm her emotions. "This is a devastating decision. But it's right. I know in my heart for Hope it's right. The Hansons are a loving couple, with strong extended families.

That was important to me. They have family. I have nothing."

Oh, Jenna. Maggie fought back the tears. Jenna was being strong and so would she. "What if you had support?" she couldn't help but ask.

Jenna shook her head. "It still isn't right. All I can give her right now is my love. I have nothing but the hope of a future to offer her. And for some that might be enough —" she broke off, then, and hugged her baby, breathing in deeply of her child.

Maggie's heart expanded with pain so explosive she thought her chest would burst.

"Do you have a camera on your phone?" Jenna asked.

Maggie nodded.

Jenna wiped her eyes and her nose. "Would you take my picture with my baby?"

Emotion clogged Maggie's throat. "Yes, I will."

Drying her eyes she pulled her phone from her pocket and took Jenna and Hope's picture.

And then she took several more.

Maggie walked out of the hospital. Disbelief weighed heavy on her heart over Jenna's decision. She told herself Jenna's baby would grow up better than either of them had. That this child would be loved. And wasn't that what was ultimately important? Not who was raising her. After all, she'd had two parents and both of them had tossed her by the wayside.

But would Jenna ultimately grow to hate that she hadn't kept her baby?

Peg and Lana had hugged Maggie when she'd come from Jenna's room. They'd reassured her that the Hansons were a wonderful couple. That the agency they used was as careful in their screening as any agency could be. Still, Maggie was stunned and her heart heavy as she and Tru walked across the parking lot.

Tru had stayed near while they were inside, not commenting a lot, but being close. It meant a lot to her to have his support. The afternoon sunlight beamed blindingly brilliant but did nothing to lift her spirits. She hurt for Jenna despite understanding what the young girl had done.

As they approached their vehicles, her own situation crowded in on her. Would she be exposed as a fraud soon? Would everything she worked so hard for be ruined?

And all because of her father. A father who obviously saw no value in her other than what he could get from her.

How pathetic was that?

25

Tru didn't know what to do for Maggie. He knew she was hurting. She wasn't saying anything and all during the time after she'd come out and told them that Jenna was giving up her baby, he'd wanted to take her in his arms and tell her it would be all right. She'd looked so stricken. As if her entire world had just come crashing down.

He felt for the kid in the hospital room holding her baby and saying good-bye. He could only imagine how hard that must be for a girl who would have kept her child had circumstances been different. How many teens were out there going through the same choice each year? Girls who were choosing life for their child even if it wouldn't be with them but with a family — like him — who couldn't have their own child.

The impact of what Jenna was doing for the Hansons wasn't lost on him. He understood the beauty of the precious gift like others couldn't.

"Maggie, are you going to be okay?" he asked when they were alone in the parking lot. She locked her arms tightly as if to hold herself together.

All she could do was shake her head and look away from him.

He stepped in and wrapped his arms around her. She sank against him, burying her face in the crook of his neck, and cried. Her shoulders shook and eventually she released the tight grip she had on her arms and eased them around his waist and clung to him.

He smoothed her hair and just held her, while his heart broke for her and for Jenna. "Let it out," he urged, resting his cheek against her hair and wishing he could absorb the pain for her.

"It's not going to be all right," she said between soft sobs. "She's so much stronger than she thinks she is. I know."

"You would know what it is to be strong as a girl alone. Yes, you would. But she is being strong, Maggie. Strength isn't always weighed the same. Can't you see the strength it's taking for her to make this decision? The unselfish strength?"

Maggie pulled away and ran shaking

fingertips beneath her mascara stained eyes. "I see it. I do. I just can't accept it."

"And that's fine, honey. It's what Jenna can accept that matters right now."

Her eyes narrowed and she studied him as if she were trying to decide if he was the good guy or the bad guy. He stared into those gorgeous eyes. "I know I'm not saying what you want me to say. But I wouldn't be any kind of friend to you if I just agreed with you all the time. Believe me, I hate having to see you mad and looking at me as if you'd just as soon I go away."

"I need to go," she said, unlocking her car.

He reached and opened the door for her. "You're okay to drive?" he asked, knowing a little time alone might be the best thing for her.

"I'm fine."

She climbed into her car and he watched as she backed out then drove away.

She'd be better tomorrow. She'd think about it all, let it settle in and she'd think more positive about it.

But as he strode toward his truck he couldn't quite convince himself that it would be that easy.

Maggie's heart ached all night for Jenna, and her mind struggled with the blackmail that her father was trying to pull off. How could so much go wrong in such a short span of hours? Though she wanted to hide in bed and cry, she couldn't. She didn't have time for that. Her life was on the line here. Her column was being threatened in a way that she hadn't anticipated until she'd started getting the letters.

If she gave him the money, she knew that her dad would have her right where he wanted her. She couldn't do that, and besides, she was far, far from rich. Her column enabled her to make a living, but that was it. She was very frugal — something good that came from her childhood life experiences. She had scrimped and saved in order to make a secure future for herself and had a little money in the bank. Her dad wasn't going to be able to extort much from her before that was gone, and then what? He'd expose her secret anyway for money however he could get it. One way or the other, sooner or later the world would know she had once helped distract people while her father stole money from them, among a few other cons that he'd made her help him with. Who would want advice from someone like that? And then there was the fear that once this was out, Shane and the really ugly part of her life would come out.

Tru had said life wasn't fair and, boy, did she know it. She tossed and turned all night long. And oddly enough . . . she wanted to go and talk to Tru about all of it. Even though he'd disagreed with her about Jenna.

She wanted his opinion. She knew it would be an honest one and there would be objectivity there that she needed desperately.

She sipped her coffee at sunrise, trying to get rid of the foggy cobwebs that had taken over her mind. Talking to Tru would mean exposing everything. What would he think of her?

It made her stomach ill, but before she'd finished the pot of coffee, she knew that Tru was the only one she trusted.

The word alone spoke volumes. She'd come a long way in the five weeks that she'd been at the Four of Hearts.

Instead of waiting until their usual six-thirty morning ride, Maggie got in her car and drove to his house up the hill from the stable. She couldn't wait.

She needed to talk before she lost her nerve.

Taking a deep breath, she knocked on the door. The sound of boots on hardwood could be heard as he walked to the door, and her nerves rattled with every step.

"Maggie," he said, surprise written all over

his expression. "Is everything all right?"

She took another deep breath. "No, Tru, I need to ask your opinion about something. I need to talk to you."

He swung the door wide. "Sure, come on in. I was just finishing up breakfast. Are you hungry?"

"No. I don't think I could eat, but thank you."

She entered his home and instantly was struck by how much it looked like him. Large and masculine, lots of tans and earth tones. But she was surprised to see the bold colors of red and peacock blue pillows used as highlight pieces. The walls had western paintings that she was almost certain were original art. Maybe at another time she would have crossed to the paintings to see if she knew the artist. But right now, she only followed him through the living area into the kitchen at the back of the house, a bright open room lit with sunshine. He pulled out a dark oak chair for her and went to fill a cup full of coffee even though she hadn't asked.

He knew she took it black with a teaspoon of sugar. She watched him stir it in, and her heart ached knowing that there might never be anything between them.

But this was about facing things. And

Maggie had decided it was time.

"So let me get this straight," Tru said, a few minutes after Maggie had sat down at his kitchen table. He stared at her as he fought to get his temper down below boiling point. For now.

"This so-called parent was a thief and a liar all your life, causing you emotional pain and providing an unstable childhood. He taught you at an early age to be his decoy and accomplice — something he should be shot for. *Then* he goes to prison where he rightly belongs and leaves you to fend for yourself in the desperate situation with your mom?"

"Well, yes," Maggie said, looking and sounding about as embarrassed as a person could get. "But — I should have told someone."

"You were a kid, Maggie. A kid. And now he thinks *you* owe *him* something. That is about the most lowdown, sleazy . . ." Tru raked a hand through his hair and, unable to remain seated, he strode to the window and stared out at the back pastures, trying to contain the anger burning through him like hot lava. Nope, it was no use. Swinging around, he stalked back to the table. "Maggie, yeah, I'm surprised to know you've changed your name. But as far as I'm concerned, Maggie Hope is your name. It's who you were meant to be. You aren't responsible for your parents. The readership of your column will not look at you as a fraud. They won't look at you badly for what happened . . . and anyone who does is out of their mind."

"But I feel dirty. And there's more."

Tru didn't know if he could handle more. He was about to blow. "What? You can tell me anything. We'll get this all sorted out."

"When I was on the streets, I met a guy who had a car and a rundown apartment. He seemed nice enough and he took me in. I was there for two days and he stopped at a convenience store, and while I was in the car he robbed the store and beat up the man behind the counter. I didn't know it until he came back and got in the car and waved around the money he'd stolen. I ran away the minute he stopped at a light. He was too concerned with getting away to chase me. And I found out later on the news that he'd hurt the clerk. I didn't know that until later. Thank goodness the man wasn't hurt badly. He recovered, but it could have been so much worse."

Tru's heart sank. Poor kid. "Aw, Maggie. I'm so sorry."

"I've never told anyone that, and it eats at

me. I guess I should have turned myself in."

"You were getting a ride from a stranger. You didn't know."

"I had information."

"Did they catch this Shane person?"

"Yes, and I looked him up later and saw that he had a substantial record."

He pulled her from the chair. "Look at me, Maggie. You have nothing to be ashamed of. Nothing. Do you have any idea where your dad is staying?"

"No, Tru, I didn't come here to have you go have a fight with him. I just came to ask your advice on how you would handle it and these other issues."

He smiled at her and cupped her face with his hands. "Honey, I'm about to show you how I'd handle it."

"But I can't have you getting into trouble. What will your sponsors think?"

"They'll get over it. There's not too many places a person can stay in Wishing Springs. I'm betting he's at the Sweet Dreams Motel, which is pretty appropriate since it's about to be lights out for him."

"Tru, you can't go beat him up. You could get into a lot of trouble. There's no telling what he'll do."

He didn't even hesitate. He pulled Maggie into his arms and looked fiercely into her startled eyes. "Maggie, I'll be fine." He kissed her then, swift and strong. Bad idea, maybe, but he was past thinking about that at the moment. "You stay here, I'll be back in a little while."

He grabbed his hat off the hat rack by the back door and then yanked open the door and headed for his truck. He hadn't been this mad since he'd learned his dad had hocked this ranch to the hilt. It had been too late then to confront his dad about that — but this . . . oh, it wasn't too late. Not at all.

Anger ate a hole in his good sense because this sorry excuse of a man was threatening the woman Tru loved. And he was about to find out just how a Texas cowboy took care of any threats to his woman.

Blood pounding, Maggie followed Tru outside. "Tru, stop," she called.

"Stay put, Maggie," he commanded and got in his truck and peeled out for town.

Maggie stood there stunned, watching dust billow behind him.

She couldn't let him do this. She'd just wanted his advice. Wanted him to be the first to know the truth.

She raced around the house and jumped into her little car. It started immediately and she peeled out. Pulling around in a wide arc, she headed down the lane in pursuit of Tru.

He was long gone.

Really? The man must have laid down hard on the gas pedal. Mind reeling, she drove as fast as her little car would carry her. "Why didn't I keep my mouth shut?" she muttered. "Why?"

She made it to town, but the motel was on the other side of town, so she had to drive down Main Street. This early in the morning there weren't too many people out and she was thankful the little town had no red lights. By the time she whipped into the parking lot of the picturesque motel, she was madder than she'd been in a very long time.

For one thing, her dad had no right to do this to her. For another, Tru had no right to deal with this like a barbarian.

He was just coming out of the office with a confused looking Pebble following behind him in her floral pink housecoat and silk slippers. Tru didn't stop as he marched straight around the edge of the motel office and stalked toward room number six.

Pebble hurried to Maggie the instant she got out of her car. "Maggie, I've never seen Tru like this. What is going on?"

Maggie took the wisp of a lady by the

arms for a quick hug. "I can't explain right now, but would you mind going in and calling the sheriff? I don't want Tru to get hurt."

"Maggie, dear, I'll go call, but I don't think it's Tru that's in danger here."

"Still, please go call."

Before Maggie could reach him, her dad had swung open the door and without even pausing, Tru had grabbed him by the shirt collar and dragged him outside and pushed him up against the wall. Though her father was almost twenty years older than Tru, he was a tall man and solidly built. Still, Tru very nearly had his feet dangling off the ground.

"W-who are you?" her father stuttered.

"I'm not your defenseless daughter, that's for certain," Tru growled.

Maggie wasn't defenseless. But she certainly wasn't Tru.

"Now, this is the way it's going to go down. I'd like nothing more than to bash in your face right now. But I'm not going to because I don't want to disturb Miss Pebble's other clientele. What I am going to do is haul you into the jailhouse and Maggie here is going to press charges against you for trying to blackmail her. Not sure how that's going to look on your parole. Because my guess is you are on parole. Right?"

"Right," her dad said, his eyes going to slits. "But, the minute you do that I'm going to tell everyone who she really is. I'm going to ruin her. So you better think hard about what you're about to do. She owes me for raising —"

Maggie heard it all and that did it. She broke him off, "I don't owe you anything. You're my father and you'll always be my father and that's just the way it is. But owe you — ha. For what? A lousy childhood?"

Tru growled and his grip grew tighter. "Seems to me you're the one that owes her a decent childhood. A life where she didn't have to run away in order to stay safe. Maybe now would be a good time to apologize for being a rotten dad, a failed human being, and a lowlife for the way you're treating her right now."

Her dad didn't say anything. Instead he struggled against Tru's grasp, only to have Tru lift him higher on the wall. "Say it. Or I'm going to lose my patience."

She wanted to turn and run and not have to look at this. Not have the reality of where she'd come from made so clear once more. But she didn't.

The sirens could be heard now, and she knew that this was going to be the talk of the town. It would become public. No matter what — the world was about to know who she really was.

Maggie Hope and all the good she'd tried to do was about to become the lead joke for many. And the object of sympathy for others.

Her life as an ambassador of hope and encouragement was about to end.

26

Sirens blaring, the sheriff arrived. Jake Morgan took his job seriously. The rugged cowboy was also a friend of Tru's. It was obvious as he climbed from his SUV that he knew Tru had things under control. Maggie realized he was also giving Tru the benefit of the doubt by not pulling him off of her dad.

"Looks like there's a bit of a problem here," he drawled, with the easy tone of a man who'd seen plenty of brawls before. "Tru, you want to speak first, seeing as you've got the upper hand?"

"Hey, he's the one manhandling me. Get me down from here," her dad yelled.

"Well, see, fact is, I know Tru here. And contrary to what you may believe, he's a pretty levelheaded individual. So, I got to ask myself. Why does he have you dangling with your back up there on that wall?"

There was nothing funny about this, but

Maggie had to suddenly bite back the need to laugh. Thank goodness there were no photographers around. Her column had been picking up some national attention, as the network had been advertising the up-coming feature on a regular basis.

In the end her dad was carried away to the sheriff's office and Tru followed them. Maggie could barely face Pebble in her embarrassment.

"I'm so sorry," she said. The sweet lady wrapped her arm around Maggie and gave her a hug. "It would be nice if we could handpick who we're related to. But for some reason the good Lord didn't give us that option. This is not your fault."

Maggie's eyes burned and she nodded. "I know. But that doesn't make it any easier." It hit Maggie that Jenna had handpicked her baby's parents. And she'd picked them carefully. Thoughtfully. Lovingly.

Pebble smiled. "And that still doesn't make it your fault."

After that Maggie went straight to the barn and saddled Stardust. She realized that the place she felt the most peace these days was on her horse's back.

Tru spotted Maggie's car at the barn and saw Stardust was missing. He saddled up a colt and headed out to find her. All he could think about was comforting her. How had she lived with this all these years? And to be the positive, hopeful person that she was, to have risen above what the world had thrown at her. She deserved the best and he knew he wasn't right for her. But right now he couldn't think of anything but being the one who made her life easier. The one who protected her. Supported her. Reassured her. Loved her.

He followed the fresh tracks toward the pond and, sure enough, there he found her. She had tied Stardust to a tree and stood beside the pond. Her long blonde hair glistened in the soft morning sunlight as she stared into the distance.

It wasn't even nine o'clock yet and they'd already had a full day.

"So, busy morning, huh?"

She spun. "Tru." She came to him, and he folded her in his arms. It was getting harder and harder not to hold her.

"I was worried you were going to get into trouble. And that it would be my fault. I should have known that a person's past always catches up to them."

He lifted her chin with his finger, and the worry for him that he saw in those marvelous green eyes of hers almost undid him.

"If a man can't take care of his girl, then he's not much of a man. That goes for a dad too. If a dad can't be there for his family, then he's not much of a dad. I'm sorry for you on that front. But not sorry that I got to be the one who helped fix the situation for you." It had hit him that she'd trusted him enough to come ask for his help.

It was an honor he wouldn't ever forget.

She looked up at him and he kissed her gently. There was no hesitation in her response — sweet torture like nothing he'd ever experienced.

"What did the sheriff say?" she asked, pulling away and placing a few feet of space between them.

"They found a billfold of stolen credit cards and are looking into them. He's in trouble and it's out of your hands." Even if she didn't press charges, her dad was going back to prison for breaking his parole and the new charges that would be brought against him. "And he said he'll want to get some information from you about the robbery you told me about, but that he doesn't see you having any legal problems with that — the statute of limitations being what it is and you not being aware of what was happening — he'll still need you to come in and make a statement."

She nodded, relief rushing her like a linebacker, but not wiping away all the emotions she was feeling. "Whatever he needs."

Tru hated the pain he saw in her eyes.

"Maggie, I can't believe you've lived with this secret all these years. With your attitude and what you've accomplished — you are an inspiration. This story is going to come out, you won't be able to stop it. But I believe *you* should break it. Talk to Amanda about it. She'll know how to help you do that. And I can almost guarantee it's going to have the complete opposite effect on people than the one you've been fearing. People — the ones who count — are going to find you more of an inspiration. More of a voice of hope than ever before and rather than expose what you consider your lack of credentials it's going to give you credibility."

"I don't know. I wish. I love my column. If I didn't love it so much, I would never have agreed to come here. But I couldn't just sit back and watch it die without trying to keep it alive."

He believed that. Without hesitating, he made a decision to let Maggie in on his story. "We both agreed to this because we wanted to keep something we love alive."

"What do you mean?"

"You trusted me with your secret, I think

I should trust you with mine."

Maggie needed this, and he did too, but he was doing it for her.

He picked up a handful of small rocks and threw one into the pond, thinking. He glanced at her. She had to be overwhelmed from the emotional experience with Jenna yesterday. And then her dad today.

"I think you need to know your dad isn't the only one who sold out to the worthless side. My dad was a piece of work too." He was harsh, but that was just the way it was. He told her then of the deceit and of how his father had signed away everything Pops had worked for.

"So you're saying if your dad hadn't died in that plane crash, y'all would have lost the ranch and not even known it until it was over?"

"That's exactly what I'm saying. He'd taken loans out we had no idea about and first liens, second liens — they came from everywhere. If we hadn't had a great lawyer, we would have lost it all. Everything Pops worked his whole life to build up."

She looked stunned as she processed what he'd confided in her. "I'm so sorry that happened to you and your brothers. And poor Pops. I'm so glad he had y'all to step in for him."

"You know, as bad as I hate the dementia, I can be thankful that he didn't have to know that his last living son had signed away the ranch he loved."

"Sadly, I understand what you're saying."

He tossed another rock then turned to her. "Listen. It's been an intense couple of days. We're taking the day off from practice. If you want to ride, then do it, but just relax and enjoy it. Or go do whatever you want but I think you've been through an emotional roller coaster and need a break. I don't know if you were planning to go see Jenna, but this will give you time for whatever you need to do. I'll go with you to see Jake tomorrow if you want. And then we'll get down to some hard work. I've got you entered in an amateur competition in two weeks."

"Two weeks?"

"You've got this," Tru assured her.

"Right now I don't feel like I have anything."

It took everything he had not to tell her that she had him. He'd kissed her earlier, and he knew that wasn't right. He had nothing to offer her except his love and support. And he knew that wasn't enough.

He completely understood why Jenna had made the choice she'd made. If he was as strong as the kid, then he'd keep his heart locked away and he'd let Maggie go.

Jenna stared out the window feeling numb. Empty.

She'd crept down the hall earlier and watched as her baby had been taken from the hospital by her new family. They'd come by and thanked her and told her she was welcome to be a part of Hope's life, but Jenna was torn. Could she handle seeing Hope and leaving her over and over and over again? And was that fair to anyone?

Now, Jenna wasn't sure what her next step was. Where would she go?

Maybe she could find a job in Wishing Springs.

A tap sounded on her door and Maggie came in. Jenna hadn't been sure Maggie would ever speak to her again. Her aching heart jumped in her chest seeing Maggie's smile.

Jenna hated to admit how badly she needed a smile. Would she ever be able to smile again?

"Can I come in?"

Jenna nodded.

"I hear you're going back to the home today?"

"For a little while. Until I move to a

women's shelter they've helped me find."

"Well, I came to offer you a ride, if that's okay."

Jenna nodded.

"And I wanted to talk to you about some options on the way."

"What options?"

"Well, I have a small apartment in the Houston area. And there's a second bedroom. I would love it if you'd come and stay there. You can go back to school and you're welcome to stay as long as you want. Rent free. I want my home to be your home."

Jenna blinked back tears. "Why would you do that for me?"

Maggie sat down on the chair across from the one Jenna was sitting in. "Because I'm your friend, Jenna. And friends help friends out. My friend Amanda helped me in this way."

"But I know you think I made the wrong decision about my baby."

Maggie looked sad. "I realized I couldn't make that choice for you. But I could support your choice. It was a choice of life for your baby and that's what matters. You did good, Jenna. And I want to help you start a new life. That's what Amanda did for me once and I want to do that for you. Please, at least consider it."

Jenna took a shuddering breath. "I thought you might not want to be my friend after what I did."

"You and I need to have a long talk, sometime. What do you say?"

Jenna nodded. It was all she could do.

"Whew, you have been busy since you've been down there, Mags. And that cowboy of yours sounds like a keeper. I can't wait to finally meet him."

"He's not my cowboy." It had been two tough weeks of training since she'd tried to convince Jenna not to give Hope up for adoption. Jenna's decision to go ahead with the adoption plan had been hard on Maggie but she was managing and planned to be there for Jenna.

"Whatever. I'll see myself at the end of the week. Like we discussed last week when you called to drop all of your 'secret past' on me," she said, emphasizing secret past. "We're meeting y'all in Brenham for the event, then we'll head back to the ranch for the interviews. And I'm not believing a word of this denial about Tru — I'll be ready to hear all about what's *not* going on when I get there," Amanda said with a laugh. " 'Bye now."

Maggie groaned as the phone went dead.

The idea of the competition wasn't anywhere near as scary as it had been in the beginning. She wasn't sure if it was because she had learned so much or that she'd had so much happen in the last few weeks that nothing fazed her anymore. She and Amanda would work her past into the interview, thus getting it out in the open. She'd been a little miffed about not knowing sooner, but that was just because she cared for Maggie so much.

And that was why she was so interested in what was going on between Maggie and Tru. But how was Maggie supposed to tell her friend what was going on when she didn't know herself? Tru had been the perfect teacher. Yet he had just pulled back as he'd done before and she wasn't sure what was going on.

All she knew was that when the competition was over she was finished here. And the idea of leaving was as hard as all the other things that had gone on.

Tru had withdrawn emotionally. As if he'd gotten too close to her after going after her dad and then telling her about his own father. And maybe because she'd been through so much in such a short time, she'd also retreated from him. She'd thought of him only as a ladies' man for so long that it was hard to realize that this kind champion was the man she'd come here to meet.

Driving to the stable for practice, she wondered where along the way she had fallen in love with him — because she knew she had. The truth was, there were so many different moments that she couldn't place a finger on a specific one. Maybe it was watching him with his Pops. Or his patience with her in the arena. Or helping her with Jenna. Or when he'd gone after her dad to take up for her for the first time in her life.

There were too many for Maggie to pinpoint, but she knew without a doubt that she loved him.

And she wasn't sure what to do about it.

Other than tell him . . .

27

Maggie drove back to the barn the next morning with mixed emotions. Her time here was almost over. She would be leaving soon. Leaving this wonderful ranch, this wonderful town . . . and Tru.

The thought of not being near Tru any longer was the hardest thing she'd faced since arriving — and Maggie had faced some of her toughest times during this bet.

Tru hadn't held her since the day he'd beat her father up. Not the most romantic of times, but he had held her then, and she almost wanted to thank her dad for giving her the opportunity to be in Tru's arms again. She missed him now.

Fresh alfalfa hay and feed had an invigorating scent to her, one she would miss.

Tru was in the arena already on his horse — looking better than should have been legal this early in the morning.

"Mornin'," he said, but he didn't dismount. He'd been distant and it was killing her. "You ready to work? We need to make you as set for tomorrow as possible."

"Sure," she said, trying to act as nonchalant as he was, then mounted up and the riding began.

It went on like that for over two hours and Tru maintained his distance.

Maggie fought a feeling of letdown that it had all been strictly business.

"You're going to do good, Maggie. There will be a lot of press here, I hope you realize. It won't just be *Wake Up with Amanda*."

"What?"

"Yeah, I got the alert from my agent this morning. Of course we've already anticipated this, but Frank, my agent, found out from his sources that more reporters than Amanda will be at the competition. And," he paused, "I hate to tell you but some of the trashier magazines will be here too. Your dad would have had his audience if he wasn't sitting behind bars right now."

"I guess he would have been thrilled," Maggie said, still hurt that her father would be the kind of man that he was. She should be upset knowing that the tabloids would be at the competition but at the moment all she could really think about was that she and Tru were acting like strangers, like they'd been in the beginning.

Only they weren't.

It took every ounce of willpower Tru had to distance himself from Maggie. He'd fought it for the last two weeks, but it was almost impossible to keep his feelings locked up.

Especially now, seeing the hurt in her eyes.

He was acting as if she meant nothing to him, simply because if he gave an inch, he'd pull her into his arms and tell her he loved her. But that would be a mistake.

If he loved her he would do exactly what he was doing.

"Are you mad at me, Tru?"

Tru grimaced, closed his eyes briefly, and took a second to get his head on straight before meeting her questioning gaze. *Mad at her?* Not hardly.

"I'm not mad at you, Maggie. Why would you ask that?" He held his boots firmly to the spot, when all he wanted was to close the distance between them and show her exactly how not mad he was.

"Then why are you keeping your distance?"

"I'm not."

She stalked right up to him. "You are full of bull, Mr. Monahan." Her sweet mouth was firmly drawn into a frown.

"Now, Maggie, hold on."

"Do not try to tell me I'm imagining this. A woman knows. I just can't let it go on without knowing what I've done wrong."

"You've done nothing wrong, Maggie. This between us will just never work." There, he'd said it. He'd gotten it out there. It was going to be the easiest thing for her. Well, the easiest thing would have been if he'd kept his distance in the first place. But he hadn't done that.

She stared at him as if she didn't know him.

"Maggie, I'm not the man for you."

Her forehead crinkled above startled green eyes. "What if I said you were?"

He groaned. "I'm not —"

"Tru, I love you."

His heart felt like it would explode. She loved him. How was a man supposed to bear looking the woman he loved in the eye and not telling her the truth?

"I shouldn't have been kissing you. I should have kept my distance. I led you on. This is my fault."

"Why are you doing this?" Maggie stared at him as if he were a stranger.

And that was good. "Tomorrow you're going to compete, and to be honest, you have

382

a good chance of placing high in this amateur competition. Then we'll give the interview. And after that I'll be back on the road hitting it hard with competitions. I'm not the settling down kind of guy right now, Maggie. You're looking for someone I'm not. I need my freedom on the road."

Hurt filled her eyes. "I see." Her words were quiet.

He nodded. "It's best you know that now. I like you a lot. You're a good woman, Maggie. The best. But I've just realized I led you on when I shouldn't have."

Unable to look at her any longer, he turned and strode out of the barn, got into his truck, and left. It was about the lowest thing he'd ever done. Well, selfishly loving on Maggie when he knew nothing could come of it was the worst. That was unforgivable on his part.

28

"Don't be nervous, Mags."

Maggie sat on the floor, with letters all around her and her computer open to a full mailbox. Her column had grown immensely since the bet began. There were letters about drug-addicted children, letters about spouses cheating on readers, letters from readers who were lonely and brokenhearted. And that was just the tip of the iceberg.

"I'm trying not to be." That was the truth. Ever since her catastrophic failure of a discussion with Tru that afternoon, she'd been a mess. Numbness gripped her.

"Good," said Amanda. "You've done a great job making the newspaper's readership want to know more about the men of Wishing Springs and the town itself and not just about the bet and the competition. I called to give you the last details. After the event, I want to have lunch at the Bull Barn, but we'll have time to talk without the cameras on the whole time. They'll follow us around some of the time and then we'll shoot the interview with you and Tru and then the footage of you riding."

"Okay," Maggie said, unenthusiastically. She was living a nightmare. Really, how much worse could it get? She'd just told a man she loved him and he'd basically told her to get lost. And now, she was supposed to show up and spend the day with him like they were best buds.

"So, see, it's going to be a piece of cake. Now, I have to ask again what's the real scoop on the two of you? Don't deny it like you did before — how's the romance going?"

Maggie hung her head and stared at her orange toes. "No romance, Amanda."

"He kissed you, Mags, you told me that and now you're all clammed up. That says something is going on."

"It's a bad connection. There is no romance."

Not anymore, anyway.

She wasn't sure what had gotten into her, today. She'd been able to see the conversation wasn't going to go the way she wanted it to and yet she'd still blurted out that she loved him. How dim was that? She could have at least saved herself the humiliation

385

and kept her mouth shut. But no. Her heart of hearts had pushed the words forward, wanting so badly for him to return her sentiments. But . . . what had he said? That he needed to be free on the road.

What was even more bizarre than him saying such a thing was the fact that she did not believe him.

Tru had lied to her. After she'd finally started trusting him completely, he'd lied.

And that was one of the things that hurt the most. Why had he lied?

Long after she and Amanda finished their conversation, she sat with her legs curled beneath her as she stared over the back of the chair at the moon and tried to figure out what had gone on.

But no answers came. Sometime near four in the morning, she roused and realized she'd dozed off sitting up, her head leaning against the chair back. Her legs were asleep and it took a long while to get them to have enough feeling in them that she could walk into the bedroom and crawl beneath the covers.

Needless to say, it was going to be a challenging day.

And Maggie deserved it. As she lay there in the bed staring up at the dark ceiling, it became very clear to her. She'd gotten a taste of a life she'd only ever dreamed of as a girl. She'd fallen in love with a man she knew she had no business falling for. She'd risked her heart when she knew better.

And now she was facing the consequences. If there was one thing her life had taught her, it was that all actions had consequences. Some good, some bad, but they were always there. And risking her heart, as fragile as it was, had been silly and foolish.

What had she expected anyway? Declarations of everlasting love?

Roses and violins?

How ridiculous. Why would she expect that?

Yes, the truth was she believed in hope . . . but everything had boundaries. And she'd completely fallen out of bounds on this one.

Tru was grateful that they were busy getting to Brenham, signing in and warming up for the cutting competition. There were so many different cameras there that they barely noticed when Amanda and her film crew arrived.

It was a circus. And he felt like the biggest clown in the show. If he was doing the right thing for Maggie, letting her go without telling her the truth, then why did it feel so wrong?

He knew it was his emotions trying to get him to cave in and be honest with Maggie. He ignored them.

The good thing about the competition was they were separated from the media to an extent.

She wasn't her usual warm self this morning. She was distant, and who could blame her. She'd bared her heart to him and he'd turned her away.

This was about Maggie right now, though. He wanted her to do well for herself. He could care less about any other aspect of this fiasco. He just wanted Maggie to feel good about what she did out in that arena today.

"Maggie, you can do this," he said, stopping her before she climbed into the saddle. She'd been watching the others compete and he'd seen the worry on her face. "There isn't one person out there any better than you. Remember most of them are fairly new at this, just like you. You're not competing against pros. This is all fun."

"Fun." She laughed and it sounded brittle, dry.

"Yeah, Maggie. Fun. Look at me." He took her by the arms and she looked at him. "I know you have been through more in these two months than anyone could ever

388

have anticipated. And I know that you never wanted to be here in the first place. But here you are. And right now, I want you to forget me, and everything else and every*one* else. I know that you enjoy it when you climb up on this horse right here. Isn't that right?"

She nodded.

He smiled at her, loving her so much he thought he'd explode. "That's what I want you to think about. This is you and Stardust doing your thing. Don't take your eye off the calf. And Maggie, I mean it. There is an aspect to this I just didn't think about, but there are going to be camera flashes out there and maybe some noise. Ignore all of it. Stardust will. He'll zero in on his calf and showboat, you just keep your eyes on the calf you pick, keep your hands up, and settle in."

"Piece of cake," she said, and almost sounded like his Maggie.

Not yours.

Yeah, not his. But as he watched her climb into the saddle and head into the arena he wanted her to be his with all his heart . . .

Of course everyone and their cousin showed up at the Bull Barn for lunch to celebrate Maggie coming in third place in the cutting. Maggie knew they'd have been there no matter what because of the cameras, but she was so thankful that she'd even placed. She didn't care if she ever placed again in anything she entered, but today she was relieved that she had.

Stardust had been amazing. He'd danced for her. His feet had been light and quick and he'd stirred up dust with each of his hard stops and switches. She was as glad for Stardust as she was for herself. And for Tru.

The man had given her his all when it came to preparing her for this competition and she truly felt that he hadn't cared about anything except her doing her best and proving to herself that she could do it.

Walking into the diner, she and Amanda took in the crowd.

"Wow," Amanda said scanning the packed place — and applauding hands.

Maggie chuckled, and her hand went to her heart, she was so overwhelmed.

Big Shorty had saved them Tru's booth for lunch and he led Maggie and Amanda to it as the applause continued. Maggie smiled at everyone. Maggie knew Amanda and the producers would have plenty of footage to make quite a colorful bit for the show.

Once she had given the folks of Wishing Springs their time in the spotlight, Amanda and Maggie took a seat in the booth and talked. The cameras rolled some just to get film of all the town and their excitement for her. But then Amanda let the crew off to eat and she and Maggie were able to have some time talking quietly — thanks to Big Shorty who brought them their drinks and then, with one stern look, let the others know to go about their business.

"I love this place," Amanda said first after they were officially "off" the record. "I can so see you here, Maggie."

"What?" Maggie wondered how Amanda could read her so well.

"You know you love this. They're like your peeps now."

She laughed. "My peeps?"

"Your people. They love you. And it's not just because you've put them on the map with their fifteen minutes of fame. They really like you."

"The feeling is mutual." She'd toyed briefly with the thought of moving here. But not with things so weird with her and Tru. "I do love it here," she said with complete sincerity. "It's so amazing that I came here a stranger and now there are so many who are my friends. I've enjoyed feeling really connected to a community."

Amanda smiled. Her friend had always

understood that no matter what Maggie did, she'd felt aloof and disconnected. Maggie had always said it was because of her past, and Amanda knew enough about her past to know it was because of her bad home life. When a kid was raised never knowing what would happen next, she distanced herself. And it was a hard habit to break even after all these years. And just when she'd dropped her barriers Tru had turned the tables on her . . . Maggie didn't need to think about that right now though. She still had an interview to get through. Big Shorty sent their chicken salad sandwiches over, and after they'd both taken a couple of bites, Amanda turned serious. "During the interview, as we discussed, I'm going to ask you a few questions about your past. You let me know what you're comfortable with, Mags. We're not going to make this about your past, so don't worry about that. Like you wanted, we're simply going to get this thing out in the open, and you won't ever have to worry about it again."

Maggie nodded. "Okay," she said, her voice stiff.

"Stop worrying. It will be a negative response, but I and the network and your editor believe it will only make you stronger as a columnist. Your story will resonate with readers, Mags."

"Tru said the same thing."

Amanda smiled. "Tru sounds like a very smart cowboy. But," she studied Maggie thoughtfully, "I have a feeling there is definitely something going on between the two of you that you, my friend, have not shared with your best friend. What's happened since the kiss, Mags?"

"There is nothing between us. Yes, there was the kiss, but it was a mistake. Despite that there was some attraction, there is no future in it. He is such a great teacher."

Amanda nodded. "What I know is that he puts a nice glow to your cheeks."

Maggie was in so much trouble. She loved Amanda, but she was in a hard spot. She was her friend, but she was also doing her job. There was no telling how this was going to all turn out after they got the footage back to the station.

And that was what worried Maggie.

The crew arrived at the ranch and took the place over. They filmed everything they could. Amanda had asked that his brothers be there, and Jarrod had flat refused, but Tru had talked Bo into it. Not because he was looking for a cowgirl bride or anything but because he saw the potential for advertisement for his stirrups.

And it was. Amanda stuck the microphone in front of him and gave Four of Hearts Stirrups a big shout-out.

Bo spent a lot of time at trade shows and had himself been interviewed several times about his business, he was no rookie. And the stirrup business was a big part of how they paid their debt down on the ranch. So that was his reasoning.

Amanda did a great job with the interview. She was a caring person and not up to tricks, though everyone knew going in that the viewers were looking for romance between Tru and Maggie because of what had happened in the interview Maggie had done. He should never have placed his hand over hers but he'd not only been attracted to her, though he'd wanted to deny it, he'd also felt protective of her. And he still was on both counts. Amanda seemed protective of Maggie too and thus hadn't been too intrusive.

Amanda had chosen to set up chairs at the edge of the arena so the barn and the round pens were in the background. They'd taken their seats beside each other and while he answered questions and often glanced at Maggie, she never looked at him. Tru could see Amanda was picking up on the fact that

Maggie was avoiding eye contact with him. And when she did look at him, she was distant. As if she didn't trust him.

And that killed his soul.

This was for her own good, he reminded himself. She deserved more than what he could give her.

When the interview was over and Amanda and the film crew had gone, Tru stood beside Maggie and waved as they headed out.

"She handled your past well, Maggie. It's going to be okay, don't you think?" He felt awkward. It was true. Amanda just did a very quick intro on the woman behind the "Gotta Have Hope" column and part of that was a few questions about her being brought up in a dysfunctional family with an alcoholic mother and a father who was a con artist. She asked Maggie how it felt to live in fear that people would find out about her situation as a child. And then about how it felt when her father went to prison and she'd ultimately become a runaway. Maggie had done beautifully. She'd answered the questions honestly and Tru had hurt for her. He'd also been rooting for her.

In the end, Maggie's story had been fascinating and he was certain the network had gotten far more from the special than they'd hoped.

"You do know your column is going to be a runaway hit. I wouldn't be surprised if other things didn't come your way because of it," Tru said.

She stared at him. "I hope so. If what I went through could help someone, then that's what I would like."

She'd said the same thing to Amanda.

"Thanks for what you did, teaching me," she said to him. "It . . ." her voice thickened, trailing off, "was fantastic. I'd better go."

He watched her leave, telling himself that he would be seeing her around town. "Don't be in a rush to leave the cabin. You can use it for as long as you need."

She was already at her car. "Thanks, but that won't be necessary. I'm all packed up. I'm staying at the Sweet Dreams Motel tonight."

"You're leaving today?" His heart had started pounding.

"Bye, Tru. Take care of yourself. I'll stop by and see Pops before I go."

And then she got in her car and pulled out of the drive.

Tru just stood there hurting.

29

Maggie went straight to see Jenna. She wasn't herself, but the kid was trying to be brave. Maggie was always struck by Jenna's grit.

And yet, she knew giving Hope up was always going to be a hole inside of the girl. Maggie could see it in her eyes despite the façade.

"You love him a lot, don't you?"

They were sitting on the swing on the back porch. Jenna's question startled her. There was no sense pretending. "I do. But some things aren't meant to be."

Jenna nodded and looked out toward the garden in the distance. "Some things just aren't possible."

Maggie heard no hope in her words and it was like a blow to her heart.

Would Jenna ever believe in hope again?

When Maggie left, she was exhausted. She'd hardly slept the night before and then with the stress of the day, she went straight to Pebble's motel. Since her father was still in jail she didn't have to worry about running into him.

After taking a hot shower, Maggie dropped into bed and despite all the emotions rioting inside of her, she crashed — immediately falling asleep as if she hadn't slept in weeks. Tomorrow would be a new day, she thought, putting a positive spin on the notion.

Maggie had learned a long time ago that every day started fresh. She would do it once more. Before she crawled into bed, though, she closed her curtains and that's when she saw Rand walk up to Pebble's door with a bouquet of pretty spring flowers. She watched him straighten his hat and smooth his shirt, making sure it was tucked in perfectly, and then he raised his hand to knock. But he didn't.

Instead, he held his hand in midair so long that Maggie began willing him to knock. How were those two ever going to move forward if he didn't find a way to make amends for the embarrassment that he'd caused Pebble when he'd gotten drunk and sung that awful song to her? How was he ever going to get to the real problem — his drinking — if he couldn't find the courage to reach for what he wanted?

And to accept whatever the outcome was, as long as he knew he'd at least given it his best shot.

Maggie watched him lower his hand, place the flowers on the front doorstep, then walk away.

She couldn't look away. She watched him walk down the street in the fading light and she thought of her column. She hadn't thought of it all day.

All of this had been to save her column and she realized now, though it meant the world to her, she'd experienced something here in Wishing Springs that would forever change her. Even if, like for Rand, everything hadn't fallen into place the way her heart wanted it to.

She needed sleep. She pulled the curtains closed and glanced back at Pebble's door. The flowers were gone.

Hope surged inside of Maggie like a spark from a tiny struggling flame . . .

Pebble had been watching. She'd known he was out there. And one day, maybe she would open the door.

Maggie fell asleep thinking about new days and starting fresh.

"What is wrong with you?" Bo asked him.

"Nothing," Tru growled as he pulled a

bale of hay off the trailer and walked past Bo to the storeroom.

"Don't give me that. You've been acting weird all day. Come on, Jarrod's cooking and he sent me down here to haul you up to the house if I had to."

"I'm not hungry."

"Hey, either you come up there and we talk, or Jarrod's going to come down here and talk. And big brother will not be happy. And neither will little brother, because I'm starving. And after what I had to go through today, being interviewed and tortured isn't making me your best friend right now. You owe me, buddy."

Tru glared at Bo, then dropped the hay where he was. "Fine. Let's go."

They headed up to the house and Jarrod had just placed chicken-fried steak and potatoes on the table. When they walked in, Solomon wagged his tail from beneath the kitchen table waiting for any stray table scrap to accidently drop to the floor for him — or for Pops to hand straight to him.

Pops sat at the head of the table waiting for them. He kept looking at the door after they'd entered.

"Maggie?"

All three of them stared at each other. Jarrod hiked a brow and mouthed, "Where is she?"

Tru shrugged. "Gone," he said.

"And why is that?" Jarrod asked as they all sat down at the table. "I got the feeling you were crazy about her the other day when she helped us with the calf. Looks to me like you're being a fool if you let this woman get away."

It had been a long, hard day. Tru was mad at the world and not really in the mood to talk but he could not keep his secret any longer. "I can't have kids, that's why."

"Wow," Bo said, his fork stopping mid-action. He laid it back down on his plate.

Setting his tea back on the table, Jarrod studied him. "From the treatments?"

"Yeah. Maggie deserves more than I would be able to give her."

"Tru, has it occurred to you that you should let Maggie decide what she wants?" Jarrod asked.

"Yeah, man, that's a hard blow, but Maggie's in love with you. It is written all over her face. Now I understand what was wrong with her today. Why she looked so sad every time she looked at you."

Tru glared at his brothers. "I'm doing what is best for Maggie."

Jarrod shook his head. "You're doing what

is best for you. If you don't let her choose, then you don't have to face her rejection. You need to fix this. Maggie deserves better."

That had Tru standing and walking toward the door to leave. Pops followed him, stopping by a picture on the wall of him and their grandmother. She'd been gone for over ten years, but she and Pops had had the real deal.

He pointed at her picture. "Best. For me."

Tru knew it was true. Pops patted Tru's shoulder. "Maggie."

Tru stared at his brothers and they both looked at him like he was the shortest stump in the forest.

"Only you can make the call and fix this," Jarrod said.

"Yeah," Bo added. "It's your life. But Tru, you're not being fair to either one of you. I'm not saying I'm ready to jump into the pond, but I believe you owe Maggie the truth."

Tru left then, walked out and went home. But the questions rolled in his head like thunder. Had he taken the easy way out?

And should he have let Maggie decide?

Truth was, if he let Maggie know the truth, then he had to face the hard truth that she could feel sorry for him, and that was something he just couldn't take.

Maggie woke at seven, loaded her overnight bag into her car with the rest of her stuff, and headed for home. Back to the city and her apartment.

She had a checklist of things to do.

Forget Tru Monahan was at the top of the list.

Talk to Amanda and tell her the truth. She'd felt terrible not letting her in on what had really happened in Wishing Springs — not for her show but for her as a friend.

Start getting her two bedroom apartment ready for Jenna, whom she planned on picking up the next weekend. She was encouraged that Jenna was staying with Peg and Lana long enough to make some decisions about contact with the Hansons and Hope. Adoptions were so different than they once were and Maggie felt better about Jenna's choice after she stepped back. Just like Tru told her, she had been making choices for Jenna based purely on emotion. Emotion that involved her need to keep a mother and child together, because she herself longed for her own mother to have wanted her. Maggie admired Jenna more now though than even before. Right or wrong, in her heart of hearts Jenna believed this was the right choice. And it hadn't been made lightly.

And then once more on her list: Forget Tru Monahan.

Maggie stopped at a gas station in town before heading to Houston.

She went in to grab a soda, hoping a little sugar would perk her up. And right there splashed across three different tabloids were pictures of her and Tru.

Maggie's mouth fell open at what they said. Scrawled across one: Monahan Finds True Love — Only to Be Dumped by Scheming Columnist. One claimed she was an *alien.* But the last one was of them hugging outside the hospital the day Jenna had had the baby. She was crying and the headline read: All Hope Lost — Cancer Drug Results Reveal Champ Can't Father Children.

Maggie stared at that. Then she picked it up . . .

Tru was an idiot. He'd said it before and he'd say it again.

He tore out of Pebble's parking lot and headed through town hoping to find Maggie saying good-bye to some of the friends she'd made. He figured Clara Lyn and Reba's were the first stops on his way out to

Over the Rainbow.

He was breaking the speed limit as he passed the corner gas station and caught a glimpse of her car. An electric shot of joy jolted him as he slammed on the brakes then did a U-turn and drove in front of her, blocking her exit.

She was storming out of the store as he pushed his door open.

"Maggie, we need to talk."

"That sounds like a good thing for us to do, except I think I've told you everything there is to know about me."

She was hotter than a firecracker, he realized a little late.

"Mag—"

"Nope, just hold on there. I don't know how I missed this. How I could have read all about your background and cancer at such a young age after you told me and then missed this detail." She slapped a paper at him. Her gaze singed him. "Is this true?"

He fumbled with it and saw it claimed she was an alien. He almost laughed, but something warned him maybe now wasn't the time for that. "No," he said instead.

"Good to know. How about this one?"

"Ow," he said, as she slapped him in the chest with another one. It claimed he'd dumped the scheming columnist. "No.

These things are not true, Maggie. What is wrong with you? Those rags are worthless."

Her eyes glittered and he saw tears. "How about this one?" She pushed the last one at him.

He was so startled by her tears he almost dropped the paper. He stared down at the headlines and his heart took a roller coaster ride over the edge of a cliff as the words jumped out at him: All Hope Lost — Cancer Drug Results Reveal Champ Can't Father Children.

"That one is the truth, isn't it, Tru?" Her words dripped with accusation.

He couldn't lie to her direct question. Somehow the story had been leaked or some reporter had put two and two together with childhood cancer and infertility and was simply shooting out a story that happened to be true. Either way, Maggie knew.

"Yes, it's true," he answered gently, not wanting to cause any more pain to fill her gaze.

"You love me, don't you?"

Her question startled him. "Huh?"

She slapped a hand to her hip. "Tru Monahan, I swear you had better level with me because I have just about reached the end of my patience. You *love* me." She stepped toward him. He backed up. "Say it."

He bumped into his truck and stopped. She didn't. She walked right up to him. If he lived to be two hundred, he'd never understand the female brain. "Yes, Maggie, I love you."

"I knew it! And all this time you put me through this torture." Sparks reignited in her eyes.

"Maggie, help a guy out. I came to talk to you to try and tell you the truth."

She was standing so close their toes were touching.

"You lied to me. You love me and yet you didn't tell me about the cancer drug. You didn't tell me about the children."

"The lack of children. I couldn't do that to you. You told me you loved me, but you want a houseful of kids. I can't offer you any of your dreams, and I found it out after falling for you."

"*You* are the answer to my dreams. I want the man I love first. The man I trust. The man who makes me not feel alone anymore. I need him. I need you, Tru. I need and want you first. And then we'll see what our future holds. *If* you want a future with me?"

"Do I want you?" Tru didn't wait, he wrapped his arms around her and pulled her into a fierce embrace. "Do I want you? How does forever sound? Maggie, I need you so bad. I want you like I want air and sunshine. Honey, I've got no hope without you. I'm nothing without you."

Maggie's soft lips trembled and she wrapped her arms around his neck. "Oh, Tru, I'm so in the same boat."

"Kiss her, for cryin' out loud," Clara Lyn's distinctive twang carried on the wind.

Tru looked up and Maggie turned her head and they spotted Clara Lyn and Reba standing outside the Cut Up and Roll along with several ladies in plastic beauty capes and in various stages of beauty applications. Including the formidable form of Bertha, hands on hips and a plastic cap on her head.

"Well, go on, now. Don't just stand there," Clara Lyn called, laughingly. "I've got to get this perm solution off of Bertha's hair or she'll be bald. And no one wants to make Bertha bald — it'd just make her mad."

Bertha cocked her head to the side, her lips pinched. She still looked more like a drill sergeant than a nurse. "Kiss the man, Maggie. You know you're wanting to."

Tru reached behind him, opened his truck and pulled Maggie into a semblance of seclusion. "Maggie, I want you to be my wife more than anything, but you have to

408

be sure. We can adopt. We can do whatever you want. But you have to be sure."

Maggie was smiling. She couldn't help it. This was really happening. "All I've ever wanted was to have a family that loved me. And Tru, that starts with you, and then we work our way up from there. Now, please make everyone happy and kiss me."

That amazing, beautiful smile bloomed across his dear face and warmed Maggie through and through. "For the rest of my life," he said, and then he lowered his head and kissed her. And he took his time, long and slow because they had forever . . . across the street, claps and whoops sounded and horns blared.

And flashbulbs went off too, but Maggie and Tru couldn't have cared less. They were finally home, lost in their love . . . and found because of it.

DISCUSSION QUESTIONS

1. This story begins with a crazy blunder by Maggie because she's so nervous she makes a bet and it quickly gets out of hand in the most unexpected way, with unexpected results. Have you ever had something completely unexpected and unplanned interrupt your life? How did it turn out?

2. Do you believe God never wastes a hurt? I do and passed that belief to Maggie. She was hurt in so many ways growing up, but she still believed there was hope and that God could use her. Can you describe a time in your life that God used you to help someone who'd suffered a hurt similar to something you've experienced?

3. This story is about sacrifice. Jenna sacrificed keeping her daughter

because, despite how much she loved her child she believed in her heart that she wouldn't be able to provide for her. Because of this belief she made the choice first, to give her baby life-and then, she made the choice to give her precious baby to a loving Christian couple who she'd carefully chosen to give her most precious gift-her child. How did you feel about Jenna's choice?

4. Tru also was prepared to make a sacrifice by keeping his love for Maggie a secret because he believed that was what was best for her. However, in doing that he was depriving Maggie of the opportunity to make the choice for herself. How does this relate to the choice that God gives us?

5. Because she longed to be loved by her parents and she saw how much Jenna loved her baby Maggie was obsessed with Jenna keeping her baby. But she had to realize that sometimes if you really love someone that requires sacrifice. This is a hard subject in so many ways. How do you feel about the choices that

were made in *Betting on Hope*? Have you ever experienced sacrifice in your life?

6. Which character in *Betting on Hope* did you relate to the most? Which character did you enjoy the most? Why?

7. Bo became extremely upset when he read Maggie's column about the cowboys and the firemen and the idea that women might come to town looking for love. Was he trying to control the situation? In my own life I've learned that there are aspects that I can control, but ultimately God is in control. Knowing this helps me when things don't turn out exactly as I had planned. I've learned to let it go and understand that God sees the big picture and is the one who is actually in control. Have you ever tried to control aspects of your life so much that you try to take it out of God's hands?

8. I love writing about the unexpected gifts from God. In my own life I've experienced these gifts over and over again in good times and bad times. Maggie had to and she un-

derstood that no matter what there was hope if we believe. Maggie understood that though her parents hadn't loved her that her heavenly Father did and His love is what carried her through. How do you feel about that? Do you believe? Do you have hope in your life?

ACKNOWLEDGMENT

To my father-in-law Walter (Bubba) Clopton — the cowboy I'll always love. Though your own memories have dimmed, ours haven't . . . your legacy of strength, loyalty, and love of God inspired this story as you've always inspired our lives.

To my wonderful family — I am a blessed woman to have you all in my life, and despite the times I'm buried beneath deadlines or stumbling around from sleepless nights spent talking with imaginary people of my stories, it is all of you I love and can't do without! You make my life complete and fill my well. I thank God each and every day for all of you. A special hug to Chuck, my sweet husband, who sees me bump into walls more than anyone and still loves me . . . as I love you too.

To my editor — the talented Becky Monds for her most excellent input. And for the numerous others who worked to make this

415

book a reality including my fantastic, supportive Agent Natasha Kern.

There were so many people who answered questions that helped in making this story authentic . . . any mistakes are mine!

And a special thanks to Bobby and Billy Walters — I could never, ever be as funny and as witty as the two of you, but I'm forever indebted to you for inspiring the mischievous twins in this book, Doobie and Doonie Burke — I believe they'll make my readers smile like the two of you make all of us who know you smile.

ABOUT THE AUTHOR

Debra Clopton is a multi-award winning novelist first published in 2005 and has written more than 22 novels. Along with writing, Debra helps her husband teach the youth at their local Cowboy Church. Debra is the author of the acclaimed Mule Hollow Matchmaker Series, and her goal is to shine a light toward God while she entertains readers with her words. Visit her website at www.debraclopton.com Twitter: @debra clopton Facebook: debra.clopton.5